POINT
OF
HONOR

WAR, MEMORY, AND CULTURE

Series published in cooperation with

THE CENTER FOR THE STUDY OF
WAR & MEMORY
at the UNIVERSITY OF SOUTH ALABAMA

http://www.southalabama.edu/departments/research/warandmemory/
Susan McCready, Content Editor

POINTS
OF
HONOR

Short Stories of
THE GREAT WAR
BY A US COMBAT MARINE

THOMAS BOYD

Edited and with an Introduction by STEVEN TROUT

The University of Alabama Press
Tuscaloosa

The University of Alabama Press
Tuscaloosa, Alabama 35487-0380
uapress.ua.edu

Typeface: Caslon

Cover image: *Traffic to Mont-St.-Père* (1917–1918) by George Matthews
Harding; courtesy of the Armed Forces Division, National Museum of
American History, Smithsonian Institution
Cover design: Michele Myatt Quinn

Library of Congress Cataloging-in-Publication Data
Names: Boyd, Thomas, 1898–1935, author. | Trout, Steven, 1963– editor.
Title: Points of honor : short stories of The Great War by a US combat marine
/ Thomas Boyd ; edited and with an introduction by Steven Trout.
Description: Tuscaloosa : The University of Alabama Press, 2018. | Series: War,
memory, and culture | Includes bibliographical references.
Identifiers: LCCN 2017035687 | ISBN 9780817359119 (pbk.) |
ISBN 9780817391782 (e book)
Subjects: LCSH: World War, 1914–1918—Fiction. | Marines—Fiction. |
War stories, American. | World War, 1914–1918—Literature and the war.
Classification: LCC PS3503.O9 P65 2018 | DDC 813/.52—dc23
LC record available at https://lccn.loc.gov/2017035687

Contents

A Note on the Text
and Acknowledgments

This book reproduces the first edition of *Points of Honor*, published by Charles Scribner's Sons in 1925. I have corrected several obvious errors, but retained Boyd's original archaic spellings and eccentric contractions. The latter appear most frequently in passages of dialogue, which capture the flavor of American speech (in all its variety) as it sounded one hundred years ago.

This new edition would not have been possible without the cooperation of Brainerd F. Phillipson, Thomas Boyd's grandson and bibliophile par excellence. I also wish to thank Sorina Suma Christian and Kristen Hop, both whom helped with the necessary typing; Dan Waterman, the editor-in-chief at the University of Alabama Press, who was patient and helpful, as always; Andrzej Wierzbicki, Dean of the College of Arts and Sciences at the University of South Alabama, who provided assistance by keeping my summers free of teaching responsibilities; and my friends Scott D. Emmert, Jennifer Haytock, Susan McCready, Daryl Palmer, and David Alan Rennie, all of whom offered deeply appreciated encouragement. To my long-suffering spouse and best friend, Maniphone Sengsamouth-Trout, I offer thanks and, once again, apologies for the late evenings at the keyboard.

Steven Trout

Introduction

Timed to coincide with the one-hundredth anniversary of American participation in World War I, this new edition of Thomas Boyd's short story collection, *Points of Honor* (1925), rescues from obscurity a vivid, kaleidoscopic vision of American soldiers, US Marines mostly, serving in a global conflict a century ago. It is a true forgotten masterpiece of First World War literature. When first published, the book impressed none other than the premier novelist of the Jazz Age. In June 1925, F. Scott Fitzgerald wrote to his friend Thomas Boyd to say that he was "crazy about *Points of Honor*."[1]

Fitzgerald, who published *The Great Gatsby* that same year, was not alone in his enthusiasm. Although fewer in number than Boyd or his publisher, the inimitable Charles Scribner's Sons, would have liked, reviews of the short story collection were consistently positive and often glowing. According to the *New York Times*, for example, Boyd had displayed in *Points of Honor* "the same competent craftsmanship . . . balanced point of view, and excellence of characterization that so easily distinguished his first novel."[2]

Equally effusive, the review in *The Nation* paid particular attention to tone and style and described the collection almost as if it were written by Ernest Hemingway, a writer just then becoming well known thanks to his own 1925 short story collection *In Our Time*: "Despite the passion and agony that tears through each of the tales in [*Points of Honor*], they are told in a voice bereft of emotion or experience—facts, simple unadorned episodes of war—but they smile with utter conviction."[3] The *New York Herald Tribune* judged the book "a better memorial [to Americans in the Great War] than granite monuments or Fourth of July orations."[4] And *The Saturday Review of Literature* noted that Boyd had "caught in his pages the minds of twentieth century Americans as they went to war."[5]

The author of these "unadorned episodes of war" was, for a brief period in the 1920s, a rising star in American literature, thanks in no small measure to Fitzgerald's support and encouragement. However, Boyd produced just two memorable books—namely, *Through the Wheat*, his first novel, and *Points of Honor*—before his death at age thirty-six. His idiosyncratic career choices caused his fame to evaporate quickly. Brian Bruce's well-researched biography, aptly titled *Thomas Boyd: Lost Author of the 'Lost Generation'* (2006), describes its subject as a charming but difficult man—a serial adulterer, among other things, and something of an editor's nightmare—who enjoyed few of the financial advantages held by other, better-known writers of the era. Frequently teetering on the brink of bankruptcy, a result of both economic forces beyond his control and compulsive overspending, Boyd could count as friends or acquaintances many of the leading literary figures of his time: F. Scott Fitzgerald, Sinclair Lewis, Theodore Dreiser, and Ring Lardner, among others, but bad luck and bad decisions kept him on the cultural margin. He was indeed a "lost author" who, in addition to falling into literary obscurity, never quite found his way in life.

This introduction will offer an overview of Boyd's military service and his tragically abbreviated writing career as well as a discussion of the eleven stories presented in this volume. Readers coming to *Points of Honor* for the first time should skip the latter section and proceed directly to the stories themselves; analysis of literature is best consulted after exposure to an artist's vision in the raw. Selective annotations, which I have provided at the back of this book, cover slang expressions, acronyms, and military facts from the World War I era with which twenty-first century readers may be unfamiliar.

I. US Marine, War Writer, and "Barnyard Boy"

The unhappiness and turmoil that characterized so much of Thomas Alexander Boyd's life had their origin in his difficult childhood, which he spent as a "practical orphan," and in his combat experience, which affected him psychologically and permanently weakened his physical health. According to the federal Veterans Administration, Boyd's sudden death in 1935 from a cerebral hemorrhage likely resulted, at least in part, from poison gas inhalation for which he was hospitalized in 1918.[6] As we will see, Boyd tried, in his writings and elsewhere, to put his traumatic exposure to frontline violence behind him, but, as it did for so many veterans, the war caught up with him in the end.

Born in Defiance, Ohio, in 1898, Thomas Boyd spent his first eighteen years passed from relative to relative. His father, a real estate agent originally from Canada, died several months before Boyd was born, and his mother, a nurse and hospital superintendent, suffered from morphine addiction. Unable to care for her son, Alice Boyd placed him with family members, first with his maternal grandparents in Defiance, where Boyd remained for eleven years, and then with various aunts and uncles in Chicago and nearby Elgin, Illinois. Boyd bounced among a number of schools, including military academies in Ohio and South Carolina, but never formally completed his high school education.

The future writer's unsettled childhood scarred him emotionally, as his turbulent adult relationships would later demonstrate, but also shaped him in positive ways. During his time in Defiance, he developed a deep fondness for the Ohio countryside and a fascination with the state's history, which would later figure prominently in his writing career. Among the kindest of his various guardians, his aunt and uncle in Elgin exposed him to great literary artists, like George Bernard Shaw who quickly became his favorite author, and nurtured his love of reading. Ironically, they also converted him to the teachings of Christian Science, which Boyd perhaps embraced, as Brian Bruce points out, as a form of rebellion against his medically trained mother.[7] Throughout his childhood and adolescence, Boyd would spend periods of weeks, even months, back in his mother's care, but he found her emotionally distant and their relationship never fully stabilized.

Boyd was taking classes from a local business school in Elgin when the United States declared war in April 1917. Like other young men pining for adventure, he enlisted almost immediately in the Marine Corps, which promised the quickest passage to the front, and trained at Parris Island and Quantico before shipping out for France in September, well ahead of the rest of the American Expeditionary Forces (AEF).

Too few marines existed in 1917 to form an entire division, and so Boyd's outfit, the Sixth Marines, was paired with another marine regiment to form the Fourth Marine Brigade (about 9,000 men at full strength) and simply inserted into the AEF's Second "Indian Head" Division, named for the profile of a Native American warrior that division personnel wore on their shoulder insignia. Throughout the horrific battles ahead, units of marines and US Army troops served side by side in the "Indian Head," led first by an army general, then by the legendary marine commander John A. Lejeune.

Theoretically, the Second Division was part of the regular army, which meant that it should have contained an abundance of professional soldiers from the prewar era. In reality, most of its troops, army and marine alike, were recent volunteers like Boyd. A few crusty marine veterans, some with service records stretching all the way back to the Spanish-American War, stood out here and there (Boyd writes fondly about one of these men in his story "Semper Fidelis"), but they too were novices when it came to the combat conditions on the Western Front. In short, no one in the Second Division was prepared for the inferno into which they would be thrown in the summer of 1918.

At first, contrary to the pitch made by recruiters, it appeared that the marines might not see any action at all. As Bruce relates, during "the first months of their tour in France, Tom and the other men of the sixth unloaded ships, constructed barracks, dug latrines and did guard duty."[8] Expecting to fight, everyone in the Sixth Marines resented these unglamorous duties, and Boyd later painted a memorable portrait of this frustrating period in the story "A Little Gall." Fed up with the monotonous labor and the cold, the protagonist, Corporal Lewis, gets drunk and half-facetiously threatens an officer—with disastrous results.

Amid the drudgery, rumors swirled; one piece of scuttlebutt even held that Boyd and his companions would soon be going home to train other marines. But in January 1918, it became clear that combat, as promised, was in their future. The men of the Sixth Marines moved from Saint-Nazaire, their much-hated headquarters on the French coast, to training facilities in the Vosges Mountains, where, as Edwin Howard Simmons recounts, the marines finally "received their 'tin hats' and gas masks, the telling marks of troops destined for the front lines."[9] Amid the excitement of learning that he was finally going to see action, Corporal Thomas Boyd suffered a personal setback: an officer caught him sitting and smoking while on guard duty. Reduced in rank to private, the Ohioan ultimately regained his stripes and maintained an exemplary record for the remainder of his time in the corps. He also went on to receive a medal and citation for valor.

In March, the Fourth Brigade finally took over a section of trenches near Verdun, the site of an epic bloodbath that resulted in over a million French and German casualties two years earlier. The shell-churned battlefield was relatively quiet by this point, but nevertheless serving in the legendary trenches of the Western Front left a deep impression on Boyd, just as it did on all American soldiers. His story "Responsibility" vividly describes the marines' nighttime entry into this mysterious subterranean realm: "Suddenly the men stepped into a communication trench. The duckboards were slippery and the trench narrow; the men did not walk, they floundered. . . . Somewhere ahead a signal pistol popped, and in a moment a bright light, like a mammoth glowing moth, fluttered slowly to the ground. The line halted, the men crowding against one another." Here Boyd paints a scene that might have come from any British, French, or German account of static warfare on the Western Front; however, as the battle scenes scattered throughout *Points of Honor* demonstrate, combat on open ground, not in the trenches, soon typified the American experience. As far as the fighting was concerned, Boyd's service in the AEF looked ahead to the kind of mobile warfare that GIs in Europe would encounter twenty-five years later.

In May, following several rotations in and out of the trenches, the Fourth Brigade relocated to a rest area just north of Paris. It would not stay there long. Two months earlier, flush with troops no longer needed on the Eastern Front (thanks to the peace treaty with Bolshevik Russia) and determined to force France and Great Britain to the negotiating table before the United States could fully mobilize its vast reserves of manpower, the German Army launched a series of desperate offensives in the west. The latest attack, aimed at French trenches along a notorious ridgeline known as the Chemin des Dames, resulted in a near breakthrough and brought German troops within forty miles of Paris. Suddenly the marines were needed on the frontline.

On May 31, Boyd and his comrades in the First Battalion, Sixth Marines, piled into camions, which carried them past streams of refugees and exhausted French soldiers (all moving in the opposite direction) to a position near Château Thierry, a town on the Marne River. The marines deployed in front of a boulder-strewn preserve of second-growth forest roughly a mile wide and a mile deep known as the Bois de Belleau or Belleau Wood. Over the next several days, the Fourth Brigade held its ground and helped stall the enemy's advance. It was the closest the kaiser's forces would ever come to the French capital. Then the marines received orders to counterattack and clear the woods of Germans. This they would do—at terrible cost.

Boyd survived the ensuing battle without injury, a near miracle under the circumstances. The first day of the counterattack, June 6, saw over a thousand marine casualties, the bloodiest twenty-four hours in Marine Corps history up to that point.[10] Seven days later, a barrage of poison-gas shells and high explosives landed on the already-thinned ranks of Boyd's battalion and killed or wounded 450 men.[11] Ultimately, it took three weeks of brutal fighting—often hand-to-hand—to drive the Germans out of what was left of the Bois de Belleau. The ordeal turned the once gung-ho marines (those who survived) into semifunctioning scarecrows, but Boyd's worst combat experiences were still ahead.

After a few weeks of much-needed rest, the marines joined another counterattack, this time near the town of Soissons. On July 19, the men of the First Battalion advanced across open wheat fields toward German positions bristling with machine guns. Half of Boyd's unit fell in the first hour. Boyd once again beat the odds somehow, and later, during the same battle, he even helped carry wounded marines through an enemy barrage, the action for which he received the Croix de Guerre and a citation from the Second Division.

Compared with Belleau Wood and Soissons, the Fourth Brigade's next engagement, the Saint Mihiel offensive, was a proverbial cakewalk. But then came the assault on the Blanc Mont massif in October, when Boyd's luck finally ran out. The marines' attack up the slope of this sinister "White Mountain" (regarded as impregnable by the French, who had already lost thousands of troops there) was perhaps their toughest assignment of the war and the most thankless. Pershing somehow forgot to mention it in his final report on AEF operations, and the legend that quickly grew up around Belleau Wood, a name still venerated by US Marines today, effaced the memory of this equally terrible battle.[12] Boyd's good fortune carried him through the murderous climb to the summit but failed him the next day. On October 4, he was incapacitated by poison gas and sent to a base hospital.

By the time the future writer, now a corporal again, rejoined his unit, the war was over, and the Second Division was marching into the Rhineland where it would serve as part of the Army of Occupation. Mercifully, Boyd had missed out on the Fourth Brigade's final engagement, an attack at the close of the Meuse-Argonne Offensive, where many marines died pointlessly just minutes before the armistice on November 11.

Two passages from *Points of Honor* perhaps reflect the author's mental and physical state by this point in his service. The first comes from the story "The Ribbon Counter." As his regiment lines up for a ceremony in Germany, the protagonist Sergeant MacMahon, a veteran of multiple battles, realizes that he has become a stranger in his own unit. Looking at the men around him, he asks, "How many of them had been at Belleau Wood? Or even at Soissons? Hell, you couldn't find enough in the whole battalion to make two squads." As an old-timer at age twenty-one, in a battalion whose replacement rate topped 150 percent, Boyd probably felt much the same way. The second passage appears in "The Long Shot," Boyd's bitterly ironic tale of a solder's homecoming. Initially greeted as a hero, then scorned by his wife and his employer, the main character Duncan Milner suffers from the lingering effects of mustard gas. Again Boyd writes from experience: "His gripping headache, with all the nerves at the back of his neck feeling as if they were tied into little knots that tortured, and his dry cough had now become a part of him. It was a cough that tore at the lining of his lungs."

In April 1919, Boyd returned to the United States ahead of his regiment and spent the next three months in the naval hospital at Great Lakes, Illinois. The exact nature of his malady remains unclear. In all likelihood, he was continuing to have problems with his lungs (they would, in fact, never fully recover); however, a physician's report filed on May 31 listed "nervousness" as the patient's complaint, a hint, perhaps, that Boyd was also suffering from shell shock or what we would today call Post-Traumatic Stress Disorder (PTSD).[13] In any event, by the time he finally received his discharge from the US Marine Corps on July 10, his health had rebounded, at least superficially.

Over the next several months, the former marine tried out several jobs unrelated to writing, including a stint in a machine shop, a setting that he would later use to great effect in "The Long Shot." In October 1920, still uncertain of his calling, Boyd moved to Minneapolis, Minnesota and married his third cousin Margaret Woodward "Peggy" Smith, an aspiring novelist who pushed Boyd to pursue his own journalistic and creative ambitions. The couple would have one child, Betty Grace Boyd, born the next year.

Though lacking confidence in his writing ability, Boyd found work, at Peggy's insistence, as a reporter, first with the *Non-Partisan Leaguer* (a reflection of his left-leaning political views), then with the *St. Paul Daily News*. His first big break came when, again through Peggy's influence, he became solely responsible for "In a Corner with a Bookworm," a section of the *Daily News* Sunday edition devoted to book reviews and interviews with famous writers. Almost instantly, Boyd became a person of importance in the Twin-Cities arts scene. And several months later, he took on a second job that proved equally stimulating and beneficial to his future writing career. Cornelius Van Ness, a local businessman and antiquarian book lover (to whom *Points of Honor* is partially dedicated), hired Boyd to manage the Kilmarnock Book Store in St. Paul, which "soon became a hangout for local and visiting authors."[14]

This was a heady time for Thomas Boyd. In his dual capacity as book critic and bookstore manager, he soon became personally acquainted with a host of major Midwestern writers, and it was not long before one of St. Paul's most celebrated native sons, the literary sensation of the moment, crossed his path. To escape the heat in Alabama, F. Scott and Zelda Fitzgerald moved to St. Paul during the summer of 1921 and soon became close friends with the Boyds. Although just two years older than the ex-marine, and with *Gatsby* and *Tender is the Night* still ahead of him, Fitzgerald was already recognized as a major talent by the prestigious New York publishing house Charles Scribner's Sons, and his editor was none other than the brilliant Maxwell Perkins, who would also help shape the career of Ernest Hemingway.

From the beginning, Boyd was starstruck, and as proof of his devotion to his new friend he plugged Fitzgerald's genius whenever possible on his book page. For his part, Fitzgerald couldn't hear enough about Boyd's overseas experiences in the Great War. Although inducted into the US Army in 1917 and commissioned as a second lieutenant, the Minnesotan had been one of the more than two million American soldiers whose deployment in Europe the armistice rendered unnecessary. He had missed the great adventure. Now, through Boyd, he had a chance to learn all about it from a man who had survived three of the AEF's worst battles. Van Ness later described the initial meeting between the two young men as "almost electric."[15]

In 1922, with encouragement from Maxwell Perkins and Sinclair Lewis, Boyd began work on his first novel *Through the Wheat* (1923), a poetic account of World War I combat drawn from its author's harrowing experiences in the marine brigade. The fledgling novelist completed most of the manuscript in just six weeks, often writing through the night in the backroom of the Kilmarnock Book Store. The finished product failed to impress Perkins, but Fitzgerald stepped in and convinced his editor to retract a rejection notice that had already gone out in the mail.

The book's reception demonstrated the wisdom behind Fitzgerald's intervention. Focused almost entirely on the sensations of battle, *Through the Wheat* drew apt comparisons with Stephen Crane's *The*

Red Badge of Courage (1895), sold well enough to pass through seven printings in under a year, and established Boyd as a fresh new talent in the stable of acclaimed authors identified with the House of Scribner ranging from Fitzgerald to Edith Wharton. Boyd basked in the fame that resulted from his literary debut, little knowing that it would prove short lived.

Offering a more expansive, multifaceted vision of American soldiers in the Great War, *Points of Honor* complements *Through the Wheat* perfectly and would have been a logical immediate successor. Indeed, Perkins believed that a successful first-time novelist should quickly offer a volume of short stories as proof of artistic versatility.[16] But Boyd had other ideas. With characteristically bad judgment when it came to publishing matters, he insisted, despite Perkins's repeatedly articulated misgivings, that his next book would be a historical novel set before the Civil War in the Upper-Midwest. The resulting narrative, aptly titled *The Dark Cloud* (1924), received lukewarm to dismissive reviews and failed to attract many book buyers. Fewer than 3,000 copies sold.[17] Perpetually short of funds (despite his recent success with *Through the Wheat*), Boyd found his literary career imperiled almost before it had begun.

Thus, in his next book for Scribner's, he returned to his war experience for what proved to be the last time. As promised in his foreword to the collection, Boyd never again wrote a book that dealt so directly with his service on the Western Front, perhaps because of the pain and anger that contemplating it evoked. Although half-hidden by the author's restrained, even laconic voice, "passion and agony," to quote the reviewer in the *Nation*, indeed stand at the heart of the collection.[18]

Most of the stories Boyd already had on hand. Some he had written a few months earlier while he and Peggy travelled in Europe. Others he composed following his return to St. Paul. Nearly all of the stories first appeared in periodicals, which was standard (then as now) for short fiction. Affiliated with Boyd's book publisher, though under separate editorial leadership, *Scribner's Magazine*, which competed for an upper-brow readership with *Harper's* and *The Atlantic Monthly*, accepted the majority and paid Boyd approximately $200 apiece for them. Featuring illustrations by the likes of Leroy Baldridge, a popular AEF artist best known for his work on the US Army newspaper *The Stars and Stripes*, six stories in all—"Rintintin," "Unadorned," "Sound Adjutant's Call," "The Kentucky Boy," "A Little Gall," and "Responsibility"—came out in various monthly issues of *Scribner's* between April 1924 and March 1925. The magazine *American Mercury*, founded by H. L. Mencken, published the story "Uninvited" in November 1924. "Semper Fidelis" appeared in the December 1924 issue of *The Bookman*.

Knowing that fans of his first novel would likely make up most of his audience, Boyd equipped his new book with a brief foreword that established the purpose of the collection in relation to *Through the Wheat*. While the latter, Boyd explained, focused on the experience of combat, "the heart of war," the former presented "a mass of more human happenings." This is perhaps a bit misleading. In most of the eleven stories, readers will encounter military violence and discover clues that situate most of the abundant frontline action amid many of the same battles depicted in Boyd's first novel. However, combat in *Points of Honor* is no longer a poetically rendered world unto itself. Here it matters primarily in terms of plot, as a realm where passions revealed behind the frontlines achieve their typically ironic resolution, a pattern established in the first story "Unadorned."

Bound in the same forest-green cloth as *Through the Wheat* and featuring the same gold typeface on the spine and front cover, which presented the two works as companion volumes, *Points of Honor* reached bookstores in March 1925. Despite the positive reviews, sales proved disappointing, a mere fraction of the revenue generated by Boyd's first novel. Fitzgerald, for his part, buoyed his friend's spirits with effusive praise: *Though the Wheat* and *Points of Honor*, he declared, are "about my favorite modern books."[19] But, as it turned out, this would be the last time he had anything positive to say either to or about Thomas Boyd.

The end of the once-warm friendship between the two writers occurred for several reasons and coincided with the onset of Boyd's creative decline. Indeed, in a series of often mean-spirited remarks made to Perkins, Fitzgerald maintained that the Ohioan should have understood his limitations and stuck to war literature, the only genre in which he displayed notable talent. In retrospect, Fitzgerald was perhaps right, though for the wrong reasons.

Fitzgerald adopted this dismissive view, in part, because of strongly held prejudices against certain kinds of writing. In August 1925, just four months after the publication of *Points of Honor*, Scribner's released Boyd's third novel *Samuel Drummond* (1925), a return to historical fiction, this time dealing with the post–Civil War vicissitudes of an Ohio farmer modeled after the author's maternal grandfather. Fitzgerald was appalled. He detested so-called novels of the soil in general, and in a vitriolic letter to Perkins, he described *Samuel Drummond* as a particularly miserable specimen of the genre. Boyd's new book, he declared, was "utterly lousy" and filled with rustic characters who were "almost ready for the burlesque circuit." In his personal notebook, published posthumously as *The Crack-Up*, Fitzgerald lamented that his former friend had become a "barnyard boy"—i.e. a writer stuck in the infertile, plowed-to-death terrain of regional farm fiction.[20]

Boyd's shift to Ohio subjects not only offended Fitzgerald's taste, it also wounded the great novelist's ego. Indeed, the seeds of the friendship's dissolution were perhaps there from the beginning: Fitzgerald's continued good will depended upon Boyd, a lesser talent and a younger man (albeit by just two years), deferring to his advice and following his example. Once Boyd went in his own direction, turning away from war fiction and rejecting urban America (the proper setting, in Fitzgerald's view, for serious fiction), a falling-out between the two men became inevitable. Boyd had committed heresy by choosing a career path very different from the one laid out by Fitzgerald, and in the months following the publication of *Points of Honor* it became clear that he would play no part in the Modernist peak of the mid-1920s, which saw the emergence of important experimental works by Ernest Hemingway, Willa Cather, William Faulkner, and a host of others. For the rest of his brief career, Boyd would remain unadventurous in terms of narrative technique and, at least where his writing was concerned, largely uninterested in contemporary topics. From

1925 onward, he looked primarily to the historical past for his inspiration, specifically the Colonial era.

Prejudice and vanity may have colored Fitzgerald's assessment of the "barnyard boy's" non-war-related work, but astute critical judgment also played a role, just as it did three years earlier when he championed *Through the Wheat*. Whatever his personal animosity toward his onetime friend, which only intensified once he discovered that Boyd had not cared for *The Great Gatsby*, Fitzgerald was essentially right: Boyd's presentation of modern warfare *does* have an intensity and a power that the author's other efforts simply do not. Fitzgerald sensed correctly that when drawing upon his experiences as a combat marine, Boyd tapped into his deepest and darkest creative energies, energies that make the deceptively "simple, unadorned episodes of war" contained in *Points of Honor* both enthralling and ultimately haunting.[21]

Boyd's life after *Points of Honor* formed a decade-long anticlimax characterized by movement—he lived for a time in Georgia, Illinois, Connecticut, Nevada, and, ultimately, Vermont—and recurring financial strain. The heady days of notoriety and promise that he enjoyed in St. Paul did not return. In 1929, his marriage to Peggy ended, in part because of his philandering, and later that same year he married another novelist, Ruth Fitch Mason, to whom he was also unfaithful. A handsome man with considerable personal magnetism, Boyd struggled with commitment throughout his life, a legacy, perhaps, of his emotionally wounding childhood.

Professionally, he devoted much of his time and energy to a string of competently written but ultimately forgettable biographies focused on eighteenth- and early nineteenth-century figures. His biography of Simon Girty, a notorious Tory (and turncoat) who served as a liaison between Native American tribes and the British Army, came out in 1927, followed by biographies of the Revolutionary War General "Mad" Anthony Wayne, the cavalryman "Light Horse" Harry Lee (the father of Robert E. Lee), and the steamboat inventor John Finch. The latter three books appeared in 1929, 1931, and 1935 respectively. None of them sold particularly well.

The historical novel *Shadow of the Long Knives* (1928), another Colonial-era narrative set on the Ohio frontier, fared much better, earning Boyd more royalties than any book since *Through the Wheat*. But he was unable to follow up with a comparable commercial success. His final book, *In Time of Peace* (1935), a sequel to *Through the Wheat* focused on the postwar privations of William Hicks (the autobiographical protagonist of Boyd's first novel), was another disappointment. With its depiction of a war veteran ground under the wheels of capitalism, the book fit well with the intellectual atmosphere of the New Deal era, but reviewers nevertheless found the narrative's explicitly socialist agenda clunky and unconvincing. The book-buying public (such as it was by this point in the Depression) ignored the novel altogether. Sadly, Boyd's last work of fiction was also his biggest flop, and it came on the heels of yet another disappointment, this time in the unlikely arena of politics. In 1934, Boyd ran as the Communist Party candidate in the Vermont gubernatorial election. After a "perfunctory and unsuccessful" campaign, he received just several hundred votes.[22]

The writer's untimely death on January 27, 1935, ended a sad career that saw considerably more failures than successes. However, Thomas Boyd was more than a one-hit wonder. Whenever he drew material from his traumatic war experience, he wrote with a power and intensity that still come across forcefully nearly one-hundred years later. Indeed, readers of this new edition of *Points of Honor* may well discover that some of Boyd's stories, the best of them, live in the imagination long after they are experienced initially. Something about these troubling, often despairing glimpses of human behavior in wartime *sticks*. A brief discussion of the book's central themes and the artistry on display—again, best consulted after one has first finished all eleven stories—appears below.

II. "A mass of more human happenings."

In the protagonist of *Through the Wheat*, who enters the experience of modern warfare full of confidence only to emerge (three battles later) shell shocked, exhausted, and spiritually "numb," Boyd created an intentionally nondescript everyman, a kind of World War I version of Crane's generic Henry Fleming in *The Red Badge of Courage* (1895). At first glance, the characters in *Points of Honor* seem similarly featureless, with names as indistinct and interchangeable as the government-issued serial numbers on their dog tags: John Wainwright, John Goodwin, Johnny Benner, Homer Fredericks, Duncan Milner, etc. The reader may easily be forgiven for losing track of which character appears in which story. And then there are those we come to know only as family names prefixed with rank, such as Corporal Lewis in "A Little Gall" and Sergeant MacMahon in "The Ribbon Counter." Sparser still are Andrus and Oldshaw (no first names given), the protagonists of "Responsibility" and "Uninvited" respectively.

However, the blandness of the (mostly male) characters' monikers belies their vividness as personalities. Unlike *Through the Wheat*, *Points of Honor* is populated with distinct individuals. But we seldom catch the author at character development. With just a few exceptions, Boyd avoids long paragraphs filled with background information or extended explorations of consciousness. The stories are too economical for that. Instead, he gets to the main "point," as it were, about each character as quickly as possible, typically through a few well-chosen images. For example, the protagonist of "Responsibility" comes to life via a well-described facial expression: "Andrus frowned, or, rather, the creases in his forehead deepened and the furrow on each cheek grew straight and long." In just a few words, Boyd captures this character's craggy personality and his aloofness from the new men assigned to his platoon, particularly the physically unimpressive Private Hannan, who approaches Andrus with—in a wonderful phrase—"timorous friendliness." Likewise, Captain Balder in "Sound Adjutant's Call" is instantly unforgettable, thanks to the succinct precision of Boyd's prose: "He was a thin little fellow with bowed, spindly legs, and a set expression about his thin white face from which you could surmise he was telling himself: 'Every man in this entire battalion may be against me, b-b-but I've got my job to do, and by gracious I'm going to do it.'"

Characterization in "Unadorned," the sophisticated story that opens the collection, is just as compact, even though the issues the narrative raises are complex and troubling. This story is worth examining in some detail. The opening description of the protagonist Wilfred Bird (one of Boyd's more memorably titled creations) subtly introduces the crisis that will ultimately drive the character to his death: "The lieutenant in charge of the fourth platoon was Wilfred Bird, a well-formed, graceful young man with a soft brown mustache, contemplative, hazel eyes, and features more fine than manly, as that word is currently used." Note the adjectives: "graceful," "contemplative," and "fine" versus "manly." This passage abounds with ambiguously gendered attributes that may, if the reader is so inclined, be read as clues that Bird is an effeminate man (by the standards of his time) and perhaps a homosexual (not that the two are necessarily linked). But the feature that stands out the most, a perfect metaphor, is Bird's mustache, an assertion of masculinity that is, at the same time, "soft." This single detail tells us a great deal about the character.

As "Unadorned" unfolds, we begin to understand that the tensions built into Bird's opening description will be central to the story. In the first third, the lieutenant's softness, if you will, paradoxically makes him effective in a role more typically identified with conventionally manly behavior. "[L]ow-voiced and courteous," he does not browbeat or lecture his men; instead, he displays a quiet confidence that inspires, rather than demands, respect. When it comes to his dress and grooming, Bird is flamboyantly fastidious, but rather than mock the lieutenant's preening, most of his subordinates copy his example, which earns the outfit praise from the divisional commander during an inspection. Afterwards, the narrator tells us, Bird adopts toward his platoon the "attitude . . . of a jealous father toward his children"; however, the lieutenant's gushing reaction to a toast given in his honor, as the man who "sav[ed] the reputation of the company," sounds more motherly than fatherly: "'They're really awfully nice boys. I'm very fond of them; and of course it is they that deserve whatever credit there is to be given.'"

But then comes the moment when, in a grim parody of the camp scene in Shakespeare's *Henry V*, Bird eavesdrops on the men under his command and hears "loud-mouth John Wainwright" impugn not only his valor, but also his manhood: "[Bird] ain't no guy to take a bunch of soldiers up to the front. Why, do you know what he is?

He's nothin' but a sissy, a lah-de-dah. . . . I'll bet you that when we git up there where the big ones is bustin', you'll have to hold him to keep him from runnin'. Yes, sir, hold him!" Wainwright's audience doesn't share this view, but, of course, Bird doesn't stay to hear himself defended. With diabolical precision, Wainwright has unknowingly zeroed in on his commander's deepest insecurities and, perhaps, the most closeted region of his inner self. As a result, Bird instantly assumes that every member of the platoon loathes him. And from this moment on, in a grotesque spectacle of overcompensation, the once popular lieutenant becomes a hated martinet indistinguishable in manner from the "stern, military, disapproving" major general presented earlier in the story.

Boyd might have ended the narrative at this point, having demonstrated both the corrosive effects of distrust on military leadership and the tyranny of a culturally sanctioned model of masculinity that Bird ultimately cannot resist. But what happens next takes the story to another level. When Bird leads his men into combat, he is struck in the leg by a German machine-gun bullet—proof positive of his courage and manliness—and then sent to a base hospital. Before he can fully recover, however, he learns that his regiment has just joined another battle. Acting without orders, the lieutenant limps out of the hospital, catches a ride on a French truck bound for the front, and forces the driver to pass through a crossroads targeted by enemy artillery. The story ends with a literal bang, as a German shell hits the truck dead-on.

One might read Bird's manic quest to rejoin his unit as an expression of heroic loyalty, as evidence of his bond with his platoon, but it isn't that at all: paradoxically, fear drives the lieutenant back to the frontline, fear of still being regarded as a "sissy." Indeed, by the final few pages of the narrative, Bird's desire to prove Wainwright wrong by unflinchingly facing the hazards of combat (over and over again) has become a dangerous fixed idea, a kind of madness. Ironically, as he bullies the French driver into racing across the intersection, inviting certain death for them both, the lieutenant's mind is far away: "He was like a man in a dream, living solely in the picture of himself in the first wave of the attack, at the head of his men, limping along toward the German lines." In the end, Bird throws away his life—and the Frenchman's—for the sake of an especially absurd and tragic point of honor. Had he had more confidence in his own personal version of masculinity, he might not have found Wainwright's comments so wounding or been driven to such irrational lengths to prove himself to men who never doubted him in the first place.

"Unadorned" not only introduces us to Boyd's minimalist—one might say unadorned—approach to characterization, it also functions as an opening chapter of sorts, establishing themes and motifs that recur throughout the narratives that follow. This is not to say that *Points of Honor* is a novel in disguise. The book does not have a central plot or a central cast of characters, even though some soldiers, like Andrus and the loud-mouth Wainwright, appear in more than one story. Nevertheless, as with Hemingway's *In Our Time*, the whole ultimately seems greater than the sum of the parts. Although each of the eleven stories can be enjoyed as a freestanding work of art, Boyd achieves a cumulative effect by bringing them together between two covers. As we move from story to story, we encounter a musical structure of themes and variations.

One such theme, located at the very center of this angry and often sardonic book, is conflict among fellow Americans, sometimes with a noble point of honor at stake but more often the opposite. Boyd's enlisted men play a cat-and-mouse game with the ubiquitously hated American military police, furtively snatching what modest pleasures they can. At the same time, they quarrel among themselves, sometimes to the point of physical violence. There are few moments of real comradeship, the supposed benefit of combat experience. As for the officers in *Points of Honor*—college-educated (unlike the mostly working-class soldiers in the ranks), hastily trained, and typically insecure or incompetent—few can resist the temptation to torment and humiliate their subordinates, men they obviously regard as inferiors.

While class warfare, something to which Boyd (with his socialist leanings) was always alert, surfaces throughout these stories, military violence against the Imperial German Army, the reason for the marines' presence in France, is, ironically enough, largely incidental; it often figures into the plots but never takes center stage. Indeed, the poetic intensity with which Boyd describes combat in *Through the Wheat* carries over to *Points of Honor* only in scattered places. Here the experience of battle is just as likely to come across as mechanical or even banal.

Consider, for example, Boyd's laconic description of the instant when Lieutenant Bird receives his red badge of courage: "About twenty yards from the first dark fringe [of the woods] he hastily stopped, took a step backward, and fell with his heels pointing toward the woods, the goal which he had planned to be the first to reach." In this instance, the third-person narrator presents the action as if recorded by a hand-cranked film camera. Bird moves forward, stops, steps back, and falls faceup with the jerky, abbreviated motion of a grainy figure in an early silent movie. Likewise, Captain Osborne's death in "The Ribbon Counter," a moment of great pathos, is made all the more powerful by the emotionally detached, cameralike narration, which emphasizes the inertness of the captain's lifeless body, a static figure at the center of a frame: "MacMahon saw him sprawl forward, much as if he had tripped, and go headlong on the ground. He waited, but Captain Osborne did not rise, not even with the welcoming bark of the seventy-fives. . . . Nor yet again with the support line troops, who had been ordered up to fill the gaps in the attacking regiment."

While the characters in *Points of Honor* are, by and large, perfectly capable of killing German soldiers, some with more gusto than others, it's the *American* enemies that matter, and Boyd presents us with a richly varied and often deeply ironic set of antagonists, both literal and metaphoric. In "Unadorned," Bird declares war on his own platoon. Andrus, in "Responsibility," struggles to remain indifferent to the expendable replacement troops assigned to his squad. Captain Bedford, the odious (but very brave) professional soldier at the center of "Sound Adjutant's Call," sadistically torments enlisted men in part as a way of compensating for his unimpressive physical appearance. Sergeant MacMahon, the protagonist of "The Ribbon Counter," comes to hate Captain Johnson, a martinet who claims the military honors due another officer. Johnny Benner, of "Rintintin," battles his well-earned reputation as a braggart; nearly everyone in his squad despises him. Corporal Lewis in "A Little Gall" drunkenly challenges an officer's authority and becomes a victim of so-called military justice. Homer Fredericks, the mournful hero of "The Nine Days' Kitten," spirals into misogyny when his girlfriend back home marries another; his war is against American members of the opposite sex. And Duncan Milner, the most abject of Boyd's protagonists, is a disabled veteran locked in dubious battle with three antagonists at once: an unfaithful wife, an economic system that makes no allowances for his ruined health, and a dysfunctional federal bureaucracy. Only Oldshaw, the middle-aged Graves Registration Service worker in "Uninvited," faces a non-American foe. His adversary? An elderly French widow who refuses to give up the corpses of more than a dozen American soldiers buried beneath her vegetable garden. The thematic patterning here could not be more sardonic.

However, Boyd's most intense treatment of division and violence among men who happen to wear the same uniform appears in "The Kentucky Boy," perhaps the finest short story he ever wrote. The narrative opens in an AEF base hospital where the medical staff essentially treats the protagonist John Goodwin, who has been seriously gassed, as a malingerer. Fed up with his indifferent care, Goodwin decides to make his way back to the frontline in the company of a rambunctious fellow patient, Private Hawthorne, the "Kentucky Boy" of the title. Acting without orders, the two men run the risk of being misidentified as deserters, and their quest to rejoin their two units becomes a seriocomic odyssey of rule breaking and close calls with military police and French railway officials.

Utterly fearless and indifferent to any and all authority, Hawthorne seems at first the perfect companion for this expedition. And here again Boyd does a masterful job with characterization. Hawthorne's energy and recklessness come across not through his physical appearance, which Boyd withholds from the reader, but through his speech, as when he persuades Goodwin to join him in an escape attempt from the hospital:

"Lord," Goodwin sighed. "But I wish I had my clothes."
"Git 'em," said Hawthorne with succinctness. [*sic*] "Git 'em."

Goodwin sat up, interested. "'y gosh, I believe I will."

"Go ahead," encouraged Hawthorne. "An' we'll beat it outa here."

Unfortunately for Goodwin, however, Hawthorne soon reveals a homicidal streak. When a doughboy from another unit insults the Kentuckian's division, Hawthorne hurls an iron coffee stand at the man's head, missing by just inches. And, as it turns out, this is not the first time he has nearly been guilty of murder: Hawthorne casually describes a feud with his company cook, whom he once pummeled (until his "knuckles looked like raw meat") and almost struck with an axe.

In short, with Hawthorne, everything is a point of honor, and Goodwin quickly realizes that his companion's free-floating aggression has the potential to land them both in a military penitentiary. At the end of the story, exhausted by the journey and by his efforts to keep the Kentucky boy out of further trouble, Goodwin returns his fellow traveler to his unit only to discover that Hawthorne's sole objective in escaping from the hospital was to catch up with the hated cook and "carve [his] name" in the man's face.

"The Kentucky Boy" opens in a spirit of boyish adventure and escape, a la *Huckleberry Finn*, and ends with disappointment and gloom, as Goodwin realizes that Hawthorne is incapable of "learn[ing] his lesson" and cannot help himself. In this regard, the homicidal Kentuckian is hardly alone: almost no one in Boyd's stories can help himself, whether that means curtailing destructive or isolating behavior or facing off against institutions—the US military, the federal Veterans Bureau, etc.—that crush or debase the individual. Indeed, *Points of Honor* as a whole falls squarely in the camp of literary Naturalism (literature focused on deterministic forces such as, psychology, heredity, social class, culture, etc. that deny individual free will). Throughout, the book reflects the influence of fellow Midwestern Naturalists like Sinclair Lewis and Theodore Dreiser, both of whom Boyd knew personally, as well as French novelist Emile Zola, the European progenitor of the movement.

Some of Boyd's characters seem molded from within, so locked into patterns of typically destructive behavior that they, in a sense, seal their own fate. Once fixated on the retrieval of his masculine honor, Wilfred Bird in "Unadorned" becomes just such a character; the obsession behind his crazed journey in the final third of the story makes his appointment with the German shell that kills him inevitable. Fittingly, the lieutenant's death occurs at a literal and symbolic crossroads, where he might deviate from his monomaniacal trajectory—but, of course, cannot.

In the moving story "Rintintin," Johnny Benner is likewise a prisoner of his insecurities and compulsions. Hospitalized for a minor injury, possibly self-inflicted, Benner returns to his squad on the eve of its entry into the Meuse-Argonne Offensive and shares an impossibly tall tale of having carried on a wild "affair with [a] French girl of royal blood." Accustomed to Benner's bloviating, no one trusts this story, even when he presents as evidence a miniature "Rintintin," one of a pair of French dolls (one male, one female) carried as good luck charms and as symbols of a lover's devotion.

Once subjected to the stresses of combat, Benner's preposterous persona ("He had, he said, taken degrees at half of the better-known universities in America, [and] had been to every conceivable place, from Siam to Nome") breaks down and reveals an abject creature utterly terrified of death and, even worse, of being thought a coward by his fellow soldiers. Ultimately, Benner redeems himself, as least in the eyes of the first-person narrator, by momentarily overcoming his fears (albeit with the aid of "enough cognac . . . to have run an automobile to Jericho") and advancing ahead of everyone else—right before he is killed. The narrator subsequently finds the "Rintintin" doll clutched in the dead man's hand.

Boyd might have ended the story with that striking image and left the truth, or lack thereof, behind Benner's alleged conquest to the reader's imagination. But the poignant denouement that follows only deepens the story's meaning. Several months after the armistice, the narrator and his companions perform the grisly task of exhuming their battlefield dead and reburying the bodies in a more centralized location. One of the unearthed cadavers is Johnny Benner, whom a former companion cannot resist eulogizing as "a louse if ever there was one." But after the soldiers plant a cross at the head of Benner's grave, the narrator makes a spontaneous gesture of remembrance: he attaches the Rintintin doll, which he has carried all this time, to the wooden cross piece.

Later that evening, as the men try to shake off their ghastly assignment by ordering drinks at a local café, a young woman appears, asking for "Capitain Bennair." She is, of course, Benner's lover, but not the ravishing aristocrat described by the braggart. Instead, the men confront a "tired, timid-looking girl" with "something pathetic about her." The narrator takes her to Benner's grave, where she sees Rintintin and excitedly produces the companion doll from her handbag. Then the girl crumples to the ground as if "she had been cut in two." Quietly, the narrative leaves her "sitting on the fresh grave . . . crying softly to herself."

What saves this poignant story from sentimentality is Benner's inability, shared by Lieutenant Bird and the Kentucky boy (among others), to curb patently self-destructive behavior—or, more specifically, to stop himself when presented with opportunities for prevarication. Despite his apparent victory over cowardice (rendered more than a little dubious by his intoxication), he remains, from beginning to end, a "louse" who compulsively lies to everyone, including his gullible lover left to mourn an officer who never existed. In other words, per the dictates of literary Naturalism, Benner is never anything but true to form, a form given shape, in his case, by irresistible deterministic forces that operate from within.

In some of his stories, Boyd pushes Naturalism into the realm of the absurd. In "A Little Gall," for example, a petty act of insubordination places the protagonist, Corporal Lewis, at the mercy of a military justice system that can only be described as Kafkaesque. For drunkenly telling his lieutenant that he "would give a dollar jist to take one good poke at [him]," Lewis receives five years in a penitentiary, a punishment completely out of line with any sane notion of legal proportionality.

But by far the most surreal narrative in *Points of Honor* is "The Long Shot," where Boyd's customary sardonic edge gives way to a dark cosmic irony reminiscent of Thomas Hardy. In 1930, this grim story served as the basis for one of the strangest film adaptations in

Hollywood history, which is, of course, saying something. "The Long Shot" became the early talky (now lost) titled *Blaze o' Glory*, starring Broadway actor Eddie Dowling. Bizarre song and dance numbers, among the earliest recorded for a sound motion picture, punctuated the courtroom drama of a disabled war veteran's descent into poverty and murder. Ironically, the movie brought Boyd the only revenue he ever received for film rights, but his bad luck seemed to rub off on the studio, which subsequently went bankrupt.

"The Long Shot" may offer less of a mishmash of styles and genres than *Blaze o' Glory*, but the story is hardly straightforward Naturalism. It feels more like a nightmare. The tale opens in France, where reluctant sniper Duncan Milner is urged by his commanding officer, Captain Havermeyer, to kill an unarmed enemy soldier whom he has caught in his crosshairs. Agonizing seconds go by as Milner wrestles with the morality of shooting another human being in cold blood, but then a poison-gas shell lands nearby, and Havermeyer withdraws. Unfortunately, Duncan fails to put on his gas mask in time, and the rest of the story documents, in chilling detail, the perils faced by a wounded veteran at a time when the federal government provided little assistance to returning soldiers.

At first, the protagonist seems free of such concerns. Sent home ahead of his unit (like Boyd in real life), Duncan reunites with his wife Dorothy and returns to his managerial position in the local machine shop, where his coworkers greet him as a hero. Since the protagonist served in the Illinois National Guard, his wartime comrades are all locals (in a town that looks much like Boyd's Elgin), and he affectionately greets them upon their return, including Captain Havermeyer, who subsequently becomes a judge in the county criminal court.

Then, slowly, inexorably, things begin to go wrong. Duncan discovers that a mysterious mental malady—undiagnosed shell shock—makes it impossible for him to focus on managerial duties. At the same time, he suffers from headaches and shortness of breath. The owners of the machine shop remove him from his supervisory position and put him back on a lathe, which produces clouds of steel dust that only worsen his lung condition. Eventually, he loses his job altogether and becomes a spectral figure in doctors' offices, forced to undergo an unending battery of tests—all designed to determine whether his impaired health has resulted from military service—so that he can receive paltry disability payments from the federal Veterans Bureau. Meanwhile, his wife loses interest in him and begins a series of assignations with another man.

At the story's climax, Duncan interrupts one of Dorothy's trysts with his wartime issue Colt .45 Automatic in hand and experiences a sudden flashback to the moment, years before, when he had the German soldier in his sights. This time, Duncan fires. And, by this point, we know exactly how the story must end: the judge who condemns the former sniper to death for murder is, of course, none other than Captain Havermeyer, the officer who once insisted that he take the life of a helpless enemy. Havermeyer's words during the sentencing are grotesquely ironic in a way that, again, reminds one more of Hardy ("The Long Shot" might have been called "A Satire of Circumstance") than either Sinclair Lewis or Theodore Dreiser: "'You have . . . been proven guilty . . . of the most terrible crime that a man can commit; you have taken a human life. You have broken the most holy commandment of your Maker, and you have defied the civilization which has sheltered you.'"

Arguably Boyd's most ambitious story, "The Long Shot" falls short, especially when it comes to characterization, a notable strength elsewhere in *Points of Honor*. Duncan becomes such an abject victim of pitiless economic forces and indifferent government bureaucracy that he ceases, beyond a certain point, to function as a living, breathing presence in the text. Likewise, Dorothy comes across as a necessary antagonist, never as a real woman. And Havermeyer functions more as a device than a character.

Nevertheless, the story is a masterpiece of setting and mood. We feel the world closing Duncan in, literally pushing him below ground. As his wife withdraws from him, shifting her shallow affections to another, the protagonist retreats into his cellar workroom, a sinister man cave where he stores his war souvenirs, including the pistol that he will use to murder Dorothy's lover. In one scene, Duncan contemplates these objects and concludes that the hell of combat is preferable to what his life has become since the war: "it was much better to spend his time in his workroom at his miniature lathe, or rummaging through his trunkful of scraps in which he had laid away his uniform, his helmet, gas mask, and automatic pistol. Picking up these mementoes of days at war, fondling them, trying them on 'to see if they still fitted,' he sometimes wished he was back in the service of the army." One could even argue that in the midst of his claustrophobic lair, so reminiscent of the various guardhouses where Corporal Lewis is imprisoned in "A Little Gall," Duncan becomes a version (albeit not entirely developed) of Dostoevsky's Underground Man; his character reaches back to the Russian novelist's iconic creation while at the same time anticipating scarred former soldiers like Travis Bickle, the forgotten, alienated Vietnam veteran in Martin Scorsese's *Taxi Driver* (1976). Thus, for all its melodrama and flatness of characterization, "The Long Shot" represents a significant contribution to the twentieth-century literature of the soldier's return and may be profitably read alongside, among others, Ernest Hemingway's "Soldier's Home" (1925), J. D. Salinger's "A Perfect Day for Bananafish" (1948), and Bobbie Ann Mason's *In Country* (1985).

⁓

Points of Honor closes with a narrative that might seem, at first sight, out of keeping with the rest of the collection: "Semper Fidelis" focuses on a real individual, Marine Sergeant Major and Medal of Honor recipient John H. Quirk, whose heroic actions in the Spanish-American War and World War I are matters of historical record. There is no plot, per se, in this last of the eleven stories, just a recounting of Quirk's grace under pressure at Guantanamo Bay in 1898 (originally recorded by Stephen Crane in his posthumously published book *Wounds in the Rain* [1900]) and at Belleau Wood in 1918. Boyd ends the narrative with the explicit assertion that through his unflinching performance of his duties in both situations the sergeant major realized the highest ideal of the Marine Corps: semper fidelis, always faithful. Here, at least, the author's merciless irony makes no appearance.

Boyd's other stories do not lack isolated points of honor—real honor —or fidelity, which somehow survive in the midst of pettiness and hateful conflict among fellow Americans. One thinks of Andrus, who rescues a man he despises because his conscience will not allow him to do otherwise, and Captain Osborne, who goes to his death focused on the job at hand, indifferent to the trappings of military glory that ironically mean so much to his cowardly colleague Johnson. Ultimately, however, what one takes away from this haunting collection is Boyd's vision of war as an engine of *unfaithfulness*: unfaithfulness between officers and their subordinates, between men and women, and—worst of all—between a nation and the soldiers it sends off to be broken in body or mind and then forgotten. Thomas Alexander Boyd may well remain a "lost author of the Lost Generation," but not deservedly so. In *Points of Honor* he created a work of sustained irony and overwhelming sadness, a worthy companion to *Through the Wheat*.

Steven Trout

Notes

1. Brian Bruce, *Thomas Boyd: Lost Author of the "Lost Generation"* (Ohio: University of Akron Press, 2006), 79.

2. "Episodes of War," review of *Points of Honor,* by Thomas Boyd, in *New York Times Book Review*, March 22, 1925, 9, 14.

3. Review of *Points of Honor,* by Thomas Boyd, *Nation*, August 20, 1925, 194.

4. Harrison Smith, review of *Points of Honor*, by Thomas Boyd, *New York Herald Tribune*, April 26, 1925, 11.

5. Review of *Points of Honor*, by Thomas Boyd, *The Saturday Review of Literature*, May 16, 1925, 764.

6. Ibid., 143–44.

7. Bruce, 7.

8. Ibid., 12.

9. Edwin Howard Simmons, introduction to *Through the Wheat*, by Thomas Boyd (Lincoln: University of Nebraska Press, 2000), vii.

10. George B. Clark, *Devil Dog Chronicles: Voices of the 4th Marine Brigade* (Lawrence: University of Kansas Press, 2013), 156.

11. Bruce, 17.

12. Clark, 10.

13. Bruce, 24.

14. Ibid., 35, 36.

15. Bruce, 41.
16. Ibid., 58.
17. Ibid., 74.
18. Review, *Nation*, 194.
19. Bruce, 79.
20. Ibid., 82, 83.
21. Review, *Nation*, 194.
22. Bruce, 140.

POINTS OF HONOR

BY

THOMAS BOYD

**AUTHOR OF
THROUGH THE WHEAT**

❧

CHARLES SCRIBNER'S SONS
NEW YORK · LONDON
1925

Foreword

These stories, perhaps the last upon the war that I shall publish, were written in an effort toward completion of one scene of the late war—the scene of which "Through the Wheat" served as groundwork. Now obviously the heart of war is to be found in actual combat, and as such it is more monstrous than any other phase of hostile activity. It is so immense, so engrossing, that an attempted portrayal of it must transcend the usual aims of the novelist. It cannot be only a matter of a person's facing a new and outrageous environment, nor the inter-play of characters one upon another; to the contrary it must be the hot, contagious breath of war which is personified and shown.

This, then, is what was attempted in "Through the Wheat," and the material of the narrative, chosen from experience near Verdun, at Belleau Wood, Soissons, Saint Mihiel, and Blanc Mont, was selected for a definite tincture and was made into a series of ascending episodes which characterized war rather than humanity. Battle, instead of civilization, provided the material.

Therefore a mass of more human happenings remained unused; it is the purpose of this volume to present them. And incidentally these stories may serve to correct the impression that I, as an author, hate war. That would not be my business. But it is my business not to glorify it; it is my business to perceive it truthfully and to set down these perceptions in such a way that they may be shared by whoever is kind enough to read them. Hate war! Hate the ambitious who cause the wars and the financiers who grow fat on them. Hate the people who believe sleek lies. If we must hate than let us hate causes; it is futile to hate effects.

If I hated war no doubt I should lie about it, thereby saving myself a good deal of sweat, labor, and anxiety occasioned by the endeavor to be honest.

These stories are not inventions. (For of heroes I knew many: Dan Daly, Macon Overton, W. F. Kahl, Gerald C. Thomas, Edward R. Stone, Berton W. Sibley, Fred Morf, Gunner Burns, John A. Hughes, Jeremiah Dalton, William Winter Dean, Earl Ryan . . . and of cowards not a few.) Neither are they—except in the case of "Semper Fidelis"— factual transcriptions, but rather tales of human deeds and emotions which were acted and felt either in the heart of war or beneath its long and lasting shadow.

Thomas Boyd, 1925

I

Unadorned

After they had returned from one of those practice manœuvres which had kept them standing in mud, viscous as court-plaster, for hours through the cold, black, soundless night; chilled and with that flat, dusty taste in their mouths which comes with early morning, it was not unusual for them to seek some one on whom to vent the ill feeling which their long, seemingly senseless vigil had awakened in them. In the course of which they would work in both directions from the middle. Beginning with the major, they would ascend the scale until they reached the commanding officer of the entire expeditionary force, or else they would tacitly absolve those only-heard-of deities and seek others closer to themselves.

The major, in some miraculous way, had captured their admiration, and it was only in the last extremity that anything was ever said against him. But the captain was protected by no such laudable sentiment, and, except for the men in the leading squads of the first platoon near whom the captain marched, the entire company grumblingly and mumblingly accused him of being everything from a shrewd, sharp German spy to a gibbering idiot. The words of criticism from the men would blend into a tuneless drone as they marched along the hard, gray side-road; and after a while the captain would grow tired of the noise and have the word passed back that there was to be no more talking on the march. This command, restraining only the more timorous, would leave the dissension to be carried on by the chronic grumblers. Oddly enough, the captain's command for silence would cause the men to seek a new object for their unkind remarks, finding it usually in the person of their platoon commander. If he had any regard for their health, if he wanted them to live long enough to get caught up to the front, which, after all, was what they came over to this damned country for, he would have got them out of this fool manœuvre. But he didn't care; he was just like the rest of these mail-order lieutenants; all he cared for was that Sam Browne belt, which he was so proud of that he wore it even when he went to bed at night, and that brass bar on his shoulder. Every blessed one of his men could die for all it mattered to him!

But the men of the fourth platoon would continue to grumble against the captain. For one reason, the fourth platoon was farthest away from the captain, and for another, they had nobody else to grumble about except the sergeants—and the sergeants were near enough to recognize the separate voices of the men.

The lieutenant in charge of the fourth platoon was Wilfred Bird, a well-formed, graceful young man with a soft brown mustache, contemplative, hazel eyes, and features more fine than manly, as that word is currently used. And the possession of such a likeness among a group of soldiers almost demanded that their owner have also a manner either of martinet or roué, so that by that sign the men would recognize him as practically one of themselves. But Wilfred Bird had no manner other than that with which he was born. And that was even more abundantly given him than one might think from his features. He was low-voiced and courteous; he treated each person as his equal, for that was the only way he knew how to treat him. He seriously and patiently listened to the complaints of the corporals and the privates; he was the solitary member of the younger officers who was fully at ease with his superiors—the colonel, say, or even the brigade commander.

From all of which it might be expected that he was held in contempt by the soldiers under him; he did not bluster, or force them to mean and unnecessary tasks to show his authority, and if he ever got drunk—as our sour-faced company commander got drunk—or visited brothels with the usual Saturday-night expedition, nobody ever knew about it. The strange part of it was, the bulk of his command respected him, and even the men in the other platoons, when they were discussing the comparative merits of the officers of the company, would say that So and So was this, and another lieutenant was that, but Wilfred Bird was a gentleman.

The word sounded unfamiliarly from their lips. It seemed, to a listener, as if the men ought not to have used that word. But one realized it to be the outcome of their regard for a man who was so unusual, so really fine.

And so, during those long wintry weeks in northern France when the men were training, hardening themselves for the front line, to which they were soon to go, Wilfred Bird marched doggedly along at the head of his platoon beside his right guide. The mud clung as disagreeably to his shoes as to the shoes of the enlisted men, the endless infuriating nights when the men stood motionless in some fake firing bay seemed as foolish and as unendurable to him as they did to the others, yet he remained silent, his closest approach to rebellion being a slightly worried expression in his hazel eyes. He had, however, no objection to make when his men began to curse, to say scandalous things against their officers for which the speakers could easily have been given courts-martial. This talk, this grumbling was, as Wilfred Bird had the sense to tell himself, a healthy reaction from the rigors of their training; it showed, unless it became excessive and hateful, that the men were lusty and in good spirits, that there would be gusto in their attack when they went to the front. Further, he enjoyed it for a more personal reason: keen, satiric phrases sprang out of uncouth mouths, delighting him with their unexpectedness, their original value. And then, talking occupied the men's minds, making them momentarily forgetful of the arduousness of the march.

It was only when the men began to wrangle among themselves that Wilfred Bird grew irritated. When one man would repeatedly step on the heels of the man in front of him, an uproar ensuing, the lieutenant would leave his place at the head of the division of the column and search for the trouble. When he found it he would say in a sort of a scolding fashion:

"Now you men be still; it's very dark—if the man behind you treads on your heels, O'Brien, ask your corporal to permit you to march in front of some one else."

"But, Je's, lieutenant," the usually belligerent O'Brien would begin. The lieutenant would hear him out, and offer a thoughtful suggestion.

When the battalion was back in its thin papier-mâché billets, supposedly resting, the men were required to be more careful in their appearance. They must shave daily, their heavy hobnailed shoes had to be kept free of mud, the buttons of their olive tunics must show through the proper buttonholes, their hair had to bear evidence of a recent combing, and their ordinary equipment, their bayonets, knives, forks, spoons, and aluminum mess-kits, must be kept clean and bright.

To insure themselves against the wrath of one of the inspecting officers (they had a way of visiting camps unexpectedly), some of the platoon commanders began to deliver long lectures to their men upon the observance of cleanliness. They threatened, and not ambiguously; and, to lessen the danger of having frowsy soldiers, they ordered the company barber to shave the heads of the enlisted men.

Wilfred Bird gave slight notice to all of this. He never stood before his tired platoon and addressed them upon the importance of cleanliness, nor said that cleanliness was next to godliness so for God's sake keep clean; he did not continue to impress upon the men the necessity of appearing spick-and-span before an inspector. Nor did he neglect them; simply, he made no mountain of the need for neatness. It was, he felt, something which people *were*, without any outside influence. Nevertheless, the fourth platoon was neat; whether it was because their commander was an eloquent example of carefulness in dress, or whether the men would rather shine their shoes and oil their rifles than hurt his feelings, does not matter.

One day, a little past noon, a few moments after the men had returned from a morning on the target range and had been dismissed in the company street, a frightened sentry on post No. 1 in front of the guard-house was heard to call out:

"Turn out the gyard. General officer."

And the corporal in charge of the watch kicked his heel against the side of the guard-house, and in a second, the door burst open and the whole watch rushed out, making formation in front of the building, before which a large, puffy man with silver stars on his shoulder-straps accepted the salute.

Then the streets, on each side of which the flimsy, sprawling bunk-houses were set, became suddenly energized. Orderlies could be seen running from their billets to the officers' quarters, and rushing back. Sergeants stood at the entrances and bellowed for the men to "shake it up," for the visiting major-general was on a sightseeing tour and he meant to inspect the battalion.

Rifle-butts pounded on the gravel and men hastened to the command of "Fall in," buttoning their clothing on the way and making hasty estimates of their appearance. They counted off, right-dressed, and as soon as the drawling, cautioning "steady" and the short, sharp "front" were given they stood with their chests out and their abdomens drawn inconspicuously under their diaphragms, nervously fingering the stocks of their rifles, their eyes looking straight to the front.

After a while the major-general reached the company to which Bird's fourth platoon belonged. He passed along the first platoon, the tall men; the second platoon and the third platoon, of medium-sized men; then the fourth platoon, the short men, opened ranks.

The divisional commander, with his formal retinue and the company commander, passed by. He looked stern, military, disapproving.

For once, Wilfred Bird, standing by his right guide at the end of his platoon, felt nervous, quaky, the sensation growing as the divisional commander stopped before him and looked down the side of his fierce nose.

"Lieutenant," said the major-general, "you have the most soldierly-looking platoon in the regiment."

Wilfred Bird, standing motionless, continued to look straight ahead, feeling his face color salmon to his ears.

For once his poise deserted him, even his military training threatening to go with it, for his lips moved as if to blurt out some acknowledgment of the general's commendation.

That evening at dinner, in the officers' mess, Captain Madison rose ponderously from the head of the table—he was the ranking captain and the major was not there—and with the palms of his heavy hands flat on the cloth, speaker-wise, he made a short speech in which he proposed a toast to Lieutenant Bird for saving the reputation of the company. Even the officers from the other companies joined, and Bird found himself on his feet, half stammering his gratitude.

"They're really awfully nice boys. I'm very fond of them; and of course it is they that deserve whatever credit there is to be given," he ended.

But whether the men deserved the credit or not, there remained for days about Wilfred Bird the sensation of those words, as if they were still in the air that he breathed, as a kind of elixir. And it led him to talk about his platoon; to consider the men as a very important unit composed of his special charges and not merely as so many heads, as he had considered them theretofore. It also caused him to adopt a new attitude toward the men. He would remind them that it was an unusual occurrence for a divisional commander to pick out their platoon from an entire regiment. But that which the men had done by chance must now be continued through effort. They had a reputation to maintain. So he began the inculcation of pride in them, and his attitude toward them was that of a jealous father toward his children. They were such nice boys; he had not noticed it before, really.

In the main the men accepted the change of disposition well enough. They too felt it to be a point of pride that they continued to be the neatest unit in the regiment, perhaps in the division. The eyes of the corporals grew sharper as they inspected the members of their respective squads before formation; and the privates took more care with their equipment, often spending moments of their leisure hours in cleaning the bores of their rifles, or scrubbing their underclothes and socks on the long wooden plank which rested on two small kegs at the side of the bunk-house.

But to loud-mouthed John Wainwright, who had always felt himself to be inferior to his lieutenant and who for that reason always thought Wilfred Bird was being patronizing, this sudden competitive desire on the part of the platoon commander was used as material for disparagement. He came from the lower Middle West, and the last thing he would put up with, he often said, was for one guy to think he was better than another. "Just because Bird is a shave-tail is no reason why he should go around like some damned English duke," Wainwright grumbled. "Who did he think he was, anyway? Telling people a damned sight better than him what to do! And so far as what the major-general had said went, it was the platoon that deserved the glory and not the commander. What had Bird ever done for the platoon, anyhow, besides act as if he wasn't made out of mud the same as all the rest of them was?"

John Wainwright had read the Bible; he knew that all men were made out of clay, and he also knew the proof positive that man and monkey had nothing in common.

But Wilfred Bird continued through the days of training oblivious of this disturbing element. He was very fond of his platoon, and it never occurred to him that they might not be as fond of him—which, as a matter of fact, they were with the exception of John Wainwright.

Wainwright talked very much and very loudly, and it seemed that from reveille until taps he was forever telling whomever he could find to listen to him about his exploits "out where he came from." His boisterous, callous manner and his boastful tales were engaging to some of the men, and others listened because they could not help it.

During the long winter, when the men were intensively training, they would spend their evenings in the bunk-house at cards or talking, and when Wainwright, now and again, would begin to speak against Wilfred Bird, his listeners would say: "Oh, shut up John. You'd kick if somebody give you a new rope to hang yourself with," or "Let him rest, he's a whole lot better than you are." But those mild checks never discouraged him. Wainwright's skin was too thick ever to be penetrated by jeers, unless they held an undertone of violence to himself. And then, of course, in his blustering way he would challenge his adversary to a fight, a fight which, for some reason, never came off.

With the fall of the last snow of the season the regiment finished its training, and the word began to be rumored about that the men were next to go to the front, their natural and hoped-for destination.

Wilfred Bird took it calmly, and simply. It was the thing which he had come to France to do, and a great feeling of relief came to him, now that he knew his regiment was headed in that direction. Not that he was without fear, for he was not. The front was as much the great unknown to him as it was to any other man who had never been there. He knew that he would very likely either be wounded or killed, that if he were neither he would spend the rest of his days until the war was over going from one front to another, cold, dirty, and hungry. He was healthy enough to want an occasional bath, and so he did not look toward the front as a larking-place.

With this awakened interest in his men, he felt it to be in the line of his duty that he discover the height or depth of their morale. If the men, as they sometimes phrased it, were "rarin' to go," he would be pleased; if they were in the doldrums over the thought of going to the front he wanted to bolster up their courage. To the casual eye they were anxious for the opportunity to meet the Germans, to plunge themselves into the midst of the great experience; but he knew that one could not always tell by outward appearance. One was likely to be deceived. It was the proper act for a soldier to tell his officer that he was glad he was going to the front. But to get the truth one had to find out whether he inwardly trembled as he made the assertion.

Most of the officers felt the pulse of their men through their orderlies; but Wilfred Bird's orderly, unluckily enough, was very shy and quiet, too embarrassed before his officer ever to speak unless it were necessary. Bird himself was not the sort of person ever to ask his orderly for information, and as he felt that he must find out, he chose, or rather was forced to accept, the means which was most direct.

After dinner, when it had grown heavily dark, Wilfred Bird would leave the officers' quarters and commence to walk slowly and quietly around the outside of the bunk-house in which the men of his command were telling stories or, seated around the rough board table by the candle-light with their blouses off, were playing cards or listening to Old King Cole sadly and a trifle reminiscently pick the strings of his big mellow guitar. From the bits of talk which he overheard in his secretive journey he hoped to discover what they were thinking of, how they really accepted the fact that they were soon to go to the front. And then, perhaps, he would enter the back door of the bunk-house and talk to one of the sergeants for a while; more often he would return to his own billet, a trifle ashamed that even so praiseworthy a purpose should force him to snoop, without letting the men know he had been near to them.

One evening—it was about the fifth time he had made his pilgrimage of the night, and he never did it afterward—he was walking slowly around the bunk-house, carelessly gazing through the slits in the wall where the mica windows had not been properly fitted, when he heard the loud voice of John Wainwright. He stopped and leaned forward with every nerve awake.

John Wainwright was saying:

"Course, I, myself, don't mind a-goin' up to the front. I can take care of myself with them Dutchmen, but I hate to go up with this Bird. He ain't no guy to take a bunch of soldiers up to the front. Why, do you know what he is? He's nothin' but a sissy, a lah-de-dah. . . . I'll bet you that when we git up there where the big ones is bustin', you'll have to hold him to keep him from runnin'. Yes sir, hold him!"

Wilfred Bird, standing outside the bunk-house, listened for no more. So that's what they thought of him, the dirty cads! Nothing of this kind had ever happened to him before; he had always felt the men liked him; and now it was made evident that, far from liking him, they thought he was a coward! He could hardly realize it; it seemed to stun him and when he did accept the fact that he had really heard those words, it left in his mind no doubt that the entire platoon was in agreement with the speaker. So this was the sort of men he had under him! Walking away, back to his room, he had the impulse to ask the major if he could be transferred to some other company. He really couldn't put up with these men, couldn't stand to see them. But after a while he decided it would be cowardly to leave the platoon. No, by heavens, he would stay and show the disagreeable little wretches!

From that time on, Wilfred Bird's courteous manner toward his platoon was a thing which existed only in remembrance—and then, in the remembrance of but a very few. For his brusque, uncommunicative attitude, ever regardless of the comforts of the men, drove away all of their other conceptions of him, so that he lived in their minds as an especially tyrannous shave-tail.

The Germans were engaged in their spring drive with continued good fortune, with the result that the regiment—the whole division, in fact—which had planned to go into the line near the Somme, suddenly found itself reeling and straggling in the direction of another sector. And in the hurry, the confusion, the excitement of the breathtaking rush to the front Wilfred Bird forgot what his men had said of him, forgot everything but the blind march forward.

But on the second day, when his platoon was dug in on the crest of a hill several hundreds of yards away from the forest in which the Germans were, and when the time was approaching for the counterattack to begin, Wilfred Bird remembered. Somewhere, along the long line of tense, fearful men a whistle sounded for the attack. Wilfred Bird was the first to rise, and with an overhead, circular movement forward of his long arm, a motion employed in practice skirmish, he beckoned his men to follow.

The woods were so dense they seemed to be a solid black. From them commenced a bitter, hateful pour of bullets which grew more hateful and full of venom as the men approached. The method of attack which the platoon had been instructed to use was one of sudden spurts and stops. The non-commissioned officers were supposed to locate the machine-gun nests—it was these which most imperiled the advance of the platoon—and under a barrage of rifle grenades a squad was to advance until it had reached a place from which it could hurl hand-bombs at the German gunners.

In theory, the plan was all that could be wished for. The only trouble with it was that the woods were thick with machine-gun nests, and as they were set in enfilade positions, another and unseen gun could annihilate a squad while it was attempting to creep up on the nest which it had discovered.

Still in front of his men, Lieutenant Bird continued toward the woods, biting into the leather strap of his steel helmet to keep from flinching as the bullets passed, but with his shoulders as squared as if he had been on dress parade. One bullet passed so close to him that the string which fastened his wrapped puttee was severed, the green cloth of the puttee beginning to unwind, gathering in a mass about his shoe and exposing the lacing of his breeches. But he kept on going forward, now and again glancing to his right or left to see that none of his platoon reached the woods before he did.

All along the line the attack was successful. Though the regiment had just gone in to war and were not to be compared with seasoned troops, they made up for their lack of experience by their stamina, their sheer foolhardiness.

The ranks of the fourth platoon were very sparse even when they were yet fifty yards from the edge of the woods, but Wilfred Bird, still unhurt, was among those who remained on their feet.

About twenty yards from the first dark fringe he hastily stopped, took a step backward, and fell with his heels pointing toward the woods, the goal which he had planned to be the first to reach.

His mind was very clear when he began to crawl back, and as he felt his leg, sensationless as a log, and saw the rusty stain soaking through his breeches, he knew that continued effort might mean his death from loss of blood. With his eye he measured the distance between himself and a little friendly mound of earth behind which he planned to get so that he would be shielded from the bullets. But the distance seemed too great, and, folding his hands before him, he dropped his head and waited.

Toward nightfall he was lying on a stretcher in one of those jerky little Ford ambulances, having been hastily taken from an evacuation hospital, which was already overcrowded when he arrived, to a base hospital of the Red Cross in Paris. Faint from loss of blood and nauseated from the inoculation of antitetanin, he lay on the lower tier of the ambulance, tearing at his hands to keep from crying out in pain every time the spindly wheels of the car struck a bump in the shell-torn road. The wheels of the little car seemed as if they would never stop turning, and he had the irrational fear that he might become a victim of gangrene before he reached his destination,—that and the panicky thought that the tourniquet on his leg was not efficiently fastened made his ride a delirium.

He did not remember reaching the hospital late that night, nor being carefully bathed and put in one of the high white beds in the ward on the first floor. And in the morning he was only vaguely conscious of the sunny warmth of the room, the whitewashed walls, the pleasant nurses who kept walking past the door.

Several days later a thin, irritable doctor, who had been used to taking his time with the patients he had as a practicing civilian surgeon and was now worried into illness by the hosts of wounded of whom it was his duty to take care, was standing over Wilfred Bird's bed examining the dressing on the torn leg which the turned-back covering exposed to him.

Bird regarded him questioningly for some time, and as he didn't speak he inquired in his soft voice, into which he tried to put a note of cheerfulness:

"Anything broken, doctor?"

"Broken?" answered the doctor sarcastically. "You'd know if anything was broken, all right. Just a plain flesh wound."

After which there was nothing for Bird but silence. He would have liked to ask how long he would probably remain in the hospital, but he realized that instead of bothering the doctor he should really be ashamed for having troubled the hospital with a flesh wound. You really should have a bone broken, or an eye put out, or a bullet through the skull before you went back of the lines to the hospital, he decided in mild amusement.

But it was not so amusing when he recalled that his platoon was up at the front and he was back in a hospital, lying in safety, warm, and fed as well as his condition would permit. He commenced to search his mind, to analyze his feelings when he had started to crawl back from the front. He could not decide whether he had been afraid; he did know that, possibly, he could have gone on until he reached the woods unless he had been struck again. The bullet had knocked him down, but he had not really felt pain until he began to see the blood showing through his breeches. It was a fine question: If he had not looked down at the blood might he not have been able to go on, leading his men, his men who had spoken of him as a coward? That he could not answer, with a final and sweeping No, hurt him and caused him to wonder whether there was not some truth in what his men had said about him. But he could not hold that opinion for long. He was not a coward, he fiercely told himself, and he would prove it to them!

The days of June passed by while he lay in his narrow bed. Once in a while some man from his regiment would come back to the hospital, and Wilfred Bird would hobble over to him and ask him questions about the platoon: what they were doing, if they were still where they were when he left them for the hospital. He grew restless as he listened to tales of hardship and heroism at the front. They were doing such splendid things, the reports came back, and so many of the men had been decorated. "Did Bird remember So-and-So?" one of the wounded who had recently returned would ask. "Well, he got his," the informant would continue, "trying to take a machine-gun nest single-handed." And then he heard that the regiment had been removed from the front lines for a short rest.

One morning, Wilfred Bird woke up with a fever. The nurse informed the doctor, and Bird was ordered to remain in his room without permission to see any visitors. He accepted this command as long as he could, but that was for not many days, because of his anxiety over the movements of his men. Would he get well, he wondered, before the regiment was ordered back to the front? Great heavens, he had to. He began to plead that they stay back of the lines until he could rejoin them. Just a few days more, he thought, and his wound would be all right. This worry that his men might be in the next attack without him drove him, whenever the nurse was absent, out into the main ward trying to discover if any of the new arrivals were from his regiment.

But the information of the movement of his troops was to be given him from another source. During the dressing of his wound, one morning, the doctor paused and said, by way of making talk:

"I hear your outfit's going back up to the front in about three days. You're lucky to be in the hospital."

Wilfred Bird said nothing; he just looked at the doctor dumbly, a trifle hurt. And after the doctor left he began to look around for his clothing, to get it together so that he would be able to put his hands on everything which he had brought to the hospital with him. All that day he remained quietly in bed, seeking in his thoughts the best means of leaving Paris and joining his regiment. In the morning he asked the nurse to make the bandage on his leg especially secure.

Late that evening he limped out of the hospital, fully dressed, and supporting himself by a stout walking stick which he had picked up. Paris had darkened herself against the air raids, and it was confusing to be walking in the strange streets, weakly lighted by a moon which was climbing over the ragged edge of the buildings. A cab was coming. With many flourishes of his stick he caught the scurrying driver's attention barely in time to keep from being run down. "To Saint Denis," he directed the chauffeur, telling himself that among all of the machines at that supply base of the American army he was certain to find one which would be going near Soissons, where his regiment was soon to go into action.

When he arrived at Saint Denis, perhaps an hour later, an M.P. told him that no American automobiles were to start for some time but that there were several French camions which were to take supplies to Mangin's army—the army to which his regiment had been assigned.

"They say it's gonna be the big smash of the year," said the lanky M.P., "but I ain't hankerin' to be in it, sir." Bird dismissed him irritably, walking lamely to the French section.

As he explained to the driver of one of the camions that he wished to ride with him to the front to be in the attack, the driver gave his shoulders the inimitable Gallic shrug, which said: "Of course, it is beyond my comprehension why a man who can hardly walk should wish to return to the front; but if you are so mad, jump in."

He climbed into the car beside the Frenchman. The motor commenced its angry chugging and the trip began. Through the night Bird sat rigidly in the front seat, both hands clasped over the crook of his stick. The camions passed along the smooth white country roads, rumbled through the towns, as Bird sat there thinking of the morning, wondering whether he would arrive in time to go over with his regiment. Already his mind saw the men advancing toward the enemy, their bayonets slanting skyward, and he smiled proudly as he saw himself abreast of them. They would never think him a coward again, he thought hotly. The sky was growing lighter as the camions left the outskirts of the Châlons sur Marne, and from off ahead came the ominous rumble of exploding shells.

Now it was daylight, and from the seat on the camion Bird could see the huge, camouflaged ammunition dumps at intervals along the road, covered by a mottled green and yellow. At one place, a battalion of men were resting on the grass beside the road, their rifles and combat packs sprawling about them. Farther on, a battery of long, black-snouted six-inch guns, poking their noses toward the German lines, were unlimbered close to the roadside; and beside them the sweating artillerymen were leading off the horses and arranging the shells. A short distance ahead the seventy-fives had gone into position. That a first-aid station had just been established was evident from the fresh red-cross sign tacked conspicuously to a tree. Yes, Bird decided, they were getting near the front and he would be in time.

Farther on he saw a cross-road, and as the camion neared it a shell hurtled over and struck squarely where the two roads met. Warily the driver slowed up the car. Bird grasped the man's arm, calling: "Non! Non! Vite!" The driver pressed harder on the accelerator and the camion spurted ahead. Another shell struck close to the place where the first shell had exploded. But Bird did not seem to mind the shells which were bursting in front of him. He was like a man in a dream, living solely in the picture of himself in the first wave of the attack, at the head of his men, limping along toward the German lines.

Now they were almost at the crossroads. From somewhere along the farther fringe of the enemy lines a long-distance gun emitted a huge black shell which speared its way through the quiet air. It struck and exploded; an immense cloud of black smoke spread above the blue camion on whose shattered floor lay Wilfred Bird.

II

The Kentucky Boy

The letters S O S, so grouped, have a multitude of meanings. Coming from a ship at sea they are a signal of distress and a plea for help; used in common speech they apply to subjects which have become distasteful through repetition. But to John Goodwin those letters described the hellish invention of some especially adept fiend.

Draw a wavering line from Verdun through Château-Thierry, and in the area south of that line, from Toul to Marseilles, you will have Goodwin's S O S. It was a maze of training camps where men were taught to load a rifle; warehouses of food, clothing, and ammunition; general and sectional headquarters; military police; and hospitals—the service of supplies. And all of it filled Goodwin with a sharp disgust.

He would have said, as he lay in one of a row of white iron beds and glared at the swarthy hospital apprentice who was trying to bluster a wounded man into taking hold of a broom, that he had always hated the S O S, hated it instinctively from the moment he had heard of it. But this would not have been true. There had been a time, from March to June, when the service of supplies seemed a desirable place to be. Unexplored, it was greatly preferable to standing in a muddy trench four hours out of every eight, sleeping in a watery dugout, and eating corned beef and canned tomatoes. It had made Goodwin anxious for a minor wound which would take him to a bed with sheets and dry blankets, where his food would be cooked and served on a plate, and toward the middle of June, as he crouched in a shell hole, to the left of Vaux, his desire was fulfilled by the German artillery. One moment he heard a softly whirring noise, an explosion, and then through a cloud of thick, pungent gas he had rolled from his shelter, choking and gasping.

There was this to be admitted in favor of the S O S: at the evacuation hospital Goodwin had been given a bath and a clean suit of pajamas. And on the hospital train the Red Cross had given him a bar of chocolate. Other than that, nothing was to its credit. He had been made to stand in line for his food, his unlaced shoes sinking in the mud, a blanket thrown over his shoulders. He was told to make his own bed. The hospital attendants were bullies and thieves, the nurses were inattentive to the privates, and the doctors couldn't have been less slip-shod in their treatment of the patients.

"All right, soldier. Snap out of it. Almost time for inspection."

Goodwin looked up, prepared to scowl, to curse, if necessary. But it was Hawthorne, so he asked with interest: "Got a cigarette?"

"Sure, I got a carton but what good does that do? Yuh can't smoke in here." Hawthorne thrust his big brown hand in his jacket pocket and exhibited a package of cigarettes.

"Lord," Goodwin sighed. "But I wish I had my clothes."

"Git 'em," said Hawthorne with succinctness. "Git 'em."

Goodwin sat up, interested. "'y gosh, I believe I will."

"Go ahead," encouraged Hawthorne. "An' we'll beat it outa here."

"Gosh—"

"Attention!" The hospital apprentice in charge of the ward shouted warning of the inspector's approach. A row of heads on either side of the room looked sharply toward the door; the patients in uniform stood stiffly by the foot of their beds, nervously smoothing out the wrinkles in the counterpane, and the medical officer, with a nurse and a sergeant following his bulbous hips, marched sternly into the room.

Goodwin, lying with his feet together and his hands flat at his sides, wondered whether Hawthorne would go, or whether he had only spoken lightly. A trip alone through the network of the S O S, with its military police and its railroad-transportation officers, would be disagreeable, but with Hawthorne to accompany him he could have "a hell of a lot of fun." And Hawthorne, even from the little he knew of him, was not the sort of person to say what he didn't mean. The inspecting doctor was approaching and he had to decide quickly.

"Sir, can I get my clothes?" He tried to work his features into an expression of health, eagerness, of a burning desire to fight in a holy cause.

The hips wedged in between the two beds, wedged out again, and from the wide aisle the sergeant wrote out a requisition and handed it to Goodwin, leaving him to wait, restlessly, until the undignified formality was finished for the day.

"Carry on," called the hospital apprentice as the inspecting officer left the ward. The bodies relaxed, turning to one another to rid themselves of pent-up speech. Hawthorne approached, pushing his unloved overseas cap to one side of his bed.

"D'ja git it?"

Goodwin showed him the slip of paper.

"Come on, then. We'll see what we kin talk outa the quartermaster. You wanta take everything you can lay your hands on."

"Do you mean it, sure enough to go back to the outfit?"

"Mean it? Hell, yes, soldier. Jist watch me." And with this assurance they walked out of the ward to the commissary, indistinguishable from the other buildings in its sallow complexion, its tarred roof, its eight little windows cut in the side, and the setting of drab mud where neither trees nor grass could be seen. Only officers, nurses, and important-looking non-coms of the medical corps strolled in twos and threes, planning dances at the hideous Y.M.C.A. or reminiscing over reckless supper-parties in the near-by town.

Inside the quartermaster building a bespectacled youth and a red-faced corporal stood behind a rough plank counter on which were articles of clothing. Goodwin handed the paper to the corporal, who passed it to the youth with spectacles.

"Size blouse ya wear?" asked the corporal.

Goodwin knew; he wasn't to be tricked into accepting ill-fitting garments. "Blouse, thirty-eight; underclothes, thirty-six; hat, seven and a quarter—"

"Matter a damn about that, buddy. I asked ya what size blouse you wore."

"I wouldn't let him call *me* buddy," Hawthorne seriously advised Goodwin. "I'd tell 'im the story of the apple and the—"

"Hey, let them pants alone," admonished the youth to Hawthorne, who was examining the stack of breeches on the counter. But Hawthorne imperturbably continued: "Git a good pair while you're at it, soldier. Here—" He drew a pair of whip-cord breeches from the pile and handed them to Goodwin. "Regular officer's britches, and they're jist your size. Now we'll pick out a blouse."

Half an hour later the pair walked out of the building, enjoying the luxury of cigarettes.

"How do I look?" asked Goodwin.

"Well, the hat's ridin' a little high an' the britches look like they was full of bricks, but the coat an' leggin's fit you fine." Hawthorne regarded him closely. "Pull up the britches and tear the band outa your hat an' you'll look like a Jigadier Brindle."

Goodwin unbuttoned his new blouse and pulled at his breeches until there was an unbroken line between the end of his spiral puttees and his hips. "Guess I'll throw away that raincoat," he said, tearing out his hatband.

Hawthorne took the rain-coat from him, drawing off in an attitude of surprise. "Soldier, you hurt me when you talk thataway. Why, that there raincoat's good for forty francs any place in this country."

"You mean sell it?" asked Goodwin.

"Sell it? Not if we seen some pore ol' woman with ten orphans standin' out in the rain without anything to eat an' no place to go. No, we'd give it away then. But if we don't see this ol' woman, the forty francs is ourn."

Godwin chuckled, "An' this extra pair of shoes ought to bring fifty."

Before the thought of their departure, its risks, the danger of arrest, the highkeying sensation of travelling alone through foreign countries, outwitting M.P.'s and officers, and the prospect of arriving again among their own, everything else dissolved in a mist. On other days the meals were grumbled over, but today the dinner's bad qualities, the lumps of tomato, the uncooked pieces of beef, were unnoticed. And in high excitement, they dipped their mess-kits in the lukewarm water, dried them on a borrowed towel, and marched busily to the extreme end of the camp, vaulted a wall, and were on the highroad, bursting with deviltry and joy.

This highroad would have conquered less robust spirits. For miles ahead of them and behind it ran a straight course. The mud was an inch thick, and very slushy; under their feet and out on the brown stubble of grass, large chunks of it had been thrown by the wheels of passing cars. In rear of them, Goodwin heard the chug of a heavy motor, and he looked in vain for a spot on which he might stand and be safe from the mud. The truck came on.

"Wait," said Hawthorne. "Let's ask 'em for a ride. Look and see if there's an officer in the front seat." There was none, nothing but red cords; and both men signaled wildly. The truck slowed down, and they climbed over the end gate and were hauled abroad.

"Hello, Artillery." Hawthorne's voice was neither high or deep. It was rather a voice, medium to begin with, which had acquired terrible clarity through sounding over long fields and wide valleys. "How far ye goin'?"

"Le Mans," said the sergeant in charge.

"Where's that at, Artillery? On the way to Paris?"

"It's on the way, as you might say," answered Artillery. "You can take a train from there."

"That's the place we'll go; huh, Goodwin?"

They settled down in the end of the bumping, careening truck, smoking cigarettes until they could hold the shortened stubs no longer, and staring restively at the flat, damp ground on either side of the road. A few miles ahead, Le Mans was already to be seen, the buildings gray in the afternoon light. It had the appearance of great size, and Goodwin wondered if the entrances were patrolled by military police, who, no doubt, would arrest them when they were discovered to be without travelling orders. But they could do nothing but chance it now.

The truck rolled over the pavement of the city, past the steep-roofed houses, and stopped at the beginning of a row of small shops. "Far as we go," said Artillery.

"Much obliged," said Hawthorne. They climbed down from the truck and walked along the street. To the right and left and on the main thoroughfare Le Mans was filled with American soldiers who lounged in doorways, swaggered along the sidewalk, explored narrow streets, overflowed the bakeries and cafés, until it seemed unlikely that room could be found for two more.

"This is no place for us," said Goodwin. "Let's find the railroad-station."

"Let's have a drink first."

"There'll be a café near the station," said Goodwin nervously. "I don't like this town myself."

They walked on, unnoticed in the throng, until they saw the railroad tracks, two pairs of them on a black, cindery bed which rose above the street.

A picket fence secured the station from trespassers, but it was low and easily surmounted, Goodwin noticed with gratification. Nevertheless, it would be better to wait for evening to get a train. There were bound to be officers about the station. And the inevitable M.P.!

"There's the café," announced Hawthorne. "Now where's the drink?"

"Let's guess," said Goodwin, striding after Hawthorne's long legs, which were rapidly shortening the distance to a dilapidated brick building with musty windows.

The front room of the café was deserted, but in the rear a group of soldiers sat about a rectangular table, their blouses unfastened, their hats pushed high on their foreheads, with small glasses before them. One man, whom baldness had visited early and whose remaining hair grew about the scalp like a horseshoe, was talking with a great deal of smugness:

"Yes, and why shouldn't we be the best division in France? In the first place, we're selected men, and, in the second place, we're from New York. There's no bums among us. We didn't have to come into the army to make a livin'; we made ours in business."

Hawthorne sat listening, his drink untouched before him. He seemed very grave, as if he were intent on understanding all that was being spoken. Finally he asked, curious: "How long you been over here?"

The bald man stopped talking, smiled knowingly about the table, and answered: "Oh, about as long as you have, I guess."

"Have you ever been up to the front?" asked Hawthorne calmly.

"If we had you'd a seen our names in the paper, brother," said the bald man.

"What outfit did you say you was from?"

"New York's Own—selected division," said the man proudly. "What division are you from?"

"The First Division of Regulars," said Hawthorne.

"Oh," said the bald man superiorly. "You with them yellowbellies?"

Hawthorne got slowly to his feet, reached for the iron coffee-stand, and threw it deliberately at the bald spot. The iron weapon struck the wall, jangling harshly to the floor a moment after the bald head disappeared under the table. "Why, damn you," said Hawthorne. He started to climb over the table, but Goodwin encircled his waist and coaxed: "Come on, Hawthorne. Let the poor fool alone. Can't you see he don't know any better? He don't mean anything; he jist ain't got any sense." Goodwin breathed hard through his exertion, but his arms remained straining about Hawthorne's narrow waist.

The bald head appeared at the corner of the table nearest the door, then ran. Hawthorne lunged to free himself, to reach the door, but Goodwin held on fast as the bald head bobbed out of sight.

"Gosh," said Goodwin, "I never seen anybody git under cover as fast as that in all my life."

"Damn lucky he did or I'd a brained him."

"Damn lucky he did or you'd be in jail long after the war is over." The consequences of such an act struck a cold chill down Goodwin's spine. "Gosh!" he shivered. "That iron thing would a killed him sure." In that event he too would have had to go to jail!

Madame came in to light the lamps, frowning over her task, every one of her movements showing disapproval of what had happened. She, too, would have been affected if the coffee-stand had struck the bald man. She would have been arrested by the American officers for selling cognac and her café would have been closed.

Goodwin pushed his glass away. "Let's git outa here."

In the street the evening made outlines of houses and shadows of doorways. A bell from the railway station, somewhere over the raised ground and beyond the picket fence, struck up a warning of an approaching train. "Let's hop it," said Goodwin. He led the way up the grassy embankment, and grasping hold of the top bar climbed over the fence. There were red and green signal-lights, and men with lanterns moving about on the platform of the dimly lighted station. Then the train rushed in, throwing up a maze of ruddy sparks out of the mouth of the squat chimney. Goodwin, between the two tracks, followed the waiting line of coaches to the first-class compartments. "Hurry up," he called, unfastening the door, "We'll ride in style." It swung open and they hurried inside as the shrill little whistle made infuriated noises. The wheels turned and the train rolled out of the station.

Through a thick, concave glass inset in the roof of the compartment, the electric lights gleamed coolly on the gray covering of the seats, each with its triangular bit of lace for a headrest and separated from its neighbor by a padded arm. There were six seats in the compartment, three on each side, but Hawthorne and Goodwin were the only passengers. They sat facing each other by the window. Goodwin smoked, but Hawthorne gazed out at the hurtling scene like a shy but eager child. Colored lights on the railroad track, pin-points of gold through the darkness, clusters, fields of blinking lights in the distance, pale faces of girls outside the compartment as the train stopped for a moment, then went on. It was all very fascinating and mysterious. He grinned.

"Gosh!" Goodwin unexpectedly remarked. "Gosh, but I got a good outfit. A fine bunch. Why, we wouldn't have a guy like that skunk in the café around us for more'n two minutes."

"So've I," said Hawthorne. "There's only one fellah in the whole lot that I can't git along with."

"Who's that?" asked Goodwin.

"Our damn mess sergeant."

"Oh," said Goodwin. "That's the way with all mess sergeants."

"No." Hawthorne slowly shook his head, as if he had fully considered Goodwin's explanation and found it lacking in truth. "No, soldier, I don't think so. Now you take our mess sergeant when we was up in the trenches last February. We had it pearty tough up there, standin' watch four on and eight off, sleepin' in the mud and bein' et up by cooties, but do you think that damn mess sergeant'ld ever send us down warm chow? No, sir. It wasn't that he couldn't a. The kitchen was in a forty-foot dugout where they had plenty of wood and plenty of greaseballs to keep things hot. But whenever I sent up a coupla men from my relief to git the chow, they'd always bring it back cold. No damn sense in it at all. So one day I goes up there with the chow detail. He was settin' down eatin' a big pie. 'Lenz,' I says to him, 'Lenz, how come we never get any hot chow? He looked at me and mumbled: 'I guess your chow's hot enough.' 'Lenz,' I says, 'you're a damn liar and you know it. An' I'll tell you something else: if our chow's not hot to-day I'm gonna raise hell.' Well, he stands up at that and begins to git excited. 'Don't you call me a liar or I'll put ya out of here.' That made me peeved. I never liked 'im anyways. 'Lenz, you come here,' I said; and when he didn't come I went after 'im an' we tangled. I pounded that guy until my knuckles looked like raw meat, an' then I set out to kick hell out of 'im. I'd a done it too if they hadn't a ganged up on me, but what kin ya do aginst four greaseballs and a damn lieutenant?" Hawthorne made a deprecatory gesture with his big, brown hands, his first movement since he had begun his story. In fact, he made no expression of any sort, his voice remaining at the same droning pitch.

"Je's," said Goodwin. "Too bad you didn't wait till some dark night. I suppose they socked you in the hoosegow?"

"Sure they did. 'You'll fight the war from the bull-pen, Hawthorne,' says the lieutenant. 'Yes, sir,' I said, 'and it's a damn good thing for that Lenz too, because if I ever git at 'im agin you won't have no evidence left to try me with.'"

"Gosh," said Goodwin, "you oughtn't to have said that. I'll bet that one crack put three more months on your sentence. No, sir, I wouldn't a said that, Hawthorne."

Hawthorne grinned, "So they put me in the bull-pen, an' it was a hell of a sight better'n doin' four on an' eight off. It was at first, anyways, 'cause I didn't have any work to do. Then we moved back to a rest camp where the rest of the gang drilled an' dug trenches all day long. I was jist gittin' used to settin' around again when they sticks me in front of a guy with a bayonet, give me an axe an' puts me on the wood-pile, splittin' rails for the kitchen stove. An' there wasn't nothin' else to do but swing that axe all day. Then on the second day I was out there at work with that sentry behind me an' I saw Lenz comin' along. He didn't see me at first, an' I went right on choppin' until he got within about ten feet of me. He was walkin' along, lookin' at the ground, and all at once he looks up an' sees me. He laughed, so I jist let loose of that axe an' shied it at 'im."

"Je's," said Goodwin, horror-struck. "Did it hit 'im?"

"No, damn it. Only the handle. An' off he limped to report me to the O.D."

Goodwin shook his head. "That'd mean a general court in my outfit. We've had guys sent to Leavensworth for less than that."

"It's a general in ours, too," said Hawthorne coolly. "An' I'd a got it except that we got shoved up to the front again. The day before we left, the captain comes in the bull-pen an' says: 'Hawthorne, we're goin' up to the front to do a job that'll make that other time we was in the trenches look like a sewin'-bee. Now you can take your choice: you can stay back here in the guard-house or you can go up in the front line an' let me see what you're made of.' 'All right, sir,' I says, 'I'm rarin' to go, but you better keep me away from that damn Lenz or I'll take him for a Squarehead.' 'Lenz won't be up there, you needn't worry about that,' says the captain, an' the next day we broke camp." Hawthorne paused.

"I guess your outfit wasn't up with us at Cantigny, was it?"

"No," said Goodwin. "We was up around Château-Thierry."

"Well, anyway, we went into the trenches at Cantigny the next day, an' them Squareheads seemed to know the minute we got there. They throwed everything they had at us: sea-bags, Jack Johnsons, whizz-bangs, Lord only knows what. An' there we was, in that old muddy trench, listenin' to them shells bustin' all around. Pow! pow! powie! they went, an' when they stopped an' we struck our heads up over the firin' bay there was a nice thick line a Dutchmen pokin' along up to our trench. Y'ever seen 'em come over? They don't look human, do they? Maybe it's them long gray coats or maybe it's them funny-lookin' helmets that come down over their heads like flower-pots, but they sure don't look human. Then it might be the long bayonets—" Hawthorne speculated carefully: "Well, I don't know, only I say they don't look human. 'N'en I got a crazy feeling that they was goin' to come right over an' step right down in our trench an' chase us out. 'Cause you couldn't kill nowheres near all of 'em even if we did smoke up the old barrels of our rifles till they was too hot to hold.

"But as I was gonna say, on they come, an' it looked like good night for us, when our own artillery opens up and lays down a barrage so thick it looked like rain. You could see the Squareheads sort of stop an' break up a little an' then come on agin, but our machine-guns caught 'em in an enfilade fire, an' the first thing we knowed somebody blowed a whistle in our trench an' everybody started yellin' 'Forward.'

"'So it's up an' at 'em!' I says to Crawford in a kind of a joke, but he hadn't anything to say. Something had walloped him in the head. Well, it was tough work gittin' outa that trench. The mud was so soft an' the trench so deep an' the barb wire so tough I thought I never would git out. An' then we starts over that yellow ground, dodgin' into shell holes and gittin' up an' runnin' like rabbits toward the Square-heads' trench. I got about halfway there an' that was all. They got me jist below the knee with a machine-gun bullet." Hawthorne stopped talking, bent over, and carefully unwrapped his cloth puttee. Between the calf and the knee was a bandage, already soiled around the edges, in the centre of which a crimson bit of rust was showing.

"Gosh," said Goodwin, "you better be takin' care of that dressing or you won't have any leg left." He paused, staring down at his hob-nailed boots in a bewildered manner. "You sure was lucky, Hawthorne. You got away with murder," he said slowly. Of course it was Haw-thorne's own business if he wanted to carry on in that way, but Good-win could not approve of it. There was something about Hawthorne's experience that flouted natural laws. It was almost an insult to the whole body of soldiery that he could pummel a non-com, be arrested, and, while under guard, deliberately throw an axe at the same non-com, and then not be punished for anything. But Hawthorne had learned his lesson; no doubt about that. . . . Poor old Hawthorne. He sure would be in bad if he and Goodwin were taken up by one of the military police. Why, with his record, he would get life imprisonment. He never should have gone with him on this escapade. He wouldn't if he had known the trouble Hawthorne had been in. But now that he had gone, had abetted him, almost, it devolved upon him to keep Hawthorne from the clutches of the M.P.'s.

"Hawthorne," he said earnestly, "I don't think we oughta go to Paris. It's too damned dangerous. I guess it's a great city, all right, but we ought to see it from the picture-cards this time."

"Soldier, you don't wanna miss Gay Paree. It's a bon *sector*. That's where everybody goes."

"I know it is. The M.P.'s is there, too."

"How will we git back to our outfits if we don't go to Paris?"

"Well I didn't mean not to go there, exactly, Hawthorne. Course we got to go there to change trains. But there'll be a lot of M.P.'s at the station we come in at, an' I thought we could jump off at a suburb an' take a street-car through town to the other station."

"I s'pose it's all right," said Hawthorne, "but I'd like to see some of the town."

"Well, we can see it from the street-car."

"Lord, soldier, I don't mean thataway," said Hawthorne gloomily. "Besides, they'll see us at the station we go out at, anyways."

"Yeh," considered Goodwin. "But they don't bother yuh if you are goin'; it's only when you're comin' in that they pick yuh up."

"I thought you wanted to see Paris, soldier?"

"I did." How strongly he wanted to see Paris, how long he had been fascinated by tales of the Café de la Paix and the Folies Bergère, the Apache district! For a moment he weakened, but a moment only, for at the end of this merriment he saw Hawthorne in Saint Anne's Prison, with a service record that was black as ink, and charged with being absent without leave. "I don't want to now, though."

"Cold feet?" asked Hawthorne.

Goodwin gulped: Cold feet! But the train was speeding to Paris, Saint Denis was the next stop, and the matter must be decided at once. "Yeh," admitted Goodwin.

"All right," grinned Hawthorne, "I won't ditch ya, soldier. When do we git off?"

The train was slowing down, and before it had fully stopped they had jumped from the compartment to the cinder walk where an Ancient in a horizon-blue cape patrolled the premises with a swinging lantern.

Before them was a five-foot fence which terminated in a gate beside the brick wall of the station. The sign, Sortie, was above the gate, and before it stood the ticket-collector taking slips of pasteboard from the passengers.

"Don't let 'im stop us," cautioned Goodwin. Stepping quickly, with a sense of onslaught, they approached the gate, smiled at the collector, and—were halted. A ticket was demanded.

"Americain soldat," answered Hawthorne.

The explanation did not serve. Barring the exit, the collector repeated his demand.

"What?" asked Hawthorne, leaning over the Frenchman, as if he thought distance to be all that prevented him from understanding.

"Ticket, comme ça, comme ça!" The Frenchman, growing irritated, held out a ticket which he had taken from another passenger, to show what he wanted.

"No savvy. I don't git ya, mister." Hawthorne slowly shook his head.

The collector danced in his exasperation over these Americans. "Ticket, ticket," he shouted.

"I don't know what you mean!" Hawthorne's voice was yet louder. "Here, how's this?" He reached in his pocket, withdrew his hospital order for a wound chevron, and held it forth.

The Frenchman violently shook his head.

"Tell 'im we're goin' back to our outfit, Hawthorne. Mussear, Bosche! Bing, bing! Toot sweet! Allemande. Knock hell out of the whole bunch!" Goodwin gritted his teeth at imaginary Germans, lunged with an imaginary bayonet, pressed an imaginary trigger, and smiled ingratiatingly.

The Frenchman cursed, waved his hands, and despaired. They passed out into the street, gay in their achievement.

No street-cars were to be seen, but an English soldier whom Goodwin hailed piloted them to the Metro and gave them directions to the Gare de L'Est. And so, while the stage of the Folies Bergère was a tantalizing mist of gauze and flesh, while a field clerk paid for the dinner of a cocotte at the Moulin Rouge, while a respectable line-officer lay prone on a bench by the Sacre Cour, and while the military police sleuthed the streets, Goodwin and Hawthorne rumbled through the bowels of Paris—the city of their latter dreams—to take the train for Toul.

Goodwin saw the dawn from a third-class coach in which he sat half-smothered by a detachment of French soldiers. He wondered how it was possible for Hawthorne to sleep. His charge was sprawled on the floor of the coach, his head resting on the feet of a snoring poilu and his legs serving as a pillow for another. Not that Hawthorne's position was too uncomfortable for rest. Goodwin himself had lain that way innumerable times. His wonder was that Hawthorne could forget about his peril. He was, as Goodwin saw it, in a dangerous position. If the least thing happened to him to cause his arrest, his past record would certainly be the cause of his going to jail. At this instant, if they were seen by a military police, a railroad-transportation offier, in fact, any commissioned man, Hawthorne would be arrested, and when the court-martial board saw his record he might be tried for desertion. How could he explain that he was going back to the front? Goodwin worried, looking out the window at the green and brown rectangular fields, the gray farmhouses, the villages clustered on the quiet hilltops.

Soon they would arrive in Toul, and if they got off the train and through the city without being challenged, Hawthorne would be comparatively safe. But Toul was a divisional headquarters. Officers and soldiers would be at the station. It would be useless to attempt to pass the ticket-collector. But they could, by leaving the train by the left side instead of the right and walking across the tracks, avoid the collector completely. So Goodwin schemed for the welfare of his friend while the friend slept on, in a mass between the seats, ignorant of Goodwin's scheming.

Toul tells its mediæval story by the thick walls, the moat which surrounds it, the turrets, with long slits for the archers, rising above the walls and looking out over the calm, fertile country of wood and farm. Goodwin saw it from the window; shook Hawthorne by the shoulder. "Get up, Hawthorne, here we are," he called.

"Huh! Where?" Hawthorne disentangled himself and sat up, staring at Goodwin.

"We'll be at Toul in a minute an' we'll have to git off the minute the train stops."

Hawthorne grinned. "All right, soldier, I guess I kin say 'No savvy' to the Frogs."

"I gotta stunt, Hawthorne. When the train stops we'll get off on the wrong side an' beat it while the coaches are still standin' between us an' the station."

The train slackened, jerked, the bumpers of the coaches struck and recoiled. Goodwin raised the latch and opened the door.

With Goodwin leading, they trotted across the tracks, cleared the fence, and followed the street which led through the outer gate at the north. Suddenly Hawthorne halted.

"I don't know about you, soldier, but my leg hurts and I want some chow."

"Come on, Hawthorne," Goodwin coaxed. "We're nearly there now. We'll be at our outfits by noon. Maybe we can find a farmhouse along the way."

"Hell," said Hawthorne skeptically, "we won't see our outfits afore night, an' you know it. Besides, it's nearly all evacuated district between here an' the front."

"Come on, Hawthorne. The streets'll be full of soldiers in a minute an' we'll git run in," Goodwin pleaded.

Hawthorne resigned himself. "An' me with a gimpy laig," he said.

They walked under the heavy gateway to the road, a white ridge bending along green slopes past the walled town and through a wood where the ground levelled. There, the road was straight, with an appearance of coolness beneath the overhanging boughs. They walked without speaking. Hawthorne, because of the not-quite-healed wound in his leg, employed a kind of ploughing gait, and from time to time Goodwin would regard him stealthily, jealously, then look straight ahead again to the point where the road narrowed into nothingness. He was satisfied with himself, pleased with his success in bringing Hawthorne back to his outfit safely. If it hadn't been for him, Hawthorne would certainly have been arrested. And with his record! He would have been thrown in jail for the rest of his life. But now Hawthorne could go back to his outfit and live down his attack on the mess sergeant. At any rate, Hawthorne had learned his lesson.

In rear of them the revolutions of a motor sounded, and as they looked back they saw an ambulance speeding toward them. The brakes tightened, the rubber seared, skidding on the gravel, and an obliging driver stopped.

At the back of the car they sat facing each other on the long, leather-covered seats. Signs of the front grew more numerous each moment. The evacuation hospital, the camouflaged supply dump, the long-range guns hidden in a cellar and covered with leaves, the mended road, the concrete machine-gun emplacement—they passed all of them.

At a crossroad the ambulance stopped. To the left was a shell-raked farmhouse, headquarters of the brigade to which Hawthorne belonged. To the right, far beyond the blue-black woods, lay Goodwin's troops. Goodwin held out his hand.

"Well, Hawthorne, what'll you do when you git back to your outfit?"

"Hell," said Hawthorne, tightening his webbed belt and grinning, "I'll report for duty an' then carve my name all over the face of that Lenz."

"Who?" asked Goodwin.

"Lenz, the mess sergeant."

"Oh," said Goodwin dully, far down in his throat. . . . "Well, so long, Hawthorne."

As he turned to the right he was sickeningly aware of the distance he had yet to go and the fact that he was very hungry.

III

Responsibility

During the day the Marne was green, but at twilight the soft haze of falling evening obscured its face with a film of blue, like smoke from an autumn bonfire. Lighter, though soaked in the same shade, the houses of Nanteuil were quiet in the July dusk; the windows were darkened, and the chimneys unused. On those two streets which terminated at the river—one ending at the foot of the low iron bridge—or on those three thoroughfares which ran parallel with the Marne, nobody was walking. It was as if the town had become suddenly depopulated in some horrible way and now was tightly hugging its ghost.

But inside the houses, had you been enabled to peep through the carefully boarded windows or to halt on the threshold of the stone doorway, you would have seen in the dwelling which stood on the corner nearest the bridge a number of soldiers whose shadows, in the candlelight, were enormous on the bare, white walls of an unfurnished second-story room. That they were formed into two separate groups was noticeable; perhaps five of the men were drawn closely together by the door, seated uncomfortably on the heavy marching-order packs which they had not yet unrolled. With eyes which gazed hesitantly about, sometimes lowering deliberately, and always wandering (except for the one man who looked blankly ahead), they could not have appeared less at their ease. They were members of the fourth replacement battalion which, after travelling by rail, camion, and foot from Brest, had reached Nanteuil that day. The other occupants of the room seemed very much at home. Andrus, the oldest, was stretched out on the floor, with blankets spread for the night, his blouse folded into the shape of a pillow, his shirt open at the neck, and his sleeves rolled above the elbows. About him khaki haversacks were placed by the makeshift pillows, and on each muddy, greasy carrier rested an aluminum mess-kit, the upturned canteen cup holding a fork or a spoon. These belonged to the men who had endured a month of Belleau Wood, where attack and counter-attack were engaged in under a continuous bombardment, a bombardment that might grow light or heavy but never entirely cease. They had seen, in the course of the month's siege, the trees stripped naked, the limbs grotesquely like the shattered arms and legs of men, and the grass browned by poisonous fumes. That morning they had come back to Nanteuil, several kilometers from Belleau Wood, to lie in support of the division which had relieved them. They had been told that they had saved Paris—a city known to them only by report—and they believed themselves to be on their way to a rest camp.

Andrus, with the sweat stains on his face, watched John Wainwright lounging against the wall, dribbling yellow flecks of tobacco into the trough of white paper which he held in his hand. Wainwright wet the end of the cigarette, caustically inquiring before his lolling tongue had reached the edge of the paper:

"How long you boys been over from the States?"

There was a shifting of feet while restive eyes besought one another to make the shameful confession—shameful because through some peculiar reasoning of the older men a recent arrival in France was a person to be scorned.

"'Bout two weeks, I guess. We'd of been here sooner if they hadn't stopped us back in that camp at Chatillon." The voice of the new man whined dully, apologetically. Andrus looked at him, thinking: "Lord, what an awful specimen!" He was: one eye fixed sternly on the ceiling, the other stared straight before him, and his hands, palms upturned, were like gloves stuffed with cotton. Among those five tyros he was the least prepossessing, yet certainly the most striking; to be sure he would not have been assigned to pose for one of those preposterous recruiting posters which shows a young man with a Grecian nose and a bronze throat relentlessly charging the enemy. He was a sorrowful sight, and he made Andrus feel that, in letting him in, the service had abandoned all physical standards in its eagerness for recruits.

But Wainwright was talking. "Well, sir," he said significantly, "you'd of better stayed where you God damn was. Boy, it's hell up there." Sadly he shook his large, unkempt head. "Nawsir, I hate to think of what them Squareheads done to pore old Heck after they captured him. Boy, you wanna look out; don't be hankerin' to git up to the front. Them Dutchmen's mean; if they ketch ya they cut ya where ya don't wanna be cut an' you come home whinnyin' like a colt. Ain't that so, Rainey?"

"Yes, sir," said Rainey emphatically. "If you see they've gotcha on the hip there's on'y one thing to do: put the old Springfield to your nose an' let 'er flicker. You gotta be careful of their damn liquid fire, too"—Rainey wanted to play the painter on his own account—"They sneak up on ya in the night an' spray it over your back. It burns right into your bones. W'y, I couldn't count the guys I seen up there that's bones was burnt right to a cinder!"

"But them G.I. cans are the worst," said Wainwright, leaning forward and lighting his cigarette from the candle. "You wanna step high an' wide when they're makin' a call. W'y, I've seen 'em make holes in the ground so big that you could hide a house in."

Andrus saw the new men unconsciously bunching together, as if their solidarity might defend them from these awful fates. Their movements were jerky, awkward, and he knew they were afraid to speak. He grew angry with Wainwright. What did the damned fool get out of scaring these new men? He wasn't very much of a wildcat himself, but to hear him talk . . . ! Not, of course, that Belleau Wood wasn't bad enough. That was just it: the front was so bad it couldn't stand any embroidering. He said: "Come out of your hop, Wainwright. There's no use in your lyin' when the real dope's bad enough."

Wainwright grinned widely, then puffed out his cheeks as if he were about to say "Blah." His voice blustered—it was habitual with him—"All right, grampappy. I won't scare none of the boys."

Andrus scowled, not at Wainwright (for he was good-natured enough) but at the position of defender in which his remark had thrust him. Already the manageable eye of the sadly pottered youth gleamed a thousand heartfelt thanks to Andrus. And Andrus, who had spoken only because he was irritated, did not want them—least of all from their present source. And now the new man got to his feet and crossed the room toward Andrus. Halfway there he worked his oddly shaped hand into the pocket of his blouse and brought out a package of cigarettes. Beside Andrus he stopped, held out the package, and sat down. And in his dully whining voice, like the sound caught and held by a music teacher's tuning-fork, he said: "Have a cigarette—I guess they're pretty scarce up around the front, aren't they?"

Andrus wanted to smoke badly. He had long since used all of his own tobacco—used it, not given it away—and the nearness of this Turkish leaf had a fascination for his fancy. He could almost taste the inhalation, coating the roof of his mouth, his palate, then drifting sensuously outward through his nostrils. Yet he drily answered: "Better keep 'em for yourself; you may need 'em."

The youth was not troubled by the rejection of his offer. At once he replaced them in his pocket. "My name's Hannan." He waited, smiling with timorous friendliness. Andrus felt the impulse to say "What of it?" Instead, he answered in his rather grating voice: "Mine's Andrus."

Discussion would have ended there had not Hannan pursued with surprising fervor: "I'm certainly glad to know you, Mr. Andrus." He sat cross-legged on the floor, his elbows hooked over his knees, the hands limp and the fingers spreading widely apart. "What section of the States are you from?" he asked.

Andrus had lived in many places in America: he had been a country school-teacher in Pennsylvania, had worked in the factories of Pittsburgh, and drifted, as a mechanic, through Youngstown and Cleveland to Detroit. To have explained all this would have been a bother without recompense of any kind. For a while he was silent; then he said shortly: "I'm from Detroit."

"Detroit! Is that so?" Hannan was pleased, excited. "Why, I was born forty miles from there myself. What do you think of that!"

Andrus thought very little of it. The vicinity of Detroit held no particular remembrances for him. Hannan could have gained his serious attention only by affirming that he had been spat from the mouth of the Devil. Even that would not have greatly surprised him. Andrus frowned, or, rather, the creases in his forehead deepened and the furrow on each cheek grew straight and long. His expression brought silence from Hannan.

Both were quiet, listening to Wainwright's endless, boastful speech and the banter it provoked from the older men. The others sat about uncomfortably. They warily digested and selected bits of conversation as the candle, set on top of Wainwright's steel helmet, sputtered so low that the wax ran down to the floor in tiny streams. Andrus yawned and commenced to unroll his wrapped puttees.

"Got anybody to bunk with?" asked Hannan.

"No," said Andrus, continuing to loosen the leather thongs of his shoes. His answer was not spoken hospitably.

Hannan did not seem to need encouragement. "Then I'll bring my blankets over. They'll make the floor a lot softer to sleep on."

Andrus knew that bedfellows, under those circumstances, were seldom chosen to the satisfaction of each. He knew that three blankets were better than one. Because of which he was silent, watching Hannan cross the room, pick up the heavy marching-order pack and drag it back across the bare floor. He removed his hobnailed shoes, put his rolled puttees in them, and after loosening the laces of his breeches he was ready for bed. He lay down, settled his head on his folded jacket and stretched out. He was asleep by the time Hannan lay down beside him.

Bugles were not blown in Nanteuil—it was too near the front—but from the hall outside came the tramp of rough-shod feet as a sergeant walked from the door to door, bawling: "Rise and shine, you birds, rise and shine." It was quite dark in the room, not even the faintest sign of daylight showing through the boarded window, and Andrus propped himself on an elbow and rubbed his eyes, wondering how morning could have come so soon, or if, perhaps, the Germans had broken through the lines again. The rest of the men were still asleep, or in that lethargic borderland between slumber and wakefulness. Andrus sat up and reached for his shoes, wondering whether he should rouse the men. It was none of his business if they didn't get up before noon, yet if they were late the whole squad would get the devil from the platoon commander. There was nothing to be gained by that. He drew on his shoes and commenced to wrap his puttees when sounds in the adjoining room decided him. "Hey, you fellahs! Better get up," he said.

For most of the men the act of dressing was easily accomplished, because they rarely removed their shirts and breeches. But Hannan needed more time. While Andrus adjusted his gas mask and Wainwright, with his spoon, scraped the candle grease from his helmet, Hannan searched for his shirt and breeches, which he had taken off the night before. He found them and stood up, in once white underclothes which sagged and bagged depressingly. Andrus was severely silent, but Wainwright exclaimed: "For goodness sake, lady, you don't think you're on Broadway, do ya?" A few of the men tittered and Hannan, staring hard with his curiously set eyes, continued to dress. Andrus stepped into the hall and walked down the stone steps.

Fastening their clothes, some with their shoes unlaced, men were trotting from their billets to fall in line on the designated company street as Andrus passed through the outer doorway. He was seldom first and never last. To-day he struck the medium again. For less than half of the men had arrived. They were formed in two skeleton ranks, facing the Marne, a clouded emerald color, flowing primly between even banks.

Unhurriedly Andrus walked behind the fourth platoon and the third. Halfway past the second he stopped and efficiently crowded into the front rank. By the free and practiced use of his elbows he made a space between number three of his squad and number one of the squad on the left, sufficient for him to see the right guide. This was the first formation for more than a month past. The sergeant in charge, before the platoon, struggled between leniency and military duty: it was time to order his command to attention and call the roll, though if he did many would have to be reported late or absent. Andrus, being present, wanted the roll called at once and the morning exercises begun. He grew morose, viewing the hesitating sergeant, and thought: "'y gosh, here it is the first damn formation and half the company's late." Just as ever, from now on the same performance would be repeated each day. He was so accustomed to it he could close his eyes and form a correct mental picture of all that was going on: men in the front rank were surreptitiously buttoning their blouses; men in the rear rank leaned over, fastening their puttees; men in neither rank trotted hurriedly over the ground which remained between themselves and the company. And the sergeant fidgeted about what to do.

"P'toon, Chun!" shouted the sergeant, smartly dashing a slip of paper against his thigh. "Har-right dr-ss." Quickly, he placed himself beside the right guide, surveying the front rank. "Ste-eady-y—hup there, Johnson wait for the command: Stead-dy-y-y-, Fr'nt." The eyes of the men, which had been directed toward the sergeant, now turned slowly to the front, and the left arms, palms on hips, dropped weakly to their owners' sides. "Tenchun to roll-call!" commanded the sergeant, referring to his slip of paper.

"Sergeants McDermott."

"He-rrr."

"Oliver."

"Hup."

"Corporals Cook."

"Urp."

"Dunbar."

"Heurr."

"Hicks."

"Up-p."

"Kahl."

"Eeow."

"Lawes."

"Heah, suh."

"Privates Andrus."

"Hurr."

"Angell."

"Hyah."

"Archer."

"Hip."

"Boudreau."

No answer, "Late," mumbled the sergeant.

"Bullis."

"Harp."

"Carver."

"Hyar."

"Eggert." (A new man.)

"Here I am."

"Freiburg."

"Yup."

"Hannan."

No answer.

"Hannan!"

Footsteps pounded down the road toward the fourth squad.

"Hannan—Hartman."

"He-e-rr. Har."

The sergeant glanced up from his slip of paper. "Say," he said angrily, "how many Hartmans are there in this platoon?"

"Only one that I know of," said Hartman.

"Then who else was it that answered when I called Hartman's name?" He was very put out.

"I d-d-did." A breathless voice sounded from the rear rank in back of Andrus.

The sergeant elongated his neck. "Well, what in hell's your name?"

"H—private H-hannan."

"Why didn't you answer when I called it?"

"I did."

"Don't talk back. Report to Lieutenant Jones after chow. Rear rank, 'Bout face; Front rank, rear rank four paces forward, har-rch. Hands on hips, place." The morning exercises were begun and the men bent in one direction for the good of their livers, another for their kidneys, and still another as a preventive of flat feet.

After they had reassembled and been dismissed Andrus found Hannan following closely after him. He had an impulse to turn and say: "Beat it!"

For once, breakfast was plentiful. There was even guava jelly among the stores which had piled up at regimental headquarters while the battalions had been at the front fighting, with the bombardment so heavy behind them that supplies could not be got through. Andrus, with his dripping mess-kit in his hands, walked from the smoking field kitchen to his billet for a few moments' rest before drill. But he had no sooner got inside and sat down on his blankets than he remembered the order of the day was combat packs and rifles; his pack was strung out all over the floor, his blankets were not folded and his rifle not cleaned, and he was too sensible to be found at inspection with a dirty rifle or an ill-made pack. He stood up to fold his blanket, thinking: "Damn that Hannan." For Hannan's blankets were in a mass on the floor, the carrier of his pack, his bayonet, canteen, and towel were tangled in them, causing Andrus to reflect irritably that Hannan of all people was the worst to bunk with. He finished folding his blanket, dried his mess dish on a soiled towel, and picked up his rifle. He was drawing a bit of oiled flannel through the bore as the rest of the men came in.

Just, by golly, as he expected. Wainwright loudly wanted to borrow some oil, and oil was precious. "Why don't you fellahs take care of your oil?" Andrus answered grumpily. "You got as much chance to get it as I have." He went on cleaning his rifle, then put the oil back in the butt plate and commenced to make his pack for drill.

Drill formation was much more military than that for morning exercises. But Andrus was never seriously troubled by that. He had come into the army, he vaguely knew, to do his duty, and his sole object during the war was to take care of himself, not to expose himself to unnecessary danger, not to get in the bad graces of his officers and thus bring extra duty upon himself. It was for this reason that he continued to remain a private: he did not want responsibility. To direct himself was sufficient. For him it was a part of the day to clean his equipment so that the most sharp-eyed of inspecting officers could never say, "Take his name, sergeant."

At a little before nine o'clock the company, standing before the Marne, was called to attention. "Squads Left!" called the company commander, and in a column of fours they swung down the street, past the low iron bridge and out toward a cleared but unplanted field.

It was a hot day. The sky was a sheet of metallic blue through which the sun seemed to have burned a sizzling hole. The blades of grass were singed a little, and about the armpits and on the backs of the soldiers sweat showed through the olive drab shirts. But the company, divided up into platoons, continued to execute Left Front into Line,

Squads Right and Left, to oblique, and Andrus was unpleasantly reminded of the quantity of food he had eaten for breakfast. At first he thought it was the guava jelly, but as he grew aware of a small, hard lump in the pit of his stomach he included in his condemnation the whole breakfast fare: the sergeant major coffee, the stewed prunes, and fried mush. Damn! but it was a hot day.

"On Right into Line!" called the platoon commander. Ahead, Number One of the first squad pivoted sharply, marked time until the count of four, and then stepped off at a correct angle. Andrus was dizzy when the men halted on a platoon front. And during the manual of arms he handled his rifle clumsily. Once he thought he would ask if he could drop out and return to his billet, but that, with him, would have been unprecedented. He remained with the platoon until it was joined up with the company and marched back to Nanteuil.

More slowly than usual he walked up the steps of the billet, and while the rest of the men were rattling their mess-kits in preparation for the noonday meal, Andrus sat down on his folded blanket. He didn't want any chow. No, sir, this rich food didn't agree with him now. Perhaps he had got too accustomed to cold boiled potatoes and monkey meat. "Lord!" he groaned, and lay down in the now empty room.

Hannan came in, late as usual, and as he drew his mess-kit from his haversack he sympathetically prompted: "You'll be late for chow."

"What of it?" said Andrus shortly. Chow be damned and Hannan be damned! Dismally he lay face downward on the soft woolen blankets, which would not assuage his illness. The minutes dragged—he thought of the food which would be served at luncheon, and he commenced to fret because the men had not returned. It must be, he thought, time for afternoon drill! As he lay there, Hannan appeared in the doorway, holding a warm steak in his mess-kit. "I thought you might be hungry, Mr. Andrus," he said, standing above the prostrate figure. Andrus lifted his head from the dark, woolly blanket. "Don't want any chow," he said. Hannan stared perplexedly at the mess-kit.

They left Nanteuil one evening, riding in camions along the Marne and guessing whether they were going toward or from the front. Sometimes the sound of artillery would be quite close, a chain of rumbling which stretched parallel to the direction in which the camions were moving. At other times the reverberations were faint. The men would smile their pleasure at the thought of travelling to a rest area until the sharp detonations were heard again.

It was dark when the camions stopped at a cross-road. Grumbling, the men clambered to the ground and were herded into a column of twos. For several hours they marched over a bare, shell-torn road. Everywhere was an unearthly quiet, broken when the word was passed to stand fast in case an illuminating rocket was fired. Suddenly the men stepped into a communication trench. The duckboards were slippery and the trench narrow; the men did not walk, they floundered, and, floundering in the wet with their forty-pound packs to make their balance more difficult, they cursed bitterly but with restraint. Somewhere ahead a signal pistol popped, and in a moment a bright light, like a mammoth glowing moth, fluttered slowly to the ground. The line halted, the men crowding against one another. Then they stumbled on, turning to the left side into the main trench, where they stopped again. The billeting officer was assigning the men to their dugouts.

On the second evening of their occupancy of the sector Andrus was standing at his post at the extreme left of the trench, where a machine-gun squad had their emplacement. His duty was not only to guard the machine-gunners against a surprise from the rear but also to challenge all persons who entered or left the trench, since the only passage was at that spot. He had been on watch for about an hour when he heard a group of men laboriously making their way over the slippery duckboards.

"Halt! Who's there?" he asked in a low voice, pointing his bayoneted rifle at the party.

"Wiring party."

"Advance, wiring party, and give the countersign."

The wiring party, headed by a sergeant, passed by, struggling with several coils of barbed wire. Andrus recognized Hannan's ill-balanced shoulders among the men. The men filed out of the trench, walking through the black night of No Man's Land. Andrus turned to the camouflaged shelter of the machine-gun emplacement, where the crew leaned against the parapet of the trench.

Ten o'clock came, and the corporal of the guard brought the second relief for Andrus's post. Andrus mumbled the instructions of his post to the man who was to take his place, and made his way along the tortuous trench to his dugout. The dugout was perhaps fifteen feet in the ground. It had a boarded ceiling, and a boarded floor on which the water was several inches deep. He took off his blouse and his wet shoes, placed the shoes by his head and drew his blankets over him. Very tired from his watch, he was nearly asleep when he was disturbed by the sound of men stumbling down the dugout steps and splashing through the water on the floor. It was the wiring party, and one of the men was talking:

"I don't know where the hell he went. When that machine-gun opened up he was right beside me. I gotta hunch he tried to crawl into that shell hole."

"'y Gosh," said Andrus, "can't you let a fellah sleep?"

"Oh, I guess we gotta right to talk," said one of the men. The voice gathered indignation as it continued: "I guess you'd talk, too, if you had jist been out on a wiring party and had the Squareheads open up and knock off one of your men."

"He wasn't knocked off, I'd swear to that," objected the first voice.

"Who?" asked Andrus.

"Why, Hannan; who do you think we been talkin' about?"

"What's the matter with Hannan?" asked Andrus.

"Ain't we jist been tellin' you?" The voice was shrill with exasperation. "He got hit out there in front of our new barbed wire."

Andrus was silent. It was, he thought, just like the numbskull to go out on a harmless wiring party and get hit. If there was only one bullet in the whole German army and ten million men to get it, Hannan would be elected to the honor. The damn fool. He stretched out and drew the blanket over his shoulder. He supposed they were wondering why he didn't offer to go out after him. Let them! There was no reason why he should go out after him, no reason why he should even bother to think about it. Hannan meant nothing to him. Certainly he had not sought him out. He turned over and closed his eyes. But they popped wide open and he found himself on his back, staring up through the blackness. . . . They couldn't find him! Well, why in hell couldn't they find him?

Must be a pretty rotten bunch. Besides, why did they have to tell *him* about it? He wasn't the official life-saver of the battalion. A rotten outfit, not much better any more than a draft division. What the hell—he drew his blanket close against his chin and deliberately set his thoughts upon something that was delectable to him: a comfortable chair, a mug of beer, and a cribbage board and some one to play who minded his business. . . . But the blanket scratched and in place of the comfortable chair he pictured the body of Hannan lying out on the field, perhaps in that shell hole in front of the bombing post. There was the chance of its being a bad wound, one that would cause Hannan to bleed to death; in two days the sun would have bloated and blackened his body. Damn that Wainwright, why hadn't he done something? . . . Oh, hell, there was no use trying to sleep. He sat up, reached for his wet shoes and pulled them on over his thick woollen socks. Picking up his helmet and gas mask, he slipped down off his bunk, his heels striking the berth below, to the water-covered floor. He felt his way to the door and climbed up the mud-covered steps.

A pale quarter-moon, dim through the dissolving fog overhead, faintly brought out the humps in the winding trench where the bulk of the company kept watch in the firing bays, on the parapets, in the shell holes between the trench and the barbed wire. Andrus stepped cautiously over the duck-boards, apprehending the sentry's vibrant challenge, the pointed rifle thrust menacingly at his chin. To walk through the trench at night always made him nervous. There was, he thought, no telling when one of these idiots would pull the trigger on you before you got a chance to give the countersign. But he walked along encountering no such ill-luck. Even the erratic Bullis was sufficiently composed to let him pass without jabbing a bayonet into this neck, and when he got to the end of the trench the guard at the machine-gun emplacement passed him as a matter of course. He crawled into the shelter, where the gunner peered over a bank of dirt into the night. On his hands and knees beside the gunner he whispered: "S-s-st." "'Smatter?" asked the gunner, without looking up. "Where were they mending that barbed wire?" "Right out in front, in the first fence where that shell hit yesterday afternoon." "Well, don't shoot if you hear any noises; I'm goin' out." "Better be pretty damn careful," advised the gunner; "the Squareheads are keepin' a sharp watch."

Andrus crept out of the shelter and passed through the opening of the trench. He had still another place to go to. There was a bombing pit which guarded the left flank of his trench and the right flank of the trench adjoining. It was just inside the first line of barbed wire, and as he approached it he debated whether to crawl or to walk. To crawl would take too much time; now if the damn fools only didn't think he was a spy! "Hey you guys!" "Who's that?" commanded a tense, scared voice. "It's Andrus." He walked ahead, guided by their voices, and saw them crouched in a hole. "Better watch out; the Squareheads are on the job to-night," they said. Why didn't they tell him something he didn't know! "I'm goin' out in front. Jist sit tight till I git back." "What're you goin' for?" they asked, but he was already moving away toward the opening in the barbed wire.

He walked quickly over the spongy earth, his eyes staring into the darkness. To see the wire was almost impossible, and to find the opening . . . Suddenly his hand struck the wire. He drew back, startled, then felt his way along the scratching prongs until he reached the opening. He had sufficient control of his mind to reflect upon the difference the few steps had made in his feeling of security. On his own side of the barbed wire he had been safe, but now he was in No Man's Land, afraid even of the night.

His face was twitching and his hand unsteady as he groped along to the next fence. On which side was the shell hole that the wiring party had spoken of? He remembered seeing it in the daytime, now he could not remember its position. He was frightened, but to convince himself that he was not he deliberately assumed the shell hole to be on the outer side. Forward he went, tearing his body through the grasping prongs which lacerated his skin and caught at his clothing. Breathless, he worked through, and as he turned he heard a clicking noise from the German trench. He dropped to the ground as an illuminating rocket rose in the night and slowly descended, making a wide, mellow arc of light.

For a few moments he lay motionless, his eyes roving over the ground in search of Hannan. Like dice rattled in a metal box, a Maxim fired, the bullets singing through the barbed wire. Then silence. Well, he couldn't stay out all night. Crouching, his hands held before him, fingers outstretched, he felt along the ground in front of the wire. Once he ventured to whisper: "Hannan." He heard a groan, so near his body jerked upward in fright. Not daring to speak, he crawled, passing his hands over the earth, feeling the bits of rotting equipment, duds, and humanity which had lain there for months.

"Here I am," he heard a plaintive whisper, and held out his hand. Hannan was sitting. "Hit bad?" "I can walk if you help me." They stood up. With his arm about Hannan's waist and Hannan's arm about his shoulder, he plodded toward the opening in the wire. In the middle of the entanglement Hannan whimpered: "I can't make it. You go back an' let me stay here, Andrus." Grimly Andrus lifted him on his shoulders and staggered forward. His fear was gone, replaced by a white fury that made him grit his teeth and gave him strength to support his burden. He passed through the wire, the bare space which lay between it and the next, and lurched through the last gap, his puttees in shreds, his legs bleeding.

"'At you, Andrus?" asked one of the men in the bombing pit. "No, it's the Kaiser," he said sourly. At the entrance to the trench he answered the challenge. "This the guy that got hit?" asked the sentry. Andrus stopped. Together they laid Hannan down by the machine-gun shelter. "Got it in the leg. Probably smashed. Somebody'll have to get a couple of stretcher bearers," Andrus said.

Well, that was over. Now he could go back to his bunk and try to get some sleep. It was only a few hours before dawn, when the whole company would have to stand to in the firing bays in case of a morning attack. Damn it! He stumbled down the duck-boards toward his dugout.

IV

"Sound Adjutant's Call!"

Perhaps nearly every American—to limit a meandering generality to one nation—some time before he has passed into middle age has felt the desire to be a soldier. Not an enlisted man who sews his own buttons on his tunic and has fifteen dollars a month to spend, who is supposed to have gone into the army because he is prenatally lazy or because he cannot earn his living elsewhere, but rather a sworded officer who postures heroically for a day and then marches down long avenues of applauding people toward the outstretched arms of his imaginary family. The impulse may have come to him with his first box of brightly painted lead toys, and the small tin cannon, the direct discharge of which would conveniently mow down the most invincible of enemies. Or, even though he escaped the insidious appeal of the toy fighters, there was yet the flashing, gory blade of Horatius, the wooden horse of Troy, the bleeding-footed troops of Washington, the charge of the Light Brigade at Balaclava, the dispassionate curses of Andrew Jackson . . . How many youths could hold out against their first sight of a company of guardsmen clanking down the street? Or the rippling folds of a flag? Or the bugle which affects the diaphragm with its rich bleat—in short, all of those parade trappings which have become extinct in battle?

But once in a while you see a man in uniform with wonder that he happens to be wearing it. You can imagine he felt the call to arms at the age of twelve, but you puzzle futilely for the reason which sent him into the army at thirty. And to increase your bewilderment he is usually an officer of some rank, a captain if he is less than forty years old, a colonel if he is nearer fifty. This kind of man appears to be thin-blooded, reserved, fashioned in an insignificant mould. And at once you tell yourself that he should have remained a civilian, that he makes the whole army look absurd by being of it. You try to picture him sitting at some office desk, as a banker, an architect, an engineer, even a clerk. But his narrow khaki-covered shoulders and his severe campaign hat cannot be separated from him, and you realize momentarily that you could have settled his destiny no better than he.

Arthur Balder was such a man. He was a thin little fellow with bowed, spindly legs, and a set expression about his thin white face from which you could surmise he was telling himself: "Every man in this entire battalion may be against me, b-b-but I've got my job to do, and by gracious I'm going to do it."

The first time I saw Balder was in the summer of 'seventeen at Quantico, Virginia. In two months the regiment would be in France, and meanwhile the officers were trying to give the men all of the practice in close order, extended order, and bayonet drill that they could crowd into eight short weeks. The First Battalion was out on the parade-grounds after three hours of vigorous skirmishing, waiting for Major Wales, who, each morning at eleven o'clock, rode from the stables out to the middle of the broad gravel field and instructed the companies in battalion drill. There was a breeze strong enough to raise the dust, but the day was as hot as a day in Haiti, and fat old Captain Stahl, whose shirt seemed always about ready to slip out of his breeches and cover his belt, was having a hard time trying to bring the Seventy-fourth Company up onto a battalion line. He puffed like a porpoise as he waddled backward in front of his company, and when at last he commanded "Squads Left" and the Seventy-fourth came crowding up on the line, the adjoining company was given left step to make room for them.

Captain Stahl had no time to spare, because he had barely halted his outfit when Major Wales cantered out on the parade-grounds, his long legs snug against his sorrel's flanks, his broad shoulders slumping slightly forward, with that stiff-brimmed, sharp-peaked campaign hat he always wore. He rode to the front and centre of the battalion and reined in his horse, waiting. The men were also waiting, had been for fifteen or more minutes, and were growing very fidgety. Following directly in rear of Major Wales came another rider, a smaller figure, stiff in starched khaki, and bouncing in his saddle like a jack-in-a-box. His big chestnut horse made him appear even smaller than he actually was, and as he took his place by the major, Mulvaney, who was in the file-closers, chirped out:

"Je's, I didn't know the major was married."

"Nor is he," said Ryan.

"But ain't that his little boy he's got with him?" asked Mulvaney ingenuously.

Then Major Wales called the battalion to attention, the captains repeated the commands, and the troops swung off in a column of fours, passed in review by companies, practiced formal guard mount, got out of step—at which the under officers shouted—dropped their rifles on the ground or on the toe of the man next to them, and behaved in general as recruits do. After nearly an hour Major Wales hoarsely called out, "Captains, take charge of your companies!"; the battalion was split up, and the units marched off to their quarters.

Banging the butts of their rifles on the floor the men stamped into the bunk-house, while the non-commissioned officers glared blackly at them. Once inside, there was a concerted exclamation of heavy disgust.

"They certainly picked a pippin when they picked him, all right."

"The army sure must be hard up for officers when they let a little snipe like that wear captain's bars."

"What have they got against the First Battalion that they wish him off on us is what I want to know."

"I'll bet he thinks we're gonna fight with cream puffs."

"I'd like to meet him alone in a dark alley."

These and similar comments were evoked by the remembered sight of Captain Balder trotting across the parade-grounds. He had said nothing, he had done nothing, he had merely been Captain Balder; and the comments would have continued had not Corporal Harriman, hoping the ranking sergeant would notice his strict observance of military discipline, called out:

"Pipe down, you men."

To which Private Hayes, who had no desire to be other than a private, answered: "Pipe down yourself, you hand-shaker. This is no business of yours." And Corporal Harriman at once subsided.

But the bunk-house screen swung open and slammed shut as Lieutenant Bedford stepped inside. With one of those Machiavellian expressions which he had already learned to assume, which meant nothing, but which intimidated three or four of the men in his platoon, he angrily inquired:

"Here, you men! What's the big idear?"

"'Shun," fluted Sergeant Ryan from the end of the room where he was straightening his blankets. Noticeably, the men's heels clicked sharply together.

"Now you men cut that stuff out," Lieutenant Bedford advised.

"What stuff, lieutenant?" Hayes innocently inquired.

"You know damn well what stuff. I heard you men sounding off. And now let me tell you something: the next man I hear speaking disrespectfully of Captain Balder goes up for a court-martial. And I don't want that to happen any more than you do. You can say what you please about any officer who is not connected with the First Battalion, but if he is in our outfit you pay him respect. And remember that Captain Balder is adjutant of the First Battalion."

"Yes, sir," Hayes meekly answered.

The men had been standing at attention all of the time since Lieutenant Bedford had entered, but it wasn't until after he had finished talking that he noticed it. "As you were," he said, pulling vexedly at his small, blunt mustache. "Who the devil told you to stand at attention?"

That was Captain Arthur Balder's unofficial introduction to the First Battalion. And shortly afterward the command was put aboard a transport. It was just about the size to hold a company, but on it a battalion, fifty nurses, and another detachment which had been left behind when their outfit had unexpectedly sailed were crowded aboard, with the result that soldiers' heads were sticking out of every porthole in the ship. And the nurses on board made life much more difficult because only the officers were permitted to be on the promenade-deck with them. Thus the entire battalion was ordered below into the hold, allowed to be on the top side or on the poop-deck only during submarine drill, inspection, or setting-up exercises.

The ship sailed from Philadelphia on the morning of the first of September, and the next day it was riding the gentle swells in New York Harbor waiting for the convoy in the company of which it was to be taken over to France. The men were all crowded up on deck to see if any German submarines had yet been sighted, to find out where they were, and, principally, to see as much of the land as they could, for they would not see it again, at least not America, for many months. I was over by the gang-plank standing near the railing, watching New York's sky-line for the first time in my life. It seemed like some fabulously monstrous crazy-quilt, those tall, lean buildings, each rising higher than the other, like steps to a very inferior heaven. There was something so unstable about it all, as if it were a modern Babylon which the next century would know only through history. I turned and looked at the famous Statue of Liberty, but she was too much of the respectable German hausfrau to be gazed at long. And while I was skylarking, as our old drill sergeant on the island used to call it, I heard somebody make a sort of clucking sound with his throat, and turned around to see Billy Morrow standing beside me, staring fervently across the water to a hill on the crest of which were built a lot of solid, comfortable-looking houses.

"You're not homesick already, are you, Billy?" I asked him.

He looked at me, and I was sorry I had spoken. "That's Bay Ridge," he said slowly.

"Oh," I said vaguely.

"I live there. Look, and I'll show you our house." I followed his pointing finger with my eyes, saw the red-and-white houses, a suggestion of autumn foliage, and fancied the avenue where he used to walk along in front of the comfortable porches, very carefully dressed, reservedly twirling a walking-stick, and thinking of his career and his best girl. He must have been thinking of those things too, and the fact that he was so near to his home and yet so beastly far must have brought his family closer to him than they ever before had been. He must have thought, too, that it would be a long while before he would again walk, care-free, along the avenue in front of his home, and that meanwhile his fortunes, the plan of his career, were hatefully precarious. There was the girl, also, whom he must have thought of. . . . You know, I could see all those thoughts in his face as he turned to me without speaking and dropped his arm to his side in a gesture of pathetic resignation.

After a while I dragged Morrow below, telling him that if we didn't hurry we would miss our chow. I don't believe he wanted anything to eat, but he must have felt that it was bad for him to keep mooning over something he couldn't have. So we got out our mess-kits and stood in line before the galley, which already had begun to smell like an abattoir. There was a new messman in the galley and, as we had fallen in at the end of the line, it was a long while before we progressed to our dish of sickly-colored stew and our canteen cup of coffee. All the time Morrow kept looking out of the portholes, thinking much more about them than he thought about his food.

As we got near the galley Lieutenant Bedford came down to inspect the food, and one of the men asked him how long the ship was going to remain in the harbor before it sailed for France. We were all surprised and a little chagrined to hear him say that we would have to wait until our convoy was formed, and that might be six or seven days hence. Morrow started as if he had been struck, and took a couple of steps toward Bedford. Evidently, whatever was in his mind was thought better off, because he stepped back into the line, looking uncertain and troubled.

"Why don't you ask Bedford if you can see the major?" I asked Morrow.

"I don't know; do you think he would let me?"

"Well, if you don't see him you're crazy. He may let you go ashore on a twenty-four-hour leave if the ship is to be here a week."

Morrow's face looked like the sun coming out after a rain. "Do you really think so?" he asked, all excited.

Lieutenant Bedford had a great many faults and a great many virtues, and one of the virtues was that he would assist his men to get whatever they could. Morrow was readily given permission to see Major Wales. But when he got up to the office, that is, to the major's room, he found little Arthur Balder sitting there at the desk, pulling at one of those long, thin stogies which it was his habit to smoke incessantly.

Morrow saluted. "Private Morrow has come to see Major Wales, sir," he announced.

"Very interesting if true," said Captain Balder in the thinnest, highest voice in the entire world. "And what does Private Morrow want to see him for?"

Morrow nearly choked at that, for he would have saluted a militia lieutenant at a distance of fifty yards, he was so impressed with commissioned officers. "I want to get permission to go ashore for a few moments to see my parents, who live in Bay Ridge, sir."

"Major Wales," said Captain Balder decisively, "cannot be disturbed. You are dismissed."

Morrow got very white, saluted mechanically, about-faced, and marched out of the room.

For the next few days Morrow went about looking at the deck and not speaking to anybody, but gradually the news of Balder's actions got out. Hays said that the little devil should have had his pants kicked for interfering with the major's business; some one else announced that he would make a better ribbon-counter clerk than an adjutant of a battalion of soldiers; Sergeant Ryan mumbled that he was a cold-blooded little fish, much more so than anybody as insignificant as he had a right to be; and Pugh vouchsafed that he wouldn't let little ol' Artie Balder be private secretary to his dog. Which all helped Morrow very little and the adjutant a great deal less.

After the convoy did arrive, eight days after the transport had landed in New York Harbor, the ships set forth for France. There were two other transports, a battleship of some description, and there was said to be a submarine—of which nobody saw the periscope, and in which everybody believed—leading the way. For the first day the ships kept within sight of each other, looking very small in the distance; but after that they disappeared as thoroughly as if they had been sunk. A rough, following sea for the first two days out brought most of the men to the starboard side of the ship (the wind was blowing from the north). The entire sea appeared to be behind the transport, and each time one of the big, whale-like swells struck the stern of the boat the bow sank conspicuously and the stern tilted up toward the lead-colored sky. It had but one effect on the men crowded below in the hold, where there was no air except that which was heavy and greasy with the smell of the ship's galley and the odor of more than a thousand half-washed men. To have found fifty men on the entire boat who would have cared if a submarine had shot a hole through the magazine would have been difficult, they were so seasick.

The officers were somewhat better off; they had individual beds upon the promenade-deck; the air was fresh; they could have their meals served in their rooms by their orderlies if they desired; they had bunks to sleep on, and some one to look after them generally. But it profited them little. They were not accustomed to the ocean, and in a continually rough sea it seemed very unlikely that any of them ever would be. Lieutenant Bedford came down into the hold but once, and his case was not unique among the officers. The men, however, were required to be present at every formation.

Well, this was the morning of third day out, and I was lying near the bow on the main deck, propped up against one of those cast-iron spools they wind up the anchor with. I hadn't had any breakfast—I was glad enough to get away from that foul galley into the air without bothering about food which I couldn't eat, and I felt that each coming minute would be a little bit more horrible than the last, when the bugle blew for submarine drill. Well, my position for submarine drill was up on the poop-deck, on the sea side of one of the life-boats. I was supposed to hold a machete in my hand and, at the signal, to cut the ropes and help let the boat down upon the waves. When the bugle blew I got to my feet and staggered up the steps, weaving around like a drunken man. That life-boat which I was to stand by seemed to be at least a mile off, I give you my word, and I was sure I would never be able to get to it. But somehow I did—just before the second call sounded. And there I stood, with one arm hooked over the side of the life-boat, my feet on the very edge of the deck, my other hand hanging on to my machete. My face felt as stiff as if it had been frozen, and each time the bow of the boat dipped down toward the sea I felt as if I should turn inside out.

I hadn't shaved since the day before we joined up with the convoy and left the harbor for the open seas, and my face couldn't have been washed more than once. Several buttons of my tunic were unfastened at the throat. . . . With my hair uncombed I must have been a ghastly sight.

We had to stand in the positions we had been given until recall sounded. Meanwhile the officers poked around the ship to inspect us. I was still standing there when Captain Balder came up on the poop-deck, wearing a dark-green uniform with red piping along the seam of the trousers and on the shoulder-straps. He had on a pair of brightly polished boots, with spurs, and he tried to saunter along as if he were walking on some avenue instead of on the poop-deck of a nastily rolling ship. But his face, that thin little face of his, gave him away. Anybody with half an eye could see that he hadn't enjoyed his meals very much either. It was as wan as a faded quince. Well, when he came up to me, what did he do but halt and eye me up and down, taking me all in in that frosty, sarcastic way of his. And while he was standing there, making me feel like some Russian immigrant, he reached in the pocket of his nicely pressed blouse and drew out one of those damned long stogies, which he very calmly lighted, and calmly blew the smoke into my face. I could have killed him on the spot. It was such an uncalled-for thing to do, the sort of advantage a small man would take over a bigger one when he saw the opportunity.

The transport landed in Brest eighteen days after it had sailed from Philadelphia, and we squeezed and folded ourselves into box cars and started off over the country toward the Vosges to go into training. It was pleasant enough in the fall of the year, and even the ridiculous practice of spending an hour a day lunging with pointed bayonet at an inoffensive sack of straw, thumping it with the butt of the rifle, slashing it broadside, and pricking it to pieces was to be endured. But with winter the high, barren hills were covered with a fine snow; the long, winding roads were frozen over, and into them the wagon-wheels had cut sharp ruts. You could march for mile after mile and see only small clusters of gray cottages, lying low against the frozen, snow-covered ground. On the streets paved with colorless bricks, down the gutters of which was emptied the sewage, you might see no more than one person at a time: a woman with hands and wrists all swollen and mottled and part of a cotton petticoat tied around her chin and head, or an old man with a nose that looked like an icicle, coming out of one of the low houses beside which would be a monstrous, smoking pile of manure. Or there might be a plodding horse drawing a rickety, two-wheeled wagon. There would be the musty-appearing café with an ancient face peering out of the window as you marched past. And that would be all.

The roads were difficult to march on at best; some of the men had worn holes in their soles and were unable to get new ones; other men had been given shoes, those heavy, hobnailed boots that were large enough when you wore cotton socks but much too small when you wore thick woolen ones. Some of the shoes were of that straight kind issued to the English soldier, which may have been all right for the Tommies but which the doughboy could not wear at all. Over this desolate country, where there was not even the sight of a tree, the First Battalion, in their long green overcoats which reached to their shoe-tops, their cold steel helmets, their pair of gas masks, French and English, their combat packs on their shoulders, and the metal butt of their rifles freezing their fingers through their shoddy gloves, dragged out mile after mile of practice marching along the rutted roads which climbed one hill only to descend another.

One morning the men lined up in front of the tar-paper shacks in which they were billeted and which the French army had not used for two years, and started off down the road on a manœuvre. Major Wales had left to teach military tactics and the machine-gun at Gondrecourt, a school for American officers, and the battalion had got a new major in the absence of Wales. They marched along for about three kilometers, where they came to a crossroads. And there a new major, Adamson his name was, and his adjutant, Captain Arthur Balder, stopped their horses directly in front of the first platoon. The major drew a map from his pocket and proceeded to scan it as if he had never seen a map before in his life. The men began to kick the toes of their shoes against the ground, to let their rifles slip from their shoulders to the ground so that they could warm their hands by clapping them together. Captain Balder continued to sit on his horse, which was slowly backing into the leading squad, prim as a little old maid in his big saddle, and with his mouth screwed up in a knot as if he had eaten a lemon. Finally, as the major continued to gaze at his map and Captain Balder's horse continued to back into the first squad, big Ellis, in exasperation, stuck his thumb into the flank of the chestnut and made a clicking noise.

Without turning around Captain Balder straightened still more in his saddle and cried out in his high, thin voice:

"Major Adamson, one of your men went tch, tch, at my horse!"

Ellis guffawed loudly and the rest of the men commenced to laugh.

That was the last time I saw Captain Balder, for I contracted some unheroic illness, and when I was discharged from the hospital I was sent to another battalion. And it was not until five years later that I learned more about him. It was in New York, in March, and the rainfall, which I believed would exhaust itself in a mild spring shower, became a drenching downpour before I had walked three blocks. Through the meagre illumination of Broadway arc lights, pale in the wet night, I looked about for a scudding taxicab, but there was none to be seen, though I had noticed many when I left the theatre and stepped out onto the streets a few moments before. As I made out the sign-post of Fifty-seventh Street under the corner lamp, I recalled that within less than a block I would be at the armory, and if a light were burning in the tower window, I could as well go there as to go to my hotel farther up the street. Colonel Bartlett's room was lighted, and as I approached the large, semicircular brick entrance I fancied the warm fire, the bottle of Scotch, and the colonel sprawling in an armchair and dropping cigarette ash on the thick, dark-red rug.

Except for the ink and paper which I had not bargained for and which rested on the flat-topped table, the mental visualization of the colonel's contiguous surroundings was perfect. And above this scene of cigarettes, writing material, a bottle and a siphon rose the colonel's large but compact shoulders.

"You should keep your windows darkened if you don't want late callers," I said.

The colonel's lively face was good-humored as he stretched out a large hand. "Dry yourself at the fire until I finish this letter, and we'll have something that will warm you up inside."

I crossed the room and stood with my back to the open fire, listening to the scratch of the colonel's pen on the crinkly paper. It was nice of him to have invited me to stop whenever I saw a light in the office of the armory. It was much better than going on and getting soaked to the skin.

"There, that's finished." The colonel breathed with relief. Writing was not easy for him. He stood up, and with two tall, thin glasses before him poured from the bottle a quantity of liquor into each. "Come away from the fire; I hate to drink alone."

We drank.

"I was finishing up a letter to Balder when you came in." The colonel slowly drained his glass. "You know him, don't you?"

"I can't say that I know him. I didn't get close enough to him for that. But I know who he is. He was adjutant of the First Battalion, wasn't he? Little Artie Balder we used to call him."

"That's the baby," affirmed the colonel in his grotesque, out-of-date slang.

"Where is he now?"

"He's down at Washington with a soft billet at headquarters."

"So! Somehow, I can't imagine him as still being in the service."

"What do you mean? . . . I can't conceive of him doing anything else." The colonel accurately aimed a stream of seltzer at his glass.

"Well, I never could think of him as a soldier. I always thought he needed a nurse more than a horse."

The colonel laughed. "He was a damned good soldier, though." And then after a pause:

"You young fellows know everything in the world, that's the only trouble with you," Colonel Bartlett began. "Just wait until we polish off the rest of this bottle and then I shall try to tell you something." The colonel's blunt-edged fingers fumbled for a space among the cigarettes in the tin box on the table. He lighted a cigarette, inhaling deeply, luxuriously, then blew the smoke out of his nostrils in thin, gray jets, which looked like the smoke of a fiery steed.

"I don't know whether you remember it or not, but I was down at

Gondrecourt most of the first part of 'eighteen, trying to get some sense into the heads of those dumb, would-be officers. And I took charge of the regiment some time in the middle of July, coming up with Wales, who had also been down there and who was rejoining his battalion. We had a day's stop-over in Paris on the Fourteenth of July, and we saw the boys from the different armies parading under the Arc de Triomphe. It struck me at the time, the fact that we had a damn sight better looking soldiers than the rest of the outfits, but that their uniforms made our men look like ragamuffins. Then we went on up to brigade headquarters, which was just outside that town where our men had that knock-down and drag-out fight with that Alabama regiment." He paused to relight his cigarette.

"I didn't' see Captain Balder when I first came up, although I wanted to very much," continued the colonel. "I had known him for six or seven years—in fact, he was my lieutenant down in Santo Domingo. But I didn't have a chance to see anybody because I had no more than got turned around in the town than the corps commander called us all up to his headquarters for a conference. Well, of course, that meant only one thing, and I was glad it did, selfishly enough, because I hadn't been up to the front before except as observer with the British. When we came back we had the pleasant information that we were going to take another shot at the Heinies in a couple of days. I guess you remember it, all right."

I nodded. I did remember.

"The men had been pulled out of the line only about two weeks before, and I never saw such a demoralized lot in my life. Wales afterward told me that there were only about two officers in his battalion that were sober. The rest of them were running around like sunstruck antelopes, and one of the officers, who had been an old sergeant on the islands before the war and who ought never to have been promoted, was picking lizards from the trees, he had the D. T.'s so badly. I think it was all due to the bad example set by the regimental commander I relieved, but then that may be only my vanity. At any rate the day came for us to shove off for the front. I had the men lined up and sent down to the edge of the road outside of the woods they were staying in, to get aboard the camions. When the camions came, an hour or more late so as to give the Heinie air intelligence plenty of time to see us, we found that we were about one camion short to the company. Oh, the French are great in furnishing transport! Well, we got the men jammed by some miraculous means or other and started off. I saw Balder just as my driver was taking the car up to the head of the line. He was sitting on the front seat of one of the camions with the French driver, holding his hands between his legs and looking as if the weight of the whole world were on his shoulders. 'Get off of there and ride like a gentleman, Captain Balder,' I signaled him. He looked over at me quickly and nodded his head, making a movement to get out. 'Oh, hello, colonel; I'm glad to see you, sir!' 'Come on, get in with me and leave your bewhiskered, dirty friend.' He thanked me, shaking his head. 'I've got to go back to the end of the line.' 'Nonsense, are you drunk too?' I bawled out. 'No,' he said seriously, 'and that's the reason I can't go along with you.' Well, to make a long story a little bit shorter, I had to move along so as not to obstruct the traffic. Those French roads are so damned narrow that two bicycles can hardly travel abreast. So that's all I saw of Balder then. But I found out later from Wales that Balder had refused the nice fat cushions of my Cadillac because he felt it his job to follow behind the men and keep them from getting out and going up for a court-martial in consequence.

"The camions stopped early the next morning at the foot of a long, winding hill, and the men got out. They were cold and they hadn't had anything to eat since the noon before, not even a warm cup of coffee. We formed the regiment into a column of twos and started up the hill; it was about six o'clock in the morning, I guess. As we got up near the top of the hill the sun burst over the trees, and from then on the men were warm enough, let me tell you. When I passed fat Captain Stahl I could actually see the cognac exuding from the pores of the folds of his fleshy neck. And the captain of your company, sir, looked like a ghost that had been dug up. A damned worried ghost, too, because Wales had given him a bawling out that he'll never forget, and I guess had put him under arrest for drunkenness in the front line.

"We marched all that day, and at night we lay down on the crest of a hill in attack formation. I called the officers around me in the little gully my orderly had found and showed them the plan of the attack.

The First Battalion was to go over first; the Second was to be in support; and the Third was to move over to the left so that it would be half behind the infantry regiment which we connected with and half behind our own regiment. There was a level plain in front of us, according to the map, and I told the officers that we'd reach this plain in a column of twos, and that they were to proceed in that formation until they drew the enemy fire. Of course they were then to deploy. That's all there was to it. Our objective for the first day was a little town five kilometres away."

The colonel looked displeased, as if he were fighting the battle over and as if affairs were not what he thought they should be.

"We started off in the morning, myself accompanying the First Battalion to the edge of the plains. There I stopped, not wishing to get ahead of the tanks that were grunting and grinding into position in front of the infantry. In a few minutes I was joined by Wales, Balder, and the major of the second Battalion. We got out our glasses and began to look around us, wondering why the Heinies didn't open up. The infantry was slowly advancing, much too slowly, for they were held up so that the tanks could get ahead of them. We found out why they didn't fire in about five seconds. They were waiting for the tanks to appear so that they could get the direct range on the infantry, not with their machine-guns, but with their artillery, their eighty-eights, those infernal shells that explode before you hear them leave the gun. And when the tanks poked their noses into sight the Germans opened up, the first shell striking about ten yards from where Wales, Balder, and I were standing, throwing the dirt in our faces and kicking up a big plume of coal-black smoke. Then a whole bunch of shells dropped ahead of us, commencing a raking barrage. I wanted to run and Wales wanted to run and Balder looked too scared to run, but there wasn't any place to run to. They were firing shrapnel above our heads and high explosive shells in front of us. They let up for a moment, and as soon as the TNT cleared away a little I wiped my eyes and got out my glasses again to have a look at the infantry. They were still marching on in a column of twos, and Wales was cursing hotly because they hadn't deployed. While I was watching them the Germans began a steady machine-gun fire on our right flank, exactly on the flank of our infantry. One company immediately dropped into single file, but the rest of the men marched on in a column of twos. It was Bedford's company, and I heard Wales say: 'That's fine; Bedford knows his job.' And then, I'm damned if the company on the extreme right didn't suddenly halt and deploy in a straight line. That damned fool officer had literally followed instructions to deploy his men as soon as the enemy opened fire."

"Good heavens!" I said.

"Well, there the men were, about two hundred of them all lined up so that the machine-gun bullets could go in one man's side and come out through the side of the man next to him if it didn't strike any bones. And each spurt of fire would kill not one but twenty. 'My God, major,' I heard Balder cry out, 'look what Bemis is doing!' And before any of us had a chance to say a word he had left us and started through the barrage, his spindly legs taking him along as fast as he could go, and his head bobbing above the wheat tops.

"Well"—Colonel Bartlett stopped to dry the sweat which his vehemence had brought out on his forehead—"I thought Balder was gone for sure, and I turned my back so as not to see him fall. It seemed impossible that he wouldn't get hit by something. There were snipers shooting from that little town in front of us, machine-guns riddling our right flank, and high-explosive shells making a wall of black smoke in front of us. But the suspense was too great and I turned around to watch him. A shell struck in front of him, and I saw the dirt and wheat flying up into the air on top of the smoke. But in a minute there was Balder again, hurrying along to the right of the line where the men were in the worst possible position they could be in. Another shell struck near him, and I expected him to fall down or to crawl on his hands and legs if he hadn't been hit. The German artillery could see him plainly, and thinking he was a runner they were spending their shells on him.

"I'll swear I don't know how he ever got there. But he did, and we saw him taking charge of the company, raising his arms and blowing his whistle, and making them fall into sections in single file with one command. Then we saw the hand-grenade section make a dash in a right oblique toward the machine-gun nests. Oh, he is a wizard at extended order drill, and he would make a great drill-master if it weren't for his squeaky voice!

"And then the damned fool turned around and started back toward us, more slowly than he had gone. There was no reason for the Square-heads to keep on firing at him, but they did fire over enough shells to make you think Balder was a whole battalion, or an ammunition dump or something equally important. When he got back to us there was a straight row of puffs of smoke between him and the German artillery where the shells had exploded. We all gathered around to talk to him, an unwise thing to do, for a shell came over, rattling in the air like an express-train, and bursting directly beside us. It knocked me flat on the ground, and when I got up I saw Balder sitting there, fish-ing in his tunic pocket for one of those long black stogies which he buys in job lots. He took one stogie out and looked at it with a kind of puckered expression, because the cigar was broken near the middle. But he tore off the broken part very deliberately, stuck the cigar in his mouth, and put a match to it. After a couple of puffs he looked up at Wales and said in that high voice of his:

"'Major, don't you think you'd better have these things cut off? They are utterly useless to me now.'

"I looked back at him more closely. He was sitting with his legs wide apart, as a young boy sits when he plays on the floor with toys, and both of his legs were bleeding. . . . he lost one foot at the ankle, and the other leg had to be amputated just below the knee."

V

Rintintin

I do not know whether you remember them or not, or even whether you ever saw them—those strange little dolls which some of the French soldiers carried in the pockets of their tunics or wore about their uniforms? They were inconspicuous enough, no longer than your finger, made of cloth-wrapped cotton batting, with dots for eyes, a dab for a nose, and a dash for a mouth, and shapeless little arms and legs. Yet, somehow, and it might have been the sentiment attached to them and for which they stood, you never forgot them. It might have been the plaintive quality of those absurd little eyes, eyes like periods made by the point of a pencil over which the writer had paused sorrowfully, knowing that he had not put in his sentence that which was in his heart.

As I say, they were a creation of the French, and they had not a little to do with love, which is more of a wild, hectic emotion in war-time than it is at more peaceful moments. There were two of them, fastened together by a string; and of course one was male and the other female. The one which courtesy bids us name the gentler, seemed, were she alive, as if she would be a flighty-headed creature, constantly taking an attitude of rapturous abandon. Rintintin himself looked as if he had been blown silly by the winds of irresistible passion. I don't believe that the wearer ever bought them—purchase would have destroyed their charm—rather were they given by a French girl to her sweetheart at the front as a symbol that she was with him wherever he went, that she loved him and that, presumably, she would remain faithful in the course of his absence.

They were French, purely, but now and again a pair of them found its way into the American Army, carried by one of the soldiers who had been back of the lines for some time among the native people, or who had lived in France before the war. And when one of them did appear among the combat troops, brought to the rest billets by the returned wanderer, there was always a group of soldiers to gather around with jeers on their tongues, envy in their hearts, and curiosity in their manners. For it was the carefully preserved fiction that the person who had been any place but the front lines had been enjoying life to its utmost. The jeers were borne by the soldier who had not been back of the lines comparing his lot with the man who had, and finding himself to be of firmer stuff, more heroic, more deserving of commiseration. The cause of the envy is obvious. The curiosity came in the desire to know what the newcomer had seen, what he had brought along with him.

That was the sole reason for their crowding about Johnny Benner when he came back. Benner had left just after we had had our first casualty, before we had got to the front. During bombing practice one of the men had withdrawn the pin from his grenade and then, becoming frightened, had held it in his hand until it exploded. A few days later Benner fell and hurt his knee. When we returned to quarters that night we learned that he had been sent to the hospital.

That was back in March, and it was now October. A scant handful of the men of the original company remained, and some of them had almost forgotten Benner. The ever-arriving new men with whom we had filled up the company after each attack had never known him. And I remember how he stood in the middle of the main billet, his heavy pack depending from one arm, the lighted tallow candles illuminating his burly form, looking uneasily around for some familiar face to greet him. Little wonder that he did feel out of place. The first sergeant and most of the other non-commissioned officers were from replacement battalions, and the soldiers themselves, lying around in the main billet, huddled in groups, must have made him wonder whether he had not come back to the wrong company.

For my part, I would rather he had. He was simply a man I couldn't like. His eyes were impolite, they were always trying to violate your individuality, to make you feel that you would have to give room for them in your thoughts; his manner, too, was obtrusive: whenever he talked he would lean toward you, lay his hand on your shoulder, or, if you were seated at a table, he would thrust his dark face close to yours.

He must have stood there a couple of minutes before Hannah, beside me, got up and broke the silence with:

"Well, I'll be damned, if it ain't old Johnny Benner."

Shortly, nearly every man in the billet was standing around him asking questions, scanning the equipment he had brought back, wondering if he had a supply of cigarettes somewhere hidden about him. As Benner stooped over to unstrap his pack, he started to grumble against its weight and to curse at the long march which he had had to take to get back to the company.

Hannah looked at him scornfully. "If you hadn't laid back there on your dead hams ever since March you wouldn't be so soft; you'd be able to stand a little hike. You ought to have been with us, hikin' up to Soissons, or standing in the mud for two days at Saint Mihiel. You ain't got much to bellyache about."

Everybody expected Benner to protest, to sound the hardships back of the lines. In our opinion he couldn't have said much that would be valid, but we at least expected him to defend himself. He was, however, not that kind. He never defended himself, because he always tried to make you feel that whatever happened to him was better, more interesting than that which happened to you.

"You're right, Hannah, old kid, I wouldn't. I sure had one great time back there. Beaucoup chow and beaucoup cognac. I et till I almost busted. Yuh git up in the morning and have a big yellah omelette and cocoa. At noon you have steak or rabbit, and at night it's chicken. Boy, an' they know how to cook, too! Nawsir, Hannah, you're right. If I'd a been up here with you guys I wouldn't a met my little French gal neither." He thrust his hand into one of his copious pockets and withdrew it, holding triumphantly for all to see a small cloth object which dangled ludicrously from his large fist.

By this time nearly everybody had arisen and all were grouped around Johnny Benner, examining the new Enfield rifle which the quartermaster corps had issued to him, the new shoes strapped to his pack, each man covetously wondering whether they were of a size that would fit his own feet. The Rintintin, to which Benner had directed every one's gaze, looked lonely without its customary partner, but Benner didn't seem to mind that. His protuberant brown eyes glistened as he held the little thing above his head.

"See this?" he asked loudly. "From mah sweet baby Jeanne." He nodded his head as if to give weight to his assertion. "Some gal, too. None of these damned cocottes for Mr. Benner. No, sir! 'Is gal's the daughter of one of them French dukes that live in castles, an' she was waitin' all her life for her uncle John Benner. An' boy, did I cop her off! Well, did I!"

"Give him another shot and he'll say he's Pershing," suggested one of the new men with high, fine sarcasm.

Benner remained unabashed. "Do you want to know how I met her?" he challenged.

Nobody did.

"I was walkin' along one of them rue de rues one day an' I come to what I thought was a park, a great big place, an' lousy with trees and flowers. Well, in I goes, bustin' along like the lord of creation when I come to this little pond. The grass was as high as your ankles and the bushes looked like they hadn't been trimmed, an' on I steps wonderin' why the city don't keep the place in better order, when I run plumb into the little woman. She's sittin' there on an iron bench lookin' kinda absent-minded. 'Hello!' I says, 'ain't you 'fraid you'll get lost, way out here?' 'Comprends pas,' she says, straightenin' up an' shakin' her little head. 'Comprom pah pah pah?' I asks, plantin' myself beside her. Well, she give me a smile for that and the first thing I knowed we was pearty good friends." Benner paused a moment, lost in contemplation. "Some gal she was. I usta see her every day after that. She lived in a big castle an' this park was the front yard. An' when I went away she gives me this little thing." He admonished our incredulous eyes with another shake of Rintintin.

"Where's the one that goes with it?" asked Hannah.

"She kep that," smiled Benner broadly. "When this damn war's over," he broke out vehemently, "I'm a-goin' back an' git it an' her too an' take her back to my folks."

"She was probably the gamekeeper's daughter," snorted Wendell from Harvard.

Wendell could not be blamed for his skepticism. Benner's boasting, before he went away, had become notorious throughout the entire battalion. He had told of his family, of their garage full of motor-cars, their servants, their dinners, in such a blatant and preposterous way that if you believed him you had to consider him to be, at least, the son of a Midas, and also to accept as fact that the American upper middle class was more preposterous than you had supposed. He had, he said, taken degrees at half of the better-known universities in America, he had been every conceivable place, from Siam to Nome. And he was not yet thirty. He never said simply that he knew any one. If you happened to name a person of national importance he would say: "Yes, I know him. I know him personally." His pretensions were palpably false, his speech, his name, yet you always had a feeling of hesitancy in believing his tales to be lies. What if they weren't lies, you wondered. For you felt, perhaps, that anything could happen in America.

But this last, this affair with the French girl of royal blood, on which he was always elaborating as we waited back there in our billets ready to return to the front, seemed to contain no truth at all. He was unattractive physically, and his head was a hodgepodge of misinformation. His shoulders were as graceless as a half-filled sack of potatoes, his large nose splattered all over his face, and his hair was never combed. How, one wondered, would it be possible for a woman to have any feeling for him at all? We had, though, a degree of sentiment for Rintintin, so we were loath to accept the fact that Benner had bought it. It was one of those stubborn, disagreeable facts like admitting that people bought Croix de Guerre and said they had been decorated. Yet, in the end, we all did agree that Benner's story was sheer cock-and-bull. And there the matter rested.

We were supposed to have been withdrawn from the front lines to rest, but announcement of our daily activities, put up each morning on the bulletin-board on the old French house which was being used as headquarters, did away with this supposition. Reveille sounded at seven o'clock, the equivalent of taps went at nine. Between seven in the morning and nine in the evening we went through setting-up exercises, close-order drill, skirmish drill, practiced rushing machine-gun nests, washed our clothes, stood inspection—in short, our legs were given exercise and our tongues something to grumble about, making the front seem pleasant in comparison with our arduous rest camp.

One morning, as we were standing in formation in the company street, between the rows of mutilated stone houses, squatting low beneath the steel-gray corrugated sky, the command "Squads right," which sent us in a column of fours down the street to the level drillgrounds, did not come. And, shivering in the late October air, we waited, growing more restless every moment. The company had been reported all present or accounted for, the brief inspection was over, and the ranks were closed; but still we waited, moving our feet about, turning our heads to the right and left, mumbling to one another in indistinct voices. Sharply, the warning voice of the first platoon commander bawled out: "Platoon 'shun," and a scraping of feet was heard all along the line as the men straightened the company front. By tilting the body forward it could be seen that our vulturous friend the brigade commander was paying us a visit. Slowly and measuredly he tramped along our front, his chin tucked in the collar of his coat, his hands behind his wide back, his wiry eyebrows meeting in a bristling line above his bulbous nose.

Silence.

"Give your men 'At ease,' Mr. Powers," he called out to the company commander.

Reluctantly, we assumed nonchalant positions, sensing some kind of trap. "Company attention," the brigade commander called in his slovenly way. Prepared, our heels came together with a click.

The brigade commander seemed a very stern, very important personage as he stood there before us, his feet apart, one hand still behind his back, the other holding a paper in front of him, in his Napoleonic way. The manner in which he cleared his throat was ominous.

"When you men came over here, nearly a year and a half ago, you weren't fit to be called parade-ground soldiers even, except for the scant number of regulars which made up the basis of the regiment to which you belong. Eight months later, when I took charge of the brigade, you didn't look much better. But since that time, at Château-Thierry, Soissons, and Saint Mihiel, and Blanc Mont, you have had your test. You fooled us all; the Germans, too. From time to time you have been read citations of your valor, from the commander-in-chief of the American Expeditionary Force, from the divisional commander, and from French generals also. I've got a message from the divisional commander for you here now. It says:

> *Men of the Dash Division: You are about to go into action again, to action on a front where one division has already signally failed to advance one foot. . . . The eyes of every division in France are upon you.*

The brigade commander cleared his throat, placed the piece of paper in his pocket, and walked away. Shortly, Captain Powers addressed the company with the announcement that there would be no drill that day, but that we were to remain in our billets, ready to leave at any moment.

"Company dismissed." Slowly we wandered back to our billets.

In our own billet every one was so deathly still I felt that if some one didn't' soon speak it would be hard telling what might happen. "Well, it's up and at 'em again," I said to Hannah at last. But Hannah was lugubrious in the extreme, and my careful, jocularly intended little prhase struck him unpleasantly. "Yeh," he said solemnly, owlishly. "And if we come back it's up an' at 'em again. That's all we've been doin': blood and corruption ever since last April." Not to be a Pollyanna, but merely to assure myself, I suggested: "It will be winter soon and then, if the war's not over, they'll take all the good divisions down in Southern France to get ready for the spring drive." Hannah looked at me blankly, then wearily. "Be yourself," he chided. "We'll never get any rest this side of hell."

"Snap out of it," I pleaded. "I thought you were a soldier. If John Benner hears you he'll start running and never stop."

Hannah looked toward a corner of the billet where Benner was half kneeling on the floor fumbling with the straps of his combat pack.' The perception may have been false, but every contour of his Leviathan-like body seemed to be quivering with nervousness. All of the men were busy at their packing, judiciously eying their equipment in the interests of lightening their load, but Benner seemed obsessed with the task. Keeping his back to all of us in the room, he continued to play with the buckles and straps of the khaki-colored carrier, rolling and unrolling his blanket, visibly puzzling over whether he would take along his extra pair of shoes or whether he would give them to some one else.

"I'll bet his heart's between his teeth this very minute," said Hannah, and chuckled.

"The great big dummy."

Having exhausted the resources of his pack as a means for employing his time, Benner turned around while we were still unobtrusively regarding him. Fear of death was stamped as plainly on his face as if it had been kicked there by a Prussian boot.

Hannah nudged me, speaking under his breath: "He looks kinda peaked." And I thought of Hilaire Belloes verse of the bad little boy who detested being eaten by the bears.

The time came for our midday ration of blood-colored stew, but still the order had not been given for us to be ready to be on the march. We were all a little nervous. Conversation was as forced as if each suspected the other of being General Pershing in disguise. After a while talk was entirely abandoned, the men sitting stiffly and glumly beside their equipment.

It was four in the afternoon and beginning to grow dark when the order came for us to fall in within five minutes. The clatter of hobnailed shoes on the old stairways of the houses in which the men were billeted was not very brisk. And as we swung off, down the unlighted street, we were all silent except for one of the men who called out despairingly: "My God, are we going to walk!"

When midnight came and the sky, the horizon, and the earth were all welded fast into an impenetrable sable sheet, we were still on the dogged, silent march. And as we proceeded through the solid blackness—it was so dark you couldn't see the man in front of you—we heard muttering from the side of the road on which we were moving. The owners of the voices, of course, could not be discerned. The voices themselves seemed to come from nowhere, yet almost at our sides. It was irritating to hear those strange half-intelligible mutterings, to feel presences, thick about us, and not to know who they were. It gave an eerie quality to the night. And as we advanced through the black-ness, grown almost palpable, a feeling of dread, of horror, wrapped itself about us like a heavy cloak. When I would raise my foot from the ground in a forward stride I would have this peculiar sensation of something ghastly being between my foot and the ground. It made me squeamish, caused me to hesitate, sweatily, to put my foot back on the ground. Now and again some one, fearing that he had become lost from the line of march, would cry out chokingly, begging to be assured that he was near his companions. Then, too, from our right and left, and sometimes from behind us, would come the sharp red flash of a shell leaving one of our pieces of artillery and hurling over to the German lines. The ear-drum-battering explosion was fright-ening, shocking, and we would recoil, in fear, with the gun, but the flash of light would give us momentary orientation. Then blackness again, and the timorous plodding of weary feet on the road which was somewhere beneath. It was a cold night, almost November, but for some odd reason drops of sweat kept creeping down my face from the padding of my steel helmet. And, queerly, I fancied the perspiration to be red in color. When, in the name of God, I wondered, would the night ever cease? Where were we going? And from that time onward I had the illusion that we all were walking blindly into the German front line in close order.

It lightened, but no more than the suggestion of a shade. Only light enough for me uncertainly to apprehend the narrowness of our path and the tangled tree limbs clutching at one another overhead. The trees were jammed together in an unbroken wall on either side, it appeared, and the lack of air was so stifling that I felt like a man in a vault the immense door of which had slammed shut. I was brought to a sudden halt by bumping into the man in front of me, the shock of contact being so great that my throat closed and I could only whis-per: "What is it?" And while I was waiting for an answer, the com-mand was passed back for us all to stand fast. The order meant but one thing to me. That was that our guiding officer had lost his way and had just discovered that he was leading us directly and precipitately in the German lines.

You could feel the tremor and the tension of the line as it stood there waiting in the night. The damned fools, I ragingly thought, why don't they do something, why don't they give us about face and let us get out of this? And as I stood there wondering, I felt the line swaying, moving to the right of the path, and heard one of the officers coming, reiterating a command in a low voice. "Deploy in the woods and swing forward," I made out as he approached and passed me, going on down the line.

Somehow, as I prepared to follow out the order and wormed my way through the woods, I found myself beside Johnny Benner, who grasped at my arm and hoarsely asked: "What's up, fellah, what's up?"

He knew as much as I about the manœuvres, and I told him so.

"You think I'm yellah, doncha? You think I'm nothin' but wind?"

He embarrassed and exasperated me. "Shut up. I don't think it of you any more than I do of myself."

"Then why don't you tell me where we're goin'? You think I've got no guts, that's why."

"You damned idiot!" I fairly shouted. "Because I don't know where we are going any more than you do."

He caught my arm and turned me toward him, reaching out his other hand. "Shake," he said solemnly. And as he spoke, with his face close to mine, I could smell enough cognac on his breath to have run an automobile to Jericho.

"Come on," I said, "and shut up, we're on some kind of a reconnoitering party and we've got to keep quiet. Can you remember that?" By this time I knew well enough that we were in attack formation and that it was only a matter of minutes before we sighted the enemy. But I feared to tell him that.

Each moment it was growing lighter; I could now see the buttons on Benner's jacket, and in a short while it would be daylight. Ahead of us the woods thinned a little, and as Benner and I broke through the thickness we saw a second lieutenant from one of the other platoons who tightened his wabbling chin long enough to tell us to halt on the line.

There was no dawn that morning; rather the sky attenuated itself until the light showed through its thinness, the sagging sky so easily pierced by the tall-topped trees. We stood waiting for about ten minutes. I was able sufficiently to detach myself from the fear of the following to think of Benner. In spite of his drunkenness, his face was already the mask of death. It was as if he knew without doubt that he would be killed soon. Had I felt as he seemed to feel I believe I should have run like a rabbit; but perhaps not; perhaps there is a fascination, a kind of hypnotism that comes with the sign of your own death.

From off near the road came the long, shrill blast of an officer's whistle, commanding us to begin the advance. Before the piercing sound had fully died, several violent gusts of Maxim bullets tore at our line. Half gasping, screamingly fearful, I hurried through the woods with the rest of the men, with the muzzle of my rifle pointing in front of me, the stock tightened securely between my arm and side.

Undoubtedly, our attack was a surprise to the Germans. The barrage had been laid back of their support lines, cutting off any means of their sending reinforcements; the attack itself had so quickly followed the barrage and had begun at such an early hour that they were still lying unprepared, pig-like in their dumbness and amazement, when we came upon them. All of them that I could see were heads, helmets, and shoulders, massive shoulders without necks, and helmets which looked like shorn cuspidors turned upside down. Those helmets made an infuriating picture, and I was conscious of putting new clips of shells in my rifle several times before we passed their outposts. It was certain that we would soon encounter their main line of defense, the place where they had dug themselves in, and seeking friendly support I looked back for Benner, calling: "Come on, soldier, don't fall down now." But he was not behind me. It came to my mind that he had sprawled to the ground in his drunkenness or else that he had scampered back to safety. "Desertion in the face of the enemy," I thought. "Well, he'll get his for that, the big coward." It seemed strange that my mind could be so detached from the actual danger before me, so that I was regarding my own actions as if I had been the proverbial innocent bystander looking at another person charge through a wood.

I was not wrong in apprehending their strong line of resistance in spite of their surprise. Coming to a thinning of the woods where the grass grew high, our line was struck by a furious fire of bullets whining nastily about our legs. As those of us who were still unmaimed crossed through the grass we saw a short way beyond a long breast-work of yellow, freshly dug clay and, peeping over the top of the new ground, the muzzle of rifles and those thick, hood-like helmets. There was nothing to do but to go forward, to go at them, firing everything you had to fire. Though it did seem impossible that I would ever pass beyond them or that they would retreat.

But the attack had been exceedingly well planned, and admirably carried out. As we were going on, every second winging us to certain death, we heard boisterous shouting on our left, heard the snapping of twigs and the cracking of tree limbs as a great many eager-footed doughboys pushed through the woods upon the enemy in a flank at-tack. It was the Ninth Regular Infantry and as they swept in, curs-ing and yelling in a curious mixture of tongues, the Germans rose as one man with their hands above their heads, and crying "Kamerad."

The sight of the infantry was glorious, and for a moment I be-came a spectator. While they herded the quaking prisoners together, sending one American back with ten or twenty Germans, I sat down on a tree stump and looked back over the ground which we had just passed, thinking of Benner. "The damn yellow-belly," I thought, "if he had only stuck it out!" With a start, I saw an olive-drab uniformed body lying motionless not ten feet from me. There was something very familiar in the body, in the large hunched shoulders, with one arm thrown in front of him, the other doubled up under him. I turned the body over and saw the face. It was Benner, with a grin on his face that could only be described as beatific. "What the hell!" I thought, knowing now that he had got to the Germans before I had. I turned his body clear over, unbuttoned his jacket, and pressed my ear against the pocket of his khaki-colored shirt to listen to his heart. There was not the slighted murmur. Another way of determining death came to my remembrance—the mirror before the mouth. But I had no mir-ror, and, detaching my bayonet from the muzzle of my rifle, I held the blade before his blue blood-drained lips, hoping to see its whiteness become clouded. Evidently Benner was dead; there was not the least moisture on the bayonet blade although the day was cold.

I was sorry, ashamed at having misunderstood him. My only atone-ment was to collect his valuable possessions, his keepsakes, his mementos, his watch, and send them to his family with a brief account of his death. Otherwise some ghoul robber would take them himself, and Benner's family would have nothing to remember their son by, not even his watch or his bill-fold. From his inside jacket pocket I took a sheaf of letters postmarked from a lower Indiana town, and addressed, one in pencil and two in ink, in straggly, unscholarly hands. The watch in his pocket was a cheap gold plate, stopped running long ago, and fastened to the heavy brass chain was one of those nickel cigarette-lighters purchased from the French. In another pocket were two French post-cards, of broad-hipped nude cocottes, the kind that are sold in cafés by fat old hags. Where, I wondered, was Rintintin? Or was the story but a momentary fancy with him, permitting him to throw away the doll after he had exhausted its dramatic value? Something stiff and clinching about his arm, the one thrown forward in front of him, caused me to look at his hand. It was tightened into a fist, and protruding from it, the hand already blue, was this bit of gay-colored cloth unquestionably being a part of Rintintin. The button of the left pocket of his jacket was unfastened. With that to assist me I could easily visualize his last act had been to clutch at this doll, and hold it tight no matter what happened. Gently I straightened his big fingers, and dropped the doll into the khaki handkerchief into which I had deposited the watch, the post-cards, and the letters.

Nine days later the armistice was signed, the actuality of which was manifested to us only in the following ways: we knew that the artillery of both sides went silent, that we were permitted to build bonfires to keep ourselves from freezing in the damp November weather, and that we could smoke at night if we could get the tobacco. But I give you my word that the armistice meant very little to us. Where was the release from a year and a half of privation, of hunger, cold, and misery? In lying on the damp ground under shelter tents, chilled and with less than half enough to eat? In listening to new officers, recently come to the battalion from some training-school in the service of supplies, thinking up disagreeable duties for us merely to show their authority? In thinking of a lonely hard march to the Rhine while the bells were ringing in New York and Paris? No, we would rather have reached Berlin with our rifle-barrels hot and smoking.

It was not enough, apparently, that we were combat troops. At least that fact was not sufficient to prevent us from being mustered into the service of grave-diggers. Five weeks after the signing of the peace found us with picks and shovels, making deep rectangular holes in the stiff clay ground for the proper burial of the dead. Our only consolation was that we were doing it for our own men and not for the fallen of some other division.

For bleakness the day will remain unsurpassed. The sky was granite, the earth was a vast continuance of drabness, even the stones which our picks occasionally turned up were of a dull mouldiness. And on top of it all were the bodies in boxes which had been lifted from their transient graves to be put in a place of greater permanence. It was the kind of weather during which the cost of inactivity is shivering, yet it was not bracing enough for one to wish to work hard. Another discomfort was our not having gloves; the moist clay would get into the chapped places on the backs of our cold hands. The distaste, the loathing with which we regarded those wooden boxes! Most of the dead we had not known, but now and again we would find an identification disk of aluminum, fastened to the box, which bore the name of a soldier who had been with us long. And then it was worse than ever. Here was a man who was among us once—dead and gone, and we had stopped fighting apparently to dig graves.

"All right, you hear me, snap it up," called out the new sergeant, now in command of our pleasant little excursion. "We gotta git this done some time."

We continued working, plunking with the picks and scraping with the shovels, and whenever the depth of the hole satisfied the officious sergeant, we dropped our tools and lowered one of the boxes into the freshly dug grave. We continued steadily for some time, saying little, causing the sergeant to believe that he had dominated our spirits completely. As we were finishing one of the holes the sergeant commanded: "All right, that's deep enough. Drop it in."

We dropped our picks and grappled with the box. By this time we had become pretty tired, and, as we were lazily taking hold of the box, little Brown called: "Hey, wait a minute. This is got Johnny Benner's name on it. I didn't know he got bumped off."

"Then I don't know where you could have been all this time," I said. "He was the first to get it. The day we began the attack."

"The hell you say! That's too bad. I'll bet his folks'll take it pretty hard." Philosophically: "Money don't help you none if you git up to the front."

"That's the joke of it," offered Sanderson, who had just been relieved from his job of company clerk in favor of some diabetic friend of the first sergeant that had joined the company after the armistice; "he didn't have any money or any family either."

"You mean to say all that stuff he was handin' us was bull?" asked Brown.

"Well," said Sanderson, "when he kicked off there was nobody to notify but an uncle of his who wrote back that he would like to see Benner get a decent burial but that he hadn't a red to help."

"All right, you birds, get a move on," prompted the sergeant.

We glared at him sourly. Some one told him, very precisely, where to go.

"What do you think of that?" I muttered blankly. "What—do—you—think—of—that!" I felt in my pocket where my hand encountered the handkerchief which held Benner's last possessions. There was Rintintin. And the question arose as to what I should do with it. I could send the letters and the watch to the uncle, but what to do with the doll?

"I don't like to talk mean of the dead, but he certainly was a louse if there ever was one," said Kirk solemnly.

"He died jist as hard as the best man in the regiment," said Brown, as we lowered the box to the grave.

Soon shovelfuls of dirt were scattering dismally on the boards. It was covered up. A mound was made and a home-fashioned Christian cross was placed at the head. The sergeant started to nail the identification disk to the juncture of the cross.

"Here, wait a minute," I said to him. And rather sheepishly I untied the handkerchief and put the doll under the piece of metal.

"Can that," objected the sergeant, "that ain't in the regulations."

"Regulations be damned!" I said, "You leave it there."

Later on Captain Bell, wrapped in a warm army overcoat, strolled among us and, after watching for some moments in silence, ordered the sergeant to give us an hour's rest. A short distance away, halfway over the brow of the hill, was a small café out of which the Germans had been driven and which was now being gleefully operated by its original French proprietor. There was coffee, wine, and, if you knew the owner, cognac. We lost no time in getting to it.

It was warm in the café, and, seated around the rough table on a board or a three-legged stool, we were prepared to enjoy our hour. The sergeant sat alone, with no one to talk to him; most of us had a great deal in common. Brown withdrew a fifty-franc note from his pocket, flourishing it above his head. "What shall I buy?" he asked excitedly, "what shall I buy?"

"Mussear," he called to the short, fat, smiling proprietor, "Cinquante francs pour soif, tres bon, savvy?"

The proprietor clapped his hands and bowed. "Oui, m'sieur, oui, oui, toute de suite." He rushed toward the kitchen.

"Where's he goin'?" asked Brown.

He returned in a minute with three cobwebbed champagne bottles, and from his gesticulations and his pleased talk we made out that these bottles had been in his cellar ever since the Germans had taken that territory two years before but that he had kept them hidden from them.

We all were properly impressed. Brown handed him the money, which he refused with a fine gesture.

As we were sitting there drinking, the door opened. Mechanically we hid the bottles under the table. But it was a girl that entered, a tired, timid-looking girl as she stood there in the half-light of the café. In her black dress, small black hat, and small, high black shoes, half covered with mud, there was something pathetic about her, too.

"Soldat Américain, monsieur?" she asked Brown fearfully.

"Yes, ma'am," Brown answered with emphasis.

"Connaissez-vous le Capitain Bennair?"

"Who did you say?" asked Brown.

She looked about imploringly, her eyes growing brighter as the proprietor appeared from the kitchen. They talked like magpies for a minute and then the proprietor came over to me.

"Madame . . . mari . . . Capitain Américain . . . Bennair."

"Captain?" I asked blankly. Another one of his lies. The girl must have walked twenty miles. How the devil did she get through? So this was the answer. "Captain Benner?" I asked, endeavoring to be impressively polite. Brandishing one of my few French words, I added: "Certainement."

She followed me out of the café like an eager little terrier. And as we walked up the hill and she saw the white crosses she clutched at my arm several times, attaining composure almost immediately.

"Voilà," I said, as we stopped before the grave. Very gently she tiptoed to the cross, reading the name, then stopped and began excitedly to clasp and unclasp her small frail hands. "Rintintin!" she cried. "Rintintin," pointing to the doll. For a space she sought among the things in her small hand-bag, then brought out the companion doll, Ninette, which she triumphantly swung before my eyes. She looked at Rintintin again.

Suddenly she crumpled up, as if she had been cut in two, and sat down on the ground so violently that I reached out my arms to assist her.

She was still sitting on the fresh grave, her small head in her lap, her arms about her knees, crying softly to herself, when I slipped back down the hill to the café.

VI

A Little Gall

It was late November. But whether the hour was morning, noon, or nearly night could not have been told without a watch. For the vicinity of Saint Nazaire, this was not unusual. In the absence of a discouraged sun the shorn trees were sweating coldly on the hillside. The rain was seeping through the gray, heavy sky; and in a long, curving line a company of soldiers, too chilled to remove their mustard-colored tunics, bent their backs over the soggy earth. There was the subdued scrape of the shovel, the dull sound of the pick striking a stone as the men, with stiff, hampered movements, grubbed up the damp sod, making a wide, deepening path of frosty earth on which their greased cowhide shoes moved as slowly as the tedious hours.

Corporal Lewis, whose industry had taken him a little in advance of the bowed line, once more raised his pick and brought it heavily down into the moist-clammy earth. He was tired, but not with a physical fatigue; it was because his efforts had brought him nothing. Nausea was there too, and a nostalgia for either of two poles: home (which was northern Illinois), where the bands were blaring stirring music for the men who were beginning to be drafted and where young women laid their bodies on the altar of patriotism and prospective life insurance; and the front, where the goaded snort of the enemy guns, yet unheard by him, was the daily diet. But this existence in continuous dampness, of chain-gang labor—the antithesis of heroism—was difficult for him to accept. Without raising his pick he gazed toward the lank, freckled lieutenant in charge of the working party, and saw that officer attempting to warm his feet and yet to appear stoical;—as if, in addition to the other desirable perquisites of junior office, second lieu tenants never got cold! The reflection was irritating, forming a base for a pyramid of minor troubles. . . . He hadn't enlisted to dig ditches. He had *left* a damn sight better job than this to come over here and fight. And as he leaned his sturdy shoulders above the wooden handle and stared at the freckled lieutenant he grew rebellious. Hell! There was no use standing there and shivering to death. He straightened, turned, and walked away.

Saint Nazaire was a few miles distant, but halfway on the road which led to it (a road which winds slowly among pale houses and is scantily covered by frayed trees as it twists downward to the sea)—halfway to Saint Nazaire is a buvette, and many soldiers, upon seeing it, decide to go no farther. Corporal Lewis was one of the many in that he found the buvette a pleasant place to stop. It had benches with roughly made tables before them along the walls; the walls themselves were unassuming except for the one to the left of the entrance, where a few sticks of wood blazing in the fireplace drew one's attention. And then there were the shelves of bottles on the walls: four-star Boulestin, Saint James rhum, Amer Picon, Vermouth, Benedictine, cherry rocher, cointreau, and a great many others which Yvonne, whose large hands looked broiled to pinkness, did not reach for as often as she reached for the cognac. As Corporal Lewis opened the door and stood for a moment on the sill he would have had to search long to find another interior so companionable.

"Ullo corps!" A voice from the shaded part of the room informed Corporal Lewis that he was not the only soldier who had left the working party for Yvonne's buvette. Nor was he pleased with the knowedge, for the absence of too many men would be observed by the freckled lieutenant. Then, too, some one was always fool enough to get drunk and cause trouble. "Only thing I ever found that'd take this cold outa your bones," said the voice, pointing a grubby finger at an emptied cognac glass which stood before him on the table. "Corps, have a little drink." The voice was timid, anxious.

"Yeh, have a shot on me, corpril."

"Lord!" said Corporal Lewis, sliding his body between the bench and table, "it wouldn't take many more for the whole company to be down here."

"Yvonne!" called the first voice, straightening, "'incha got 'ny respect for a corporal? Give the man a drink."

Yvonne in her bedroom slippers, which she wore six days out of the week, trotted into the room from the kitchen, tying the strings of her apron around her fulsome waist. She smiled.

"Caporal, beaucoup coniac," explained the second voice, subsiding.

It was just what he needed, Corporal Lewis knew after the first glass. But as the drinks were small the liquor seemed to lose much of its warming quality before it reached the proper place in his anatomy. Lewis could feel the untouched spot, just above the webbed belt that tightly girded his solid waist, cold and grasping. This gnawing sensation quickened him to remark, "The next round's on me; fill 'em up again, Yvonne." He translated his English by describing a circle with his long index finger, a circle on the inside of which were the three empty glasses.

After a while Yvonne set the bottle of Boulestin in the middle of the table and departed with the purchase-price in her pocket.

"Now," said the first voice, "if the corps don't mind we'll settle down to a little drinking."

"I know what you fellows thought. You thought I came in here to run you into the brig." Corporal Lewis traced a spiral course with the stem of his glass on the wet top of the table.

"You're a corporal, aren't you?" the first voice significantly inquired.

Lewis leaned forward, resting both forearms on the table. He had never wanted to be a corporal, but he could not avoid the warrant. He was too self-reliant, too physically fine to be permitted to remain a private. "They wished the job on me; I didn't want to take it," he said without the note of apology which usually accompanies such talk.

"I guess I was wrong," admitted the first voice; "I thought old Bran Face had sent ya down after us."

"You know," said the second voice, suddenly grown warlike, "I'd like to see that big stiff"—the big stiff was Bran Face and Bran Face was the freckled-faced lieutenant in charge of the working party—

"come down here and try to run me in. I'd knock him for the longest row you ever seen."

"'nd so would I," Corporal Lewis assented grimly, lowering the neck of the bottle to the brim of his glass. Saffron from a black mouth dribbling in a water-white glass. It was the cognac that was grim.

"Oh, no, you wouldn't," the first soldier grinned wisely.

"Why the hell wouldn't I?" Corporal Lewis spoke so fiercely that the eyes of the first soldier were covered with a film. Nevertheless he answered:

"You got those two stripes on your arm, that's the reason."

"Let 'im live, corpril, let 'im live. He don't know what he's saying," put in the second soldier with strong contemptuousness.

"You think so, do you?" asked Lewis, speaking thickly and leaning across the table toward the first soldier. "You think these stripes would make any difference in what I said if that shave-tail came in here? Listen!" his voice rose, "I'd jist as soon take a poke at him as take another drink."

"You cert'n'y would," declared the first soldier in admiration. "Here, 'y God, I'll buy another drink."

Half an hour later the buvette door opened and the three men, their arms about one another's necks in friendly fashion, tried to reach the road at the same time. And as they precariously, but happily, made their way in the light that was neither of morning, noon, nor night toward the grounds where the company still worked they sang, to the tune of "What a Friend We Have in Jesus" the following lines:

"When this bloody war is over
No more soldiering for me;
No more dress parades on Sunday;
No more taps or reveille.
" %-&'()**)('&-%$ "??? $%
)('&-%$ "ögg?" $%'-)&(
I'll be damned if I can soldier
With a shovel, pick, and hoe."

Nearer the place where they should have been working, where their rifles were senselessly stacked in four short rows, their approach was more sober. But pretense was useless now, for they had been observed. And as they came nearer a half-covert whisper fluttered along the line of working soldiers. One straightened and frankly stared, another furiously flayed the ground with his pick, as if he himself feared punishment for the deviltry of the three intransigeants, and still another muttered ominously that "They'd get theirs." But the lieutenant had not moved; even when he summoned a duty sergeant his words were scarcely heard.

For no reason at all, unless the lieutenant's folded arms could be called a reason, Corporal Lewis found himself walking over the moist ground past the gaping men toward the waiting officer. So the duty sergeant who had come to fetch him drew back uncertainly as he marched unsteadily by. Arm's length from the lieutenant Lewis stopped and saluted, an exaggerated, slashing movement of his right arm.

"Corporal, you are under arrest." The officer drummed with his fingers on his upper arm. "You two other men go back to work, but you, Lewis—why for two cents I'd knock—"

Suddenly Lewis stopped swaying. "Hell," he said, and tried to spit contemptuously. "Why, I'd give a dollar jist to take one good poke at you."

The lieutenant's eyelids flashed upward, like unexpectedly released window-shades. From set lips he said, "Sergeant, march this man into the guard-house."

All the way back to camp, over the dreary roads, scarred by the wheels of the camions, Corporal Lewis walked beside his armed escort. A grin widened his mouth and his broad nose turned up more than ever. Altogether he appeared so blissful that one of the guards completely forgot the importance of his duty and smiled with friendliness. Momentarily, Lewis chuckled; the smiling guard grew apprehensive, and the expression on his face was that of a nice mouse who, miraculously enough, was guiding the steps of a lion. The stocky shoulders of Corporal Lewis were impressive.

They came into sight of the long, low-lying buildings of the camp and the guards straightened their rifles on their shoulders. But the prisoner continued to grin, and once, as they marched up the gravel road to the guard-house, he said in defense of his integrity, "I gave him as good as he sent, and anybody that says I didn't is a liar."

No one denied his claim. Not even the sergeant of the guard who took his cartridge belt from him and went through the formality of searching his pockets. Doubtless, he would not have heard if they had, for his head was going round in a buzzing haze and his spirit was amicable. What had he done? Nothing. All of this searching of pockets seemed as much like byplay as a kangaroo court. It was only after the barred door of his cell in the guard-house had been closed and locked that he began to remember. Then slowly, as he looked out over the dirt floor where the second relief was sleeping on soiled mattresses and saw the sergeant of the guard making out the evening report, the scene came back to him. But what had he said? Distinctly enough he saw himself standing before the lieutenant, but the rest of the picture was a blot. What of it? What difference did it make? He laughed to prove that it made none, then because his befuddled mind perceived the sound to be mirthless he laughed again. One of the guards walked uneasily to the cell door to quiet the disturbance, but Lewis had stretched out on his mattress and at once had fallen asleep.

Inmates of the guard-house were spared the before-breakfast exercises in the cold morning air. As Lewis awoke in his cell he could hear alongside the building the Seventy-fourth Company's drill sergeant calling out "Hands on hips, place!" and fancied the men in unison bending their knees, thrusting out their arms and thumping their chests in the routine manner of working the stiffness from their bodies. He looked out into the darkened room and seeing the first relief of the camp guard sleeping, waiting for breakfast, he thought, with gloomy pleasure, "thank God, I'm spared that, anyway." He had in mind both the guard duty and the setting-up exercises. After awhile breakfast was brought and Lewis's cell door was opened by a taciturn guard who set a canteen cup of coffee and a mess-kit of mush on the floor. Metallically, the door slammed, leaving Lewis to his silent meal. Life in a cell, Lewis considered, had not been so depressing when he had been a member of the guard. He had talked to the prisoners. But these fellows, why, they treated you like you were a criminal!

At ten o'clock a scared sentry in front of the building bawled, "Turn out the guard, officer of the day." But he permitted the officer to approach him too closely for the first and third reliefs to put on their belts, button their overcoats, and rush out the door before the officer came into the guard-house. "'ten-shun," angrily commanded the sergeant of the guard, suspecting a reprimand and eager to pass it on before he had received it. "Carry on, carry on," sourly ordered the officer of the day, glaring at the ensemble. Lewis could sympathize with him. When he had been acting sergeant of the guard he had always got his men out on time for inspection by the O. D., the commanding officer or any one else whose rank required the courtesy of the guard.

"Nothing new turned up?" the O. D. asked the sergeant. "Got a new man in the lockup, lieutenant." "Drunk, or A.W.O.L.?" "No charges yet, sir." Lewis looked up startled. That he had not yet been charged with a particular misdemeanor increased the uncertainty of the nature of his punishment. He tried to placate his mood by telling himself that at most he would be fined a month's pay. The lieutenant was speaking again.

"What's the man's name?"

"Corporal Lewis, sir."

The lieutenant seemed surprised. "Lewis, what's he in here for?" he asked the question of himself and Lewis saw him walking toward his cell. The lieutenant had small hands and a small, nervous face. His steps, his gestures, every movement was hurriedly made, not as if he were important, with many mission to perform, but as if he were impatient to finish his duties. "What are you here for, Lewis?" he asked sharply. "I don't know," answered Lewis, grinning. The lieutenant frowned in a preoccupied manner. "You better hurry up and get out. I want you in the intelligence section." He walked abruptly away. And after he had gone Lewis called:

"Sarge, can you come over here a minute?"

The sergeant walked to the cell door into the iron lattice work of which he twined his gnarled fingers. "What is it, Lewis? I can't let you smoke if that's what you want."

"No, I don't want to smoke now. But sarge, I tell you: If you want to git your guard out pronto next time, just have your corporal in front of the guard-house kick his heel against the door as soon as he catches sight of the O. D. Then by the time the sentry sings out, the men'll be ready to fall in out in front."

"By gosh, that's a good stunt. . . . I never thought of that. . . . Say, Lewis, if you want to smoke, go ahead."

Lewis looked hurt. "I told you I didn't want to smoke."

On the third morning of his stay in the guard-house Corporal Lewis was given a suit of dungarees, pale blue and sloppy. And with them covering his uniform and a sentry behind him with fixed bayonet, he was marched into the company street, past the men who were forming for drill. The men stared as he passed and he wrenched a grin into his face as he went by his own company. But later, as he was digging up ground for a new latrine, his hands and dungarees caked with reddish clay, and the sentry was standing over him, when his platoon marched past he looked steadily down at the earth, and the veins stood out on his solid neck with chagrin.

It was only the beginning. That, Corporal Lewis discovered a week afterward from the court-martial board which, perhaps unable to make up its mind as to what action to take, sent him back to the guard-house. He also learned that he was charged with offering violence to an officer and he began to worry about the approaching Christmas. For, obviously, with neither money nor freedom, he would be unable to send any presents back to the States. A special court-martial meant that he would lose at least the month's pay. He could, of course, write home, but it would be difficult to explain, the folks would not understand; they always believed conditions worse than they actually were. Grimly, he went through the dreary days. One evening, less than a week before Christmas, he sat in his cell until long past midnight, his hands feverishly grasped and his eyes staring sightlessly through the iron lattice work of the door.

On the morning of the third day before Christmas the officer of the day (he was second in command of the Ninety-fifth Company and the embodiment of everything that was swashbuckling) stormed into the guard-house with a heavy frown. "Dammit," Lewis heard him say to the sergeant, "bang goes Christmas. Just as I had a party all fixed up at Saint Nazaire we get orders to break camp." He pulled vexedly at his black mustache which was like two turned-up sabres. "Hell," said the sergeant, "we're outa luck, too; jist had a table put up in our bunk-house and ordered two cases of champagne." After awhile the sergeant inquired, "where we goin'?" "Oh," the officer carelessly replied, "somewhere up near the front. Better sharpen up your teeth. We may have to eat cannon-balls for our Christmas dinner." Move, thought Corporal Lewis. The battalion was going to move, and his heart behaved much as if he had been pitched from a ten-story window. What would happen to him? Would he be left here, separated from the men whom he had enlisted with? Violently, he shook the door of the cell.

The sergeant of the guard noticed him sufficiently to command, "Stop that racket and sit down."

But Lewis had to find out. "Sergeant, may I speak to the officer of the day," he called so loudly that the officer walked over to his cell.

"Lieutenant, are they goin' to leave me here or what?" the question choked him.

"Oh," said the officer of the day tolerantly, "they'll take you along all right. You needn't worry about that."

After riding in box cars for several hundred miles, from the southwestern part of Brittany to a town a few miles from Verdun, the battalion stiffly got out of the train and tried to walk on legs which had been sat on, lain on, twisted and crushed for so long a time they had got entirely out of their owners' control. In this part of the country the trees grew more erect, more militant. It was easy to fancy that soldiers' bodies, feeding the roots, had severely fashioned the trunks after ramroads. In this country were hills, pastoral hills half covered with snow, and the battalion wound among them on its way through Souilly to Somme Dieu. At its lagging tail was Corporal Lewis, the only man without a gun. But on either side of him was a guard equipped with not only a rifle, but a pistol. The slow pace irritated him, for he was less tired than the rest of the men. He had ridden in a caboose of which the only other passengers had been his guards, while the rest of the men had been herded in groups of forty into the absurdly small box cars. But his restlessness passed when the moving troops came abreast of a French hospital and some inspired young officer, though he had never before seen or heard of the place, pointed it out as the subject of the Germans' latest bombing atrocity. "The dirty dogs," thought Corporal Lewis, as he surveyed the long, white, wooden building. "Any one could see the big red crosses on the roof of the building." There was no excuse for it, the Germans had deliberately bombed a hospital! "That was a lousy trick, wasn't it?" he appealed to the guard on his left. But it was no use; the guard refused to talk to him.

Toward noon they crossed a slender river, clear as a mirror, and plodded up a slope to the battered, uninhabited town of Somme Dieu. There was a long, cobblestone street which bent sharply in the middle. On either side was a row of those soft stone houses which take their color from the weather. As the sky was a sheet of slate, the houses were ashen. From the roofs of some of the houses it was plain that Somme Dieu was familiar with the brunt of the enemy guns.

The battalion stopped, then moved forward jerkily, and Corporal Lewis discovered that the men were being billeted in the houses. As he stood there waiting, the advance officer marched down the line, slushing through the street drain with an air of looking for some one. "Oh, there you are," he said to Lewis's escort, "follow me and I'll show you the guard-house."

Sentries had already been established (one was standing before the door) and as Lewis walked inside followed by the two guards he saw that even a cell had been prepared for him. It was a larger cell than the one at the camp in Saint Nazaire. It had stone walls and a stone floor like the house of which it was a part. But the door was of wood, secured by a large padlock. Corporal Lewis went inside. As the door closed after him the lock snapped fast.

Sometimes, in those long days that followed, Lewis had the strangling fear that he would never be released. And terrifying suggestions of madness would come to his mind. The guards never took him out any more. Apparently there were no more latrines to be dug. How he wished there were! If only he could feel the touch of friendly earth. But now through the days he could only sit and stare at his strong hands with which he once had done so many things but which had become good for nothing.

Everything imaginable seemed to be happening outside the guard-house. In his mind the dreary street was like a stage set and reset for a musical comedy. He fancied girls and soldiers strolling together, men drinking in plush cafés where the orchestra played under swaying palms. But once he looked outside the door of the guard-house and saw the forlorn street he feared the battalion had moved to another town. But this he could not bear to believe. They could not go there without him. Once he pretended sickness. It got him a dose of calomel. A few mornings later he heard the officer of the day speak his name to the sergeant of the guard and saw the latter pick up the key to the cell door. Fascinated, he watched the key in the sergeant's hand. As the key slipped into the padlock, Lewis stepped forward, ready to leave with the outward swing of the door. The lock snapped and he stepped into the room.

"What is it, another trial, sir?" he asked the officer of the day.

"Not that I know of. I got orders for you to be turned loose and to see that you report back to your company."

Lewis laughed foolishly. "Gosh! Are you sure? I mean—Well, what d'ya know about that. Report back? I guess I will." He ran back into the cell and came out with his blanket, his mess equipment and his other belongings which he was allowed to keep with him. "Yes sir!" he said emphatically, "I'll find the top sergeant right away."

That night there was much laughter in the house where Lewis had been billeted. All of the men were of his own platoon and though he had no money himself Jack Pugh had plenty and some of it was used to buy wine, biscuits, and canned preserves from the French canteen. Pugh made a show of reluctance at parting with the money, but finally said, "Heeah, spend iss hunnerd francs and lemme alone. But doan ask me to tote nuthin." They sat about the bright fireplace and drank and slapped Lewis on the back and one of the men said, "Why, man, it was a blessing for you to be in the lock-up. Nothing to do and just think, you must have about four months pay coming." They did not go to bed until the sentry threatened to call the corporal of the guard.

Four months' pay coming! Nearly one hundred and fifty bucks. Lewis could not sleep for thinking of it. At the lowest rate of exchange that was six hundred francs and with that amount he could buy almost anything he chose. Green jade beads, wrist watches, bottles of champagne, women's legs, all ran helter-skelter through his brain. In this muddle of things he had not dared dream of for week after week, and somewhat dizzy from too much wine in a warm room, he fell asleep.

But in the morning his eyes were bright when reveille was blown; he was the first man dressed and out on the company street for setting-up exercises. After breakfast and morning inspection it was very pleasant as the battalion was given "Squads right" and the men swung from the cobblestone street to the fields for drill. Lewis liked the feel of the muscles as his legs stretched out; it was like getting off a boat which one had been on for several weeks.

"Hup, two, three, four; hup, two, three, four," Sergeant Ryan called in his low contralto. Then "Squads left . . . company, halt." And they were out on the drill grounds, making ready for practice with hand grenades.

The drill grounds were in a wide valley, spacious enough for a battalion to march and countermarch. At the farther end, where the valley stopped and a hill began over which could be heard the boom of guns, was the bombing pit with white targets rising out of a wide, deep trench. The company was split up into platoons and the platoons into sections. Then the day's training began, with Lewis's section the third to practice.

"You go through it by counts; first pull out the pin, then draw your arm back, shift your weight to your right foot and let it go with your arm kinda stiff," Sergeant Ryan counselled him. "Remember, with your arm stiff. If you try to throw it like a baseball you'll break your elbow."

Lewis's turn came and he grasped the heavy, corrugated grenade in his right hand. Now he was good for something, he exultantly thought. At the count of two he withdrew the pin, dropped his right foot back and held the grenade far behind him. Three, the count sounded, and sighting, with his left arm outstretched, he threw. The grenade struck the target fairly, a drumfire explosion followed as it went off.

"Good work, corporal," said the instructor to Lewis. "Now let's try it from the fifty-yard range."

But Lewis was equally successful there. His grenade struck the target from every range. His blood was singing and he felt that he could have hurled one of the grenades over the top of the hill.

On the way back to camp Lieutenant Bedford, his platoon commander, told him in a low voice, "Lewis, that was pretty good. I think I'll put you in charge of the bombing section. It'll mean sergeantcy."

One morning a few days later as the battalion was closing ranks after inspection, ready to march off down the Rue de Dieu to the drill-grounds, an officer arrived from headquarters in an automobile which stopped at the near end of the line of men. The officer, with his glistening Sam Browne belt and polished, spurred boots, got out and walked toward the major, holding up a warning hand. The two men met, saluted, and after talking a moment the major called:

"Corporal Lewis . . . front and centre."

From the first sight of the officer Lewis had been suspicious. Hearing his name was none the less such a shock that his rifle slipped from his cold fingers and banged against the cobblestones. Without picking it up he stepped backwards and, going in rear of the second company, walked toward the major and visiting officer. Halting, he saluted.

"Attention to orders," began the officer in a loud voice, loud enough for all to hear. . . . "Corporal Lewis did, on or about the 20th of November, strike or attempt to strike . . . officer . . . found guilty . . . that he be sentenced to five years in Federal prison."

VII

The Ribbon Counter

They were all the same—no difference at all between one and another so long as each wore a tin hat, an olive drab uniform, and a gasmask slung around his neck; all the same under the steel Stetson—like hell! —MacMahon was following out a generalization he had read in a soiled, month's-old periodical, picked up by chance. The writer had referred to the soldiers as "All Sammies, all the same under the tin hat," MacMahon resentfully remembered as he sat with his back against the inner wall of the old farmhouse in which his outfit was billeted.

That night or the next the regiment would move forward into the front line, and MacMahon, who had already been in four major offensives, found it better for his mental peace to view life just then through some one else rather than himself. He didn't like the little voice, somewhere inside him, which kept saying: "Five times and out; five times and out!" ever since word of this new drive had come to the men one evening after they had lain, motionless, for three days under the uninterrupted duel between the Allied and enemy artillery.

Though the news had been accepted with a stony satisfaction it was, MacMahon knew, like lying supine on an operating table, while the surgeon made lengthy jests with the nurse, and a hog butcher prepared to perform the operation with a cleaver; horrible, yet greatly to be preferred to uncertainty and complete impotence. And in addition to this relief there was more than a little pride in the mind of the regiment as it looked forward to the engagement. For three times the artillery of an entire corps had laid down a barrage, and three times the division in the field had failed to advance; ergo, the Second was now being called into action to break the Kriemhilde Stellung, the northern side of which no Allied soldier had seen since 1914, except as a prisoner of war. Like all other American divisions in France—whether they guarded warehouses or worked as stevedores—the men of the Second considered themselves to be shock troops, and their foe was the well-known and invincible Prussian Guard. That was customary.

"Five times and out—All the same under a tin hat"—the latter phrase had the upper track in MacMahon's mind, and he stared at Captain Osborne and Lieutenant Johnson, seated together on a sack of straw on the stone floor of the half-razed farmhouse, but looking toward opposite corners of the battered wall. Johnson had just returned to the battalion from officer's school, where he had been since summer; he wore a new serge uniform, shining puttees over his bulging legs, and a Sam Browne belt about his full stomach. No one could have taken him for anything but an officer. From a stranger it was he instead of Captain Osborne that would have received the salute. Beside him, Captain Osborne lost by contrast what little he had to distinguish himself from the enlisted men. There wasn't much: his uniform was of the same regulation issue as MacMahon's, and spotted with clay and grease; his cloth puttees were frayed; his steel helmet dented, and his gasmask had many times been used as a pillow. Also, he was smaller than Johnson, more spare, with compact, determined shoulders, and sober brown eyes which seemed ever to be gazing, troubledly, toward a scarce seen object.

What they said to one another that night, MacMahon did not know. But at ten o'clock when the company squirmed into its equipment and tramped through the darkness in a column of twos to join the battalion on the main road, he was sure that Johnson had stayed back with the "Twenty per cent," the messmen and the other noncombatants. For a time, as they marched along in the black night, it annoyed MacMahon; he had always suspected Johnson of being spurious in some way, but as the man had never actually been to the front, he was never able to make certain. Still, he had his private name for him: the sword swallower. It fitted perfectly, he knew. "The damned sword swallower!" he muttered viciously.

But that night there were greater troubles than Johnson. The battalion had a long way to go before dawn, and unless they hurried they would be late. The road was slippery with mud, and from time to time the weaving line would be forced to halt and wait for the machine gun company, which struggled forward, sweating under the weight of their heavy tripods and their boxes of ammunition. From the rear end of the double column the order came: "Pass the word along; the machine-gun company's not caught up." Then the line halted, and as the slack was taken up men unwittingly stumbled against those in front of them, until they were all jammed together on the road. This separated the rear end of the infantry still farther from the leading column of the machine gunners, so that there was an irritating period of waiting until the stragglers arrived. Then the hooves of a saddle-horse clumped along the road, and an angry voice cried out: "Fall out on the right of the road," or "Git th' hell outa the way!" The line of men removed the rifles which they had placed behind them (as a prop for some of the weight of their marching equipment) and staggered into the ravine between the field and the road where they sat, impervious to all physical sensation, until the moment came for them to be on the move once more.

An hour or more before dawn the thickly black night, through which they were sightlessly marching, burst, all about them, into red leaping flashes, and the following reverberations shook the muddy ground under their tired feet. The bombardment had begun, and as if it gave them speed their pace quickened while their weariness decreased. Now voices sounded on either side, some asking: "What outfit, buddy?" eliciting the gruff reply, "Second." Though no professional historian has ever marked the incident, MacMahon knew that many artillery officers, in both the division that was to be relieved and the one—the Second—which was to take its place, would either win or lose several months' pay as a result of the infantry's success in the morning.

It had seemed impossible that one division should accomplish, in one attack, what another division had failed three times to do—but when morning came, so faintly over the soggy earth, the infantry was close behind its own barrage with fixed bayonets pushing through the heavy woods, parting the low tree limbs and trampling the brush.

Captain Osborne, in the lead when the battalion broke into the woods, was the first to reach the clearing, a flat piece of ground at the base of a hill, black with trees. The clearing buzzed with the maddening, inquisitive zip-zip of the machine-guns ahead, but Osborne pushed on calmly, his shoulders a little forward, his head drawn into them so that his neck appeared shorter than it really was, and holding a Colt automatic in his hand. Strangely, MacMahon found himself following closely, with Morrow and Thomas joining. There were others, but they did not enter MacMahon's consciousness, not even when they sprawled foolishly on the ground. MacMahon saw only the few slabs of gray rock which peaked the hill, the untrampled, brown-tinged earth which led to it, and Captain Osborne and himself drawing nearer each moment to the slender muzzle of the Maxim out-thrust from a crevice in the rock. Like a rapier of a thousand blades, held by an invisible and expert fencer, the bullets of the machine-gun flashed by so closely that he could feel the scorch through his cloth puttees. Then, for the first time, Captain Osborne's pistol answered, and, as if it had been agreed upon, MacMahon shifted his rifle to his left hand and reached in the pocket of his blouse. Slowly his hand came out, grasping a grenade. For a moment he was scared, ready to fall to the ground: he could not put down his rifle, and he could not extract the pin from the grenade with one hand. His energy was draining away as he caught the pin between his teeth and twisted it out with a jerk. Calmly, his arm drew back; he aimed, and the missile, on a dead line, whined through the air, struck the top of the rock and bounced inside. He fell forward as the thing roared out in explosion, then watched the mushroom cloud of dense smoke rise above the gray slabs.

Of those who had climbed the hill but four reached the emplacement, though the machine-gun had been silenced, and as MacMahon followed Captain Osborne into the nest, where the biting smoke still hung, he saw the gunner, his face resting against the stock of the maxim, his right hand clinging to the trigger guard and his left thrown in front of his head. The loader was seated beside the water-cooler, his body limp and his head lolling against his shoulder. His face was a chronicle of ten days' fear and privation: an uneven growth of beard on his cheeks was matted with grime, yellow where the dirt had not changed it to drabness; his pale blue eyes could not have taken on much of a difference in death; the lines at the corners had been engraved by nights of waiting, by the strain of repulsing an enemy three times, and the pupils had long held the knowledge of his end.

The main line of defense would be a short distance ahead, and Captain Osborne raised the German from the Maxim and placed the machine-gun so that the barrel pointed in the opposite direction, while MacMahon was sent back to discover how far the rest of the battalion had advanced.

He ran down the hill on legs that had a strong inclination to crumple at the knees! At the base he saw the path to the clearing marked by bodies, and as he came to the edge of the woods and found another company breaking through, he cried hysterically: "Thank God, you've come!" "Just like some fool girl," he upbraided himself, a short while later.

Then, during a period that was loathsome to recall, they advanced forty-two kilometres through the deep forest. The enemy had begun an organized retreat, now that their main line of resistance had been broken, and though there were plenty of machine-guns and snipers to be killed or captured, the division advanced so rapidly that the field kitchens and the supplies could not keep up with them. At night they sometimes slept on the wet moss or fallen leaves with a ration of two blankets for three soldiers. For nine days this advance continued, and then, bedraggled with mud, chilled from the damp cold days and the colder nights, so hungry that fat, uncooked pork and raw potatoes were accepted without remonstrances, their bodies so dirty that they ceased even to itch, they arrived one morning at the edge of the woods where, in the bowl of the valley below, they could see a river wandering through untilled fields. The first man out of the woods stepped quickly back, for a volley of machine-gun bullets, sudden as hail, struck the ground in front of him. The next passed knee-high, and in an instant the whole battalion front was charged with lead. The men stopped still, the suddenness and fury of the resistance making them dumb as cattle. An officer ran along, skirting the woods and shouting: "Back, back, you damn fools, and dig in!"

MacMahon looked compassionately on those lumpheads who were digging deep holes—as if they expected to remain there for the rest of their lives. It would be "Up an' at 'em" again as soon as the attack could be formed and the position of the enemy estimated, and he, Mac-Mahon, did not propose to waste his substance in a wanton assault upon the earth. No, he had done that too often; he was wiser now, he thought. Nor was he wrong, for toward noon, after the machine-gun patter had died down and the big shells had commenced to whine overhead and burst into the woods, a section of small tanks appeared, wheeling and squirming around on the left and right flanks, and the officers and non-com's bestirred themselves, exhorting the men with cries of: "Up you come there, soldier!" and "Git your stuff together; we're gonna shove off."

Reluctantly, with a feeling of dread stiffening their legs and arms, they stepped cautiously out of the woods and advanced slowly over the brown sod, soggy in the noonday sun. From somewhere ahead, perhaps from the ridge far beyond the river and the hill which it drained, rattled the machine-guns of the enemy, feebly answered by the few Hotchkiss guns which had kept abreast of the infantry.

As the tanks struggled through the moist earth the German artillery shortened their range, the shells exploding in front of the infantry so close that great pieces of earth were thrown up, striking against the men's faces and clothing. There the counter barrage was aimed, a curtain of ripping metal with each gun firing at two-minute intervals. And when it seemed that the alternative to retreat was annihilation, the tank in front of MacMahon's company stopped still, forcing the infantry to halt with it.

MacMahon remembered Captain Osborne then, tightening the chin-strap of his helmet, which sat so closely to his rounded shoulders, and walking through the hail of bullets to the motionless tank. What was in his mind MacMahon did not know, but he surmised that it had to do with moving the tank. While he watched Osborne he forgot his own fear in the fascinating sight of a man who, knowingly, drew the brunt of the enemy fire upon himself. Why didn't he go faster, MacMahon implored, but Osborne walked on with short, quick steps, one hand at his holster to keep his pistol from flapping against his legs. He was about ten yards from the tank when Mac-Mahon saw him sprawl forward, much as if he had tripped, and go headlong on the ground.

He waited, but Captain Osborne did not rise, not even with the welcoming bark of the seventy-five's, which had got into position and were hammering at the ridge ahead. Nor yet again with the support line troops, who had been ordered up to fill the gaps in the attacking regiment.

The next morning at eleven o'clock the order came to cease firing. The war was over, somebody shouted, and the rest of the soldiers looked at him, speculating on whether to throw their helmets at him or up toward the boughs of the trees. The colonel sent out his runners with instructions that fires would be permitted, and that if the men had not used all of their reserve rations, they should be allowed to eat them then and there. At four o'clock that afternoon, as MacMahon was scraping together more wood to throw on the bonfire, the brush behind was roughly parted, and a voice called:

"Sergeant, what are you doing?"

"For the love of—" MacMahon began in exasperation, then looked up and saw Lieutenant Johnson's polished puttees and new serge suit. "Gatherin' wood for a fire," he ended sourly. He continued collecting the damp twigs, and after gathering as much as he could carry, he walked back to the place where the men were grouped, warming themselves. On his way he wondered how the devil Johnson had got up there so quickly. Though it was just like him, the sword-swallower. He was the kind to stay away from the front while there was danger, and then to pop up, like a jack-in-the-box, the moment there was peace. And his, MacMahon thought shrewdly, was the sort that made war where none was—war among his own men.

He had an opportunity to judge in the course of the long march when the division followed, forty-eight hours behind the German army up to the Rhine. Johnson was given charge of the company, and the first day on the road the new commander showed his aptitude for military tactics by making the men walk at attention instead of permitting them route step, which was customary on long hikes, and which Captain Osborne had allowed even on short ones. The second morning the company was fallen in, ready to be off before any of the others. This extraordinary zeal had caused some grumbling in the ranks, and it must have been heard by Lieutenant Johnson, for on the sixth day, at Arlons in Belgium, he delivered a speech which MacMahon learned by heart:

"Some of you men think that just because the war is over you can act pretty much as you damned please. But I want to tell you right here and now that you can't. We've all fought the Bosche together, and had a pretty hard time of it, but just because we licked them is no sign that we're going to lay down now. We're all employees of the United States Government, and it's our job to follow up these Squareheads until we hit the Rhine. And I want to say that we'll do it like a bunch of soldiers instead of a bunch of bums. From now on every man will shave once a day; he'll keep his shoes greased and all of his buttons fastened; his rifle and haversack will be kept ready for inspection. And there will be no grumbling. If any of you men have anything to complain about, tell it to me; if you start any of your damn agitating around there'll be a flock of court-martials."

The big stiff! Saying that *we* had fought the Germans. Expecting a man who slept in haymows and who hiked until long past dark to shave every day. All employees of the government! Yes, only the difference was that Johnson never made so much money before in his life, and many of the rest of the men had never made so little. If thoughts were included in what Johnson called "your damn agitatin' around" MacMahon would have spent the rest of his years in Fort Leavenworth federal prison.

In Luxembourg, where the regiment halted for two days because they had come upon the German army, and the rules of the occupation required that they remain at least forty-eight hours behind, Lieutenant Johnson received his captaincy. His celebration was carried out in rigid accordance with his nature; he invited the new officers to his billet, and set before them bottles of schnapps and German champagne, urging them to drink, while he remained coldly, gloatingly sober. He was a captain with three hundred dollars a month, and the right to demand a great deal of respect.

From the new men and the new officers whom he outranked deference was given him. The older soldiers, Morrow, Bloom, Rainey, and Galt, were silent in his presence except at such times as those when the company had to go without its chow because Johnson had not given the proper instructions to the mess sergeant, and the field kitchen remained far behind, or when the new billeting officer, gone ahead to the objective of the night to requisition places for the men to sleep, had marked out the same houses which another company had already engaged. There was plenty of heated clamor then.

But Captain Johnson had continued at the head of the company as they marched in the long, plodding line over hill and valley, and wound along the river bank of the Ahr, where the cliffs were red and copper-colored, and where a natural formation of rock, shaped like a mammoth chair and called the Kaiserstuhl, dropped its long shadow on the twisting roadside.

It was a hopeless trip throughout for the older men. Wearied from the eleven days' struggle through the Argonne, stiff and chilled from sleeping on the damp ground, wretched from insufficient and disagreeable food, they had faced the hike through three countries and a duchy. Many had continued only because of bullheaded pride, but when the company crossed the Rhine there were soldiers straggling for miles behind, victims of dysentery, influenza, and exhaustion, all with blistered feet. It had seemed a manifestation of someone's vicious brutality, that march. With the war before them, MacMahon had not minded the discomforts, the fatiguing marches with shoes whose soles had worn through. A purpose could be seen, for the enemy was at their destination. But with the war over, where was the need of killing more men in a senseless race to the Rhine?

Captain Johnson had not shared MacMahon's opinion. At the first formation in Honnigen, after the company had been billeted with the poorer of the German families, he had announced that those soldiers who had fallen out would be charged with Absence Without Leave.

And now in the great fortress of Ehrenbreitstein artillerymen of the Second Division had settled down to a routine of barracks duty. Across the river at Coblenz more Americans were guarding the bridgehead. Eastward, along the Rhine, in Neuwied, Rheinbrohl, Leutsdorf, and Honnigen, sentries of infantry companies patrolled the streets, and the units themselves, climbing steep, snow-covered hills in attack formation, were already practicing those same manœuvres which, but two months before, had cost the lives of hundreds of their members. Nominally the war was over, and people were beginning to wonder why an armistice did not mean a victory.

The first battalion of the Sixth Regiment was stationed at Honnigen, compact at the base of a hill which, though rocky and nearly perpendicular, was a cultivated and productive vineyard. Between the town and the river lay a flat stretch of ground which was used by the troops for close order drill, inspection, and parade. Each week the function of this plateau assumed a greater importance. Officers from General Headquarters, it seemed, roamed the occupied area for the single purpose of examining the soldiery—a practice for which none had the same pretext though all shared alike the sharp, inquiring eye that searched for any form which laxity of morale might take. One week there would be a review; another time the officer would inspect equipment, flat feet, or gasmasks. The men grew weary: no one but themselves knew the war was over.

One morning, MacMahon conjectured something more significant was to occur. For one proof the regimental standard had been brought out. He could see it folding and unfolding, the gold tassels and the dark blue silk spreading out in the sporadic puffs of wind. Furthermore, the companies had been especially scrutinized at drill formation. And since then they had been waiting, standing in a long, speechless line on the parade ground. From his place in the file closers MacMahon could see, over the heads and shoulders of the two ranks of men in front of him, the waters of the Rhine gliding swiftly between the wide stone banks. It was a pleasant sight, and he glanced quickly at the regimental standards close to the red and blue of the national colors. Yes, there they were, nice and clean, but with an enviable number of decorations pinned to the blue cloth. Still, MacMahon reflected, they hadn't been got for nothing; the battalion had paid for them well—a fact which would be shown by calling the origi-

nal roll and listening to the many names which would remain un-
answered.

The truth was, MacMahon decided as the four captains, tired of
waiting for their superior, formed themselves into a knot in front of
the regimental standard, the decorations on that flag didn't belong
to these men at all. Not to the men he saw before him, or at either
side. How many of them had been at Belleau Wood? Or even at Soissons? Hell, you couldn't find enough in the whole battalion to make
two squads. With this conclusion he felt vindictive, wondering why
these company commanders were so useless. Why didn't they do something? But that was the way with these new officers. Not one of them
knew his business. And as for Johnson, even though he had been of the
original personnel, he was the worst of the lot. A mighty good thing
for Johnson that Captain Osborne was pushing up daisies. Otherwise
he wouldn't be company commander, that was a cinch. Fretfully, Mac-
Mahon stared at the backs of the men who stood in line before him.
Nearly all of them had come in the fourth, fifth, or sixth replacement
battalions, and MacMahon, to whom their figures would always have
an air of unfamiliarity, instead of seeing the wearers of those steel helmets as persons, saw only the ghosts of those with whom he had come
to France and whom he had left there when the Army of Occupation
followed the enemy to the Rhine.

Unhurriedly, a large gray automobile rolled out of Honnigen along
the road to the parade-ground. At the entrance of the field the car
stopped with a smothered whine; a lieutenant spryly alighted and
opened the tonneau door for Major Shipley, an American Brigadier,
and a French colonel, whose light blue breeches with two stripes of red
at the outer seams, dark blue tunic, the bosom of which was crusted
with medals, and stiff cap held MacMahon's attention. Chatting and
grinning, the four officers swung from the rear of the battalion to a
position in front of it.

"Company at-ten-shun," bawled the captains, and as the line shuf-
fled, uncoiled and snapped into straightness, Major Shipley acknowl-
edged the concerted salute in a manner of more than ordinary brusque-
ness. And from the file closers MacMahon stared out over the heads
of the men in the rear and front ranks to the group of higher offi-

cers. The lieutenant who had helped the general out of the car, he noticed, carried a small black box, held carefully against his side. The general himself, a fat, slouchy man who, MacMahon remembered, returned salutes without troubling to remove the straight-stemmed pipe which he continually held in his mouth, had disposed of the customary wrinkles of his blouse by standing, for once, erect.

Obviously the present occasion was one of importance. Of course! Why hadn't he thought of it before? The French colonel was there to hand out some decorations. Eagerly MacMahon tilted forward as Major Shipley drew a sheet of paper from his inner pocket. He drew back, smiling contemptuously. What did these people know about war? Old Shipley was referred to all over the Division as Dugout Dan. All he knew about the front was what he saw from the bottom of a forty-foot hole. The brigade commander's claims to distinction were in no way admirable. As for Johnson—well, when he considered Johnson his thoughts, for relief, swung to Captain Osborne.

MacMahon gazed sourly out over the two ranks in front of him, past Major Shipley and the French colonel to the Rhine, on whose leaden face a barge was floating toward Coblenz. Irrelevantly, he wondered where Jen Yager had gone; no one had seen him since the attack at Soissons; he had not been taken prisoner; one moment he had been walking along in the first wave, only to disappear the next. Perhaps it was Yager's pack and arm which had risen so foolishly above the blot of smoke from that exploding shell. . . . Captain Johnson stood erect before his company. Major Shipley importantly straightened the slip of white paper grasped in his hands. Morrow, a private in the rear rank, turned round and whispered shrilly:

"They're gonna pass out some more decorations; they got a whole basketful, an' that Frog officer's promised me one if he's got any left over after the greaseballs have got their'n."

A new sergeant was frowning at Morrow, but MacMahon grinned. "Last time I was down at the head I heard a general say that Congress was gonna strike off a new medal for the M.P.'s. The Medal of Honor ain't good enough."

Major Shipley read from his paper: "Captain Walter Johnson."

Captain Johnson executed a sharp right face, strode to the centre of the battalion, accomplished a snappy column left, and marched toward the group of officers. He halted. The lieutenant placed his hand in the black box and drew out a bit of bronze. He held it, suspended from a striped ribbon. He handed it to the French colonel, who very carefully pinned it to the breast of Captain Johnson. Bold-eyed, Captain Walter Johnson about-faced, and retraced his steps.

Major Shipley glanced at his paper again: "Sergeant Joseph Patrick MacMahon."

Hesitating, a feeling of shame coming over him as strongly as if he had been stripped naked, MacMahon stared ahead. In the silence Morrow's snigger sounded loudly. His eyes grew big and his steps uncertain as he followed the path which Captain Walter Johnson so recently had taken.

VIII

The Nine Days' Kitten

From the farther and better-lighted end of the long, tarred paper bunk-house sounded the voices of the company quartette: Goodwin, Everett, Enright, and Riley Crookes. It was their favorite song that they were singing, and in it they unbosomed all of their loneliness, their grief, their longing, and their wonder at the mystery of the un-read riddle of existence. Let no one believe this song was joyous; on the contrary it was a threnody, and if the aria rose to golden heights it was but the singers exulting in their full expression of pain. Throb-bing, bleating, Riley Crookes' tenor ascended on the closing lines:

"Just a dream of you de-ea-ea-ea-ear;
Just a dream, tha-a-a-at's aw-aw-aw-awl."

As the lingering melody died out Homer Fredericks turned over on his side and wondered if the bunch intended to sing any more that night. Probably they did, for half an hour still remained before taps would be blown. A poker game, he thought hopefully, might stop them, but it was too far from pay day for anybody to have enough money to play. Dolefully he wished they would stop.

There was so much sweet agony in the words! Listening to them was like pressing a bruise: it hurt, but gracefully. For Homer had a "You Dear" to dream of. In fact, he also had her picture. It hung from a rough cross-beam above his head, and as he straightened out his body and drew the woolen blanket to his chin he looked at the small oval frame. Sighing, he said "Gosh!" in a prayerful voice. "What wouldn't he give to be back there now!" But no, such reflections were unmanly: he was over here to fight for her, to do his bit that she should be proud of him. She had eyes the color of tender cornflowers, and her hair was a careless aura of loose-spun gold.

> "Just a drea-ea-eam of you—dear
> When the lights are low . . ."

The bunch was at it again. A hearse never travelled more slowly, a hateful fate pursued with less implacability, than the voices of that quartette weaving out of their plaintive dirge. The words made young Fredericks feel the gnawing of homesickness. What a time he could have if he were back home! He would have matriculated at the university that fall, and at just about this time he would be coming home for the winter holidays. Boy! There was the new car which his father had bought as a persuasive against enlisting ("You're only eighteen, Homer; why don't you wait and see if Uncle Sam needs you?" his father had cautioned), and there was Angela, his girl—his mother and father, and the gang with whom he had played football in his senior high-school year.

Like an ineffable boon the mellow notes of taps flooded through the dark cantonment.

"All right, you men. Lights out!" shouted Sergeant Updike from his lower bunk near the door of the building. The quartette stood up, and with their arms linked, their heads bowed and close together, they finished the song.

"For Chrise sake, shut up! Do you birds want the O. D. after us again?" Sergeant Updike, for his own part, didn't care whether they yelled their heads off, but he feared a reprimand from the officer of the day.

"Pipe down, Updike; you make more noise than they do," said an unknown voice.

"Ha! ha! 'At's tellin' 'em!"

"Who said that?" stormed the sergeant.

Gradually the electric bulbs and the candles were extinguished until the entire room was black. Fredericks bunched the straw under his head to make a comfortable pillow. He fell asleep.

Photography was not well represented among these soldiers. Riley Crookes had a picture of his wife. It was a plain snapshot, cracked and blurred by time; he carried it inside his bill-fold. Billy Davidson had a camera likeness of his sister; but for the most part the observance of carrying a loved one's picture was honored in the breach. This was due not to disinclination on the part of the soldiers, but to inexorable necessity. Men who carry all of their belongings on their back, who toil in the hot sun, wade through streams and sleep often under a leaky sky have little place and little security for perishable mementos.

Young Fredericks, then, was distinguished not only by possession of a tangible copy of the girl who kept his heart, but by the silver frame as well. The frame was dented in several places. It had been first marred one day on the rifle range. He carried it in the pocket of his olive-drab shirt, and as he lay down to fire from the six-hundred-yard range, he had pressed it against a stone. The glass, which once protected the face, was broken, and the likeness itself was soiled and stained from being carried in the breast pocket of his blouse. To an unprejudiced observer the picture was no longer the attractive thing it had been when Fredericks had come into its ownership.

That night was one for remembrance. He had told her that he was going to enlist, and they had sat together on the piano bench until very late. Now and again he had furtively imprisoned her hand, then choked too much to speak. She loved him and she knew he was going away, possibly to be killed. The silence, one of communion at first, was painful later. Finally they rose and walked toward the door. And then, mutually impelled as if by magic, he found his arms about her, his lips against her lips, and saw a troubled, yet happy emotion mirrored in her blue eyes. A curious kiss; he had known her throughout her school days, had, in grave reverence, walked home beside her with her books countless times, but this was the first. And it was a shock. He had no notion that anything could inspire so much awe as did her lips. A goddess always, the fact that she could kiss made her still more wonderful. "Angela, will you—if I come back—wait, will you?" he had besought and with a low, expanding laugh she said "Yes." Then she had gone up-stairs and returned with a cabinet portrait. He had left with the photograph under his arm, and the following day he bought the frame, silver and oval, not much larger than the palm of his hand. Mindfully, he had cut the head from the picture and placed it in the frame. The rest of the portrait he put away in a trunk in the attic, assuring it that when the war was over he would make it whole again.

Fredericks carried it through the training camp and to the crowded boat which brought his regiment to France. At working parties, on long hikes, drills, or leave, it was with him—ever. He fancied its contact made him better; assuredly it fired in him the desire to be a corporal. Also, it kept him from engaging in many of the futile pursuits with which soldiers occupy their spare moments. For, when he had nothing else to do, he would go to the Y. M. C. A. hut and write long letters to Angela. It was enough that her answers were as frequent as the delayed mails. He kept all of the letters, in a bundle fastened by a soiled blue ribbon.

Reveille shattered the stillness of the morning. Sergeant Updike thrust his head outside his bunk and called: "All right, you men; rise and shine." Like a jack-in-a-box the head popped back again.

Fredericks sat up in his bunk, drew on his thick woolen socks, and pulled at his heavy hobnailed shoes, whose stiffness was not being alleviated by a daily application of machine-oil. He swung his body over the ledge of his bunk and dropped to the dirt floor, buttoning his blouse as he hurried outside where the men were beginning to form for morning roll-call.

He was very alert as he stood in the shuffling, restless line. There was zealousness in his brown eyes, zealousness and a kind of chiding stare at those who were arriving late. Morning formations were not loathsome to him, no matter how grim the sky or how mean the wind.

"Squad leaders' report," commanded Sergeant Updike.

Fredericks was proud to be enabled to say: "Third squad all present." Perhaps he would be given the next sergeantcy in the platoon.

"Squads right, hrrch; double time, hrrch," came the orders. The platoon wheeled in a column of fours and charged briskly along the cindered road toward the red clay drill ground.

"Hup, two, three, four; hup, two, three, four." Updike gasped the cadence out, and the platoon's hobnailed shoes pounded against the earth. "To the rear, hrrch." The ranks loosened, became a sea of confusion, then reformed and double-timed back to the bunk-house.

"Squads right, hrrch, platoon . . . halt."

As the men came up on a line somebody in the rear rank snickered.

"What's the matter back there?" called Sergeant Updike. "You're not dismissed."

"You got us hind end first," said Andrus, who spoke his mind.

Several of the men laughed.

"All right, Fredericks, that's enough outa you." Sergeant Updike was growing nettled.

"I didn't say anything," expostulated Fredericks. He hadn't.

"Shut up or I'll run you up for a shoot."

Fredericks stared, uncomprehending. Why, what the devil had got into Updike? *He* hadn't done a thing, and yet Updike threatened to report him! For what?

The platoon was dismissed and the men hurried into the bunk-house for their mess-kits. Fredericks walked to his bunk, found his plate and cup and followed the stream of olive-drab uniforms past the long row of tarred-paper buildings toward the field kitchen, across the main road, from the chimney of which a gray wisp of smoke was curling toward the dank sky.

A few weeks before Christmas he went into town and bought her a present. Many of the men were buying those gaudy silk handkerchiefs with "Souvenir de Guerre" embroidered of them, but these did not strike his taste, so he searched until he found something more to his liking. It was a small wrist-watch. Very carefully he wrapped it and sent it away.

Then he was gloomy, wondering whether the gift would reach its destination, whether she would like it, whether it was the proper sort of thing to send. It had seemed to be while he was choosing it, but somehow girls were curious.

Christmas came, and as Fredericks stood in line in the company street, his shoes unlaced and his blouse partly unbuttoned (for reveille had just blown), the first sergeant announced that there would be no other formation that day except guard mount in the evening.

"Dismissed!" commanded the platoon sergeants, and the men stampeded whoopingly to their bunk-houses. Liberty all day! Nothing to do till to-morrow! Fredericks alone had a solemn face—and that even with the prospect of the Christmas dinner before him. Turkey had been purchased from the mess fund, candy had been supplied by the Red Cross, and champagne had been bought with the money from the company canteen.

At noon the men sat about a table, made of rude boards, long enough to seat thirty soldiers on each side. The messmen entered with large pans of dismembered turkeys, cranberry sauce, apples, dates, and nuts, potatoes, and galvanized containers of creamed and sugared coffee. Knives, forks, and spoons rattled on the boards from the sheer exuberance of the diners. Wine was drunk in great quantities, and toward the end of the meal many of the men commenced to sing. There were no snow, no holly, and no presents. It didn't seem very much like Christmas, but it certainly was a good feed. Even Fredericks, when questioned, had to admit that.

Enright was emptying a bottle of champagne, holding it to his mouth, when the door opened and Lieutenant Bedford, the platoon commander, walked in.

"Cheese it!" some one warned excitedly.

Lieutenant Bedford smiled jovially. "Carry on, carry on! If you men run out of booze come up to the officers' quarters. We got enough to float a ship." He grinned. "Is Fredericks here?"

Moodily, Fredericks looked up. "Yes sir," he said.

"Got a piece of paper for you," said Lieutenant Bedford, advancing.

Fredericks examined it,—a cablegram! What the devil could be in it, he wondered as he tore it open. He read:

"Merry Christmas and much love.
          Angela."

Flushed and choked with pleasure, he looked up at Lieutenant Bedford. "Thank you, sir. I guess I couldn't have had a better Christmas present than that."

"Fine," said Bedford. "Drink up; nothin' to do 'til to-morrow." He walked out.

Fredericks sat down, beaming. "Say, this is some Christmas dinner, ain't it?" he said to Everett.

"You poor stiff. I told you that a long time ago."

Gosh, he was a pretty damn lucky guy to have a girl like that. He'd bet that not another soldier in a million got a cablegram for a Christmas present. A cablegram! He had read of them in stories about very important people, but it was the first he had ever seen. . . . After dinner he put it away with the little bundle that was her letters.

For days afterward Fredericks wished that the battalion would be sent immediately to the front so that he might distinguish himself in some way that would be pleasing to Angela. He might even get a medal! That would be nice to show her. He could write and say, in an off-hand way, of course, "I did some little thing out on a raiding party in No Man's Land last night, and they're going to give me a medal for it." Or, perhaps it would be better to keep silent and let her first read of it in the newspapers. Wouldn't she be surprised!

But the battalion showed no signs of moving up to the front. Current rumor had it that the organization was to be split up and sent to different parts of the country for guard duty at the various warehouses. So Fredericks, with an enthusiasm to excel, showed Lieutenant Bedford how well he could drill a squad, showed him the fervor he could put in the lunge of a bayonet.

There had not been a delivery of mail from America since Christmas, and Fredericks was growing worried. Several weeks passed and no letters came. And some one had the explanation (whether true or false) that fifteen sacks of mail had been lost with the sinking of a transport on its way to France. Then one afternoon, as they were returning from drill, the lieutenant's orderly appeared in the doorway with an armful of letters.

Sergeant Ryan, then in charge, gave them rest while he read off the names. There were letters for everybody but himself, Fredericks thought worriedly, as the pile continued to dwindle. Finally, the last letter disappeared, and the platoon was dismissed.

His only solace was to reread the old letters and to stare at the cablegram. Which he very frequently did. But even the most pleasant letters can grow stale by too close scanning, and toward the last of February he found himself loath to go back to them. Besides, there was supposed to be a great batch of mail at divisional headquarters, and it would arrive shortly.

It came, and Fredericks was among the first to welcome it. He stood well forward in the mob of men, so close that he could see the writing on the envelopes which the company clerk held in his arm. "Sergeant Ryan, Corporal Hayes, Corporal Cook," the clerk read off the names and flung the letters toward their owners. Flinching, Fredericks heard him out. "Corporal Fredericks." "Here," Fredericks gasped reaching for the letter. It was from his mother. He put it in his pocket and once more fixed his eyes on the diminishing pile.

"That's all, *fini*," said the company clerk. The men dispersed, and Fredericks went over to the corner of the bunk-house and opened his letter. He was glad to get it, very glad, but it did not make up for the one he had vainly expected. Opening the letter, he read of what the home service organizations were doing to help the boys, of his mother's fear over his safety, that his father had decided to keep the old car until Homer returned, and then—

At first the words were no different from those of which the entire letter was composed; yet something caused him to scan them again, and as he did so there occurred a curious tightening about his heart, wholly physical. Then his eyes distinctly saw: "Mrs. Stratton has announced Angela's engagement to Harold Spratt. The paper says they will be married the first week in April." "Yes, oh yes," he thought dully, looking for the strange words again. But the paper was a blur before his eyes, and his breast had become as lead. His head up, his eyes unaware of the scene before him, he walked along the company street. Mechanically, he folded the letter and dropped it in a pocket of his blouse. She—she, why she was going to be married to someone else!

It was too astounding for belief. There must be some mistake. But that clamping, leaden feeling made him doubtful that what he had just read was false. Then it was all over between them: she wouldn't write, he wouldn't write, it was just as if they had never met. But no, that wasn't it, for she had a part of him which he would never be able to reclaim. And of her he had—

Batlike, he pushed forward along the main road which led from the camp to the town. That night he went away, he recalled. Was she only making a fool of him then? Probably she never really thought anything about him: that kiss, likely enough, meant no more to her than a dirty franc note meant to him. There was no use trying to be anything now. Who cared whether he was a corporal or a captain or a private? Nobody.

"Halt!" It was the sentry on post number nine, guarding the exit of the camp. "Where th' hell d' ya think yer goin'?"

Fredericks stopped. He saw the sentry, his rifle at port arm, facing him.

"If ya wanta git out show your pass."

"I don't wanta git out," Fredericks mumbled. What did he want to get out for? Why did he want to go any place since each had become the same? Now his steps were laggard as he walked back over the main road toward the long, dingy-looking bunk-houses, squatting low against the stale, colorless earth. He passed an officer, but failed to salute; nor was there a rebuke forthcoming to deter the wandering of his mind.

He turned to the left at his own company street and walked past the closed doors where the first and second platoons were housed. At his own abode he entered, stumbling over the door sill. Sergeant Ryan was curling his reddish moustache between slim, white fingers. Sergeant Updike, the conscientious, was applying an oiled rag to his rifle which lay, like a baby, across his knees. Georgie Hayes drawled out information of the Pittsburgh blast furnaces where he had once worked. But Fredericks neither saw nor heard them. He went on until he reached his bunk, placed his foot on the bed beneath and climbed up. Hanging from a nail in the rafter was the oval-framed photograph.

Carefully, he unfastened it, then fumbled about among his few belongings until he found the package of letters. He slipped both in the pocket of his blouse and climbed down.

There was a kind of resolution in his step as he left the bunkhouse and tramped out over the plain. The clay was sticky, but he laid his course straight ahead for the woodpile, where logs were chopped up for fuel for the field kitchen. Here he stopped and, bending over, picked up the dry, white splinters, forming them into a tinder little pen, under which, one by one, he placed the sheets and envelopes of the letter paper. They had his name on them: Corporal Homer Fredericks, and the address by which his battalion always could be reached. They were his, certainly. In them she had said that she loved him. Yet they were his no longer. He sighed and, kneeling on the clay, struck a match.

The match flamed palely. He watched the wood kindle, watched the paper turn from white to brown, and from brown to an ashen gray while the letters which her pen had made writhed and struggled boldly against extinction. When the splinters blazed he put the photograph on top of the heap, and gazed on it until the metal blackened and the pasteboard charred.

Bitterness over her infidelity found expression in his denunciation of himself: why had he been so big a fool as to believe her? He had nobody to blame but himself. Since all girls were the same, he hadn't. He should have known. . . . Girls! Hell! What had he left to fight for now? Here he was, over in France, fighting (or going to fight) to make her safe—from what evil he scarcely knew—and she showed her gratitude by marrying some one else! But they were like that. All of them. The days dragged past, each like the one preceding, and thus he thought.

Such preoccupations could not help but have their effect upon his actions. In the mornings, when reveille sounded, instead of hastening his squad to formation, he was often the last to arrive. His shoes unlaced, his hair uncombed, he would crowd into the line, sometimes after his name had been called. Then Sergeant Updike would glare at him and say: "Fredericks, the next time you're late you'll lose your liberty for a month." Liberty! What did he want with liberty?

One evening his name was called out for duty as a corporal of the guard. It meant that he would have to clean and grease his shoes, polish his rifle, and make up his pack for heavy marching order. Standing in line, staring past Sergeant Ryan and at the closed bunk-house door, he thought of the little time he had in which to get ready before guard mount. That was the way with the outfit, these days: they never let you know what you were supposed to do until about ten minutes before they wanted you to do it. And then they bawled you out because you weren't ready.

"Dismissed," called out the sergeant. Fredericks strolled into the bunk-house.

"You better snap it up or you won't be ready in time for guard mount, Fredericks," said Andrus, who was already rolling his pack.

"I guess I've got plenty of time," he said shortly.

He sat on the edge of his bunk with his legs hanging over the bed beneath and formed his blankets into a semblance of the shape prescribed by the infantry drill regulations. He brushed the straw from his haversack and the attached pack-carrier, and made up his heavy marching order. There was little time left to clean his rifle, so he did not swab the oil from the bore—it would be too dark that evening for the inspector of the guard to notice.

By the time he was ready the guard had formed. The men were standing in two ranks in front of the second platoon bunk-house, and as Fredericks advanced he saw Sergeant Updike talking to the new officer of the day. He had a sense of foreboding at the sight of Updike. The twenty-four-hour duty, for Fredericks, would not be easy with him as sergeant of the guard. He quickened his step.

"Hurry up, we're waiting for you, Fredericks," said Lieutenant Jones sharply.

"Take the second squad," Updike told him.

Sergeant Updike called the guard to attention, called the roll and relinquished his charge to Lieutenant Jones. Lieutenant Jones commenced to inspect the rifles. When he came to number three of the second squad Fredericks brought his rifle up to port arms, sharply, hoping that the verve of his action might dissuade the officer of the day from inspecting him. But while he was thus hoping he felt the piece suddenly snatched from him, saw the lieutenant swing the butt toward the sky and look through the bore. Then the rifle plunked against his chest, and he heard the lieutenant say: "Better get after that bore, Fredericks, as soon as you get to the guard-house."

The ranks were closed and the guard, in a column of squads, marched along the company street to the main road.

"Column left . . . march," called Lieutenant Jones. The men swung along the road, past the old guard and halted, facing the empty fields. The old guard marched down the road and the new guard fell out.

Inside the guard-house the men unslung their heavy packs. The nine men of the first relief unfastened their haversack straps from their cartridge-belts, shouldered their rifles and filed out the door. Fredericks drew a soiled straw mattress over by the wooden cells where the prisoners were kept, and commenced to make up his bed for the night. He wouldn't have an opportunity to use it before midnight but, he thought, it was well to secure a dry place on the guard-house floor. . . . Finished, he lay back, smoking until chow call blew.

At a quarter to six he was standing outside the guard-house with the second relief. A damp wind was blowing and the sun had disappeared behind a black horizon. A nasty watch, from six to eight, he thought: it meant that he would have to get up at midnight for the second turn.

"Call off, second relief." He waited until the men had finished. "Know your general orders?" he asked perfunctorily. As no one admitted ignorance, he said: "Right shoulder arms; right face; forward, column left march." And the men, out of step, filed down the road on their way to take over their duties as camp guards.

Fredericks posted the last man, listened to the exchange of special orders, and started back for the guard-house. He wanted to smoke a cigarette, and as the night was dark he decided he wouldn't wait until he got back. Stopping, he rested the butt of his rifle on the ground, reached in his blouse pocket for tobacco and cigarette papers. Leisurely he made the cigarette, lighted it, and shouldering his rifle continued his journey.

He walked along the main road, inhaling the smoke and blowing it out, thinking that it would be his luck for the rain to commence during his next watch. As he drew close to the officers' building he saw two figures moving toward him. Quickly he plucked the cigarette from his mouth. But too late.

"Halt." It was Sergeant Updike. Fredericks stopped, flustered, as the men drew closer.

"Oh, it's you, is it, Fredericks?" asked Updike. Lieutenant Jones said, sarcastically: "Is this the way you post your relief? Smoking cigarettes?"

Fredericks gulped. "No, sir."

"What do you mean: 'No, sir?'"

"I think a court-martial will teach him better, sergeant," Lieutenant Jones said drily.

Fredericks saluted and walked off. He was in disgrace. In the very depths of it. And soon to be court-martialled.

He plodded back to the guard-house and sat down on his straw mattress. About him the men of the first relief were lying, endeavoring to sleep now so that they would be able to remain awake when they went back on watch at ten o'clock. Fredericks rolled another cigarette and lighted it. Well, he thought, it was better for the court-martial to come early than for it to come late. He didn't want to be a corporal, anyway.

Wretchedly the night and the next day passed. When the guard was changed and the men marched back to their quarters he found that several among the platoon already knew of his misfortune.

"I won't pity you," Everett told him; "if you get busted and lose three months' pay. It's your own damned fault. You know what kind of a guy Jones is; you know he'll stick ya the first chance he gets. . . . Besides, Updike was down on you."

He did not lose any of his money except the extra seven dollars and some odd cents to which his corporalcy entitled him. But one evening, just after the time for guard mount, he was ordered to the guard-house. He went there quickly and stood in front of a small detachment while the new officer of the day read off the charge of his misdemeanor and then sheared his chevrons from his sleeves with a pocket-knife.

Mail deliveries no longer meant the same to Fredericks. Once he had been conspicuous in his eagerness to hear the names on the letters read. He had wedged himself deeply into the mass of expectant soldiers. But no longer. Though he could not hear the cry "Mail-ho!" without some response.

One day, a week after he had been reduced to the ranks, he stood outside the bunk-house and watched the company clerk approach, carrying a large bundle of letters and packages. He started forward, involuntarily, then drew back against the wall. The door was open and inside the men were playing cards and talking. They would be very anxious to know of the arrival of mail. He turned his head toward the door and spoke in a monotone:

"Hey, you guys, there's a lot o' mail out here."

"Come out of it. Don't kid like that," Goodhue answered. Nevertheless he looked to see if Fredericks was speaking the truth, and in a moment the door became a thing of paper against the rush of the men, impatient to learn their fortune.

"Take your time, take your time!" said the company clerk, as the men crowded about him.

"Crookes," he read off.

Crookes grasped the letter, tearing it open.

"Hartman," continued the clerk, naming the owners of the letters.

"Whoopee, it's a boy!" Crookes suddenly exclaimed.

"What's a boy?" asked Enright.

"My wife's just had a baby, you dumbbell; it's a boy." He seemed ecstatic.

"Ha, ha-hah!" laughed Fredericks. "Ha, ha-hah!" That was a good one! At once he thought Crookes' wife had been unfaithful. Of course: all women were unfaithful; they were bound to be. Hadn't Angela been unfaithful? A cuckoo, that's what women made of men. Here Crookes had been away from home for ten whole months, and his wife writes him she's had a baby. Crookes was a damned fool: he ought to know better than to trust women. They were all false. Crookes, the big boob! *He'd* never let a woman pull that stuff on *him* and get away with it. No sir.

But hadn't a woman done just that to him? Though not so bad. No, she had been unfaithful before she was married. But Crookes. . . .

Poor old Crookes. Suddenly Fredericks felt deeply sorry for him. Yep, he thought, he and Crookes were in the same boat. They'd have to get together and talk things over.

"Je's waddya know about that," Crookes was saying. "Here I been a father for two months and didn't know it. She wrote this letter—let's see," he looked at the post-mark, "wrote it six weeks ago."

"I'd sue the damned government if they held up *my* mail like that," counselled Enright heatedly. "That lousy administration at Washington—"

That evening, from the farther end of the bunk-house, sounded the voices of the company quartette: Goodwin, Everett, Enright, and Riley Crookes. Throbbing, bleating, Riley Crookes' tenor ascended on the closing lines. And now and again the singers stopped to drink from a large bottle of cognac which Crookes had purchased for the celebration.

IX

The Long Shot

Duncan Milner was a good shot, an expert rifleman. For this distinction the government had given him a medal and, each month, allowed
him an extra five dollars to spend in whatever way he pleased. Being
a qualified marksman he had been chosen to be one of the four in the
battalion to act as sniper. And thus, while the rest of the men had the
shelter of the trench, the duty of Duncan Milner led him into un-
protected places.

He lay in a shallow scoop of half frozen mud, looking down the
long gray slope at the trench beneath, where members of his company
stood on the slippery duckboards on sentry duty, or sprawled near the
mouths of their dugouts, smoking cigarettes, scraping the plastered
dirt from their puttees and breeches. Beyond the zig-zag trench, with
its parapets and firing bays, rolled No Man's Land, bleak and ghastly
with tufts of dead grass, cuplike shell holes, rotting pieces of equipment, and rotting the men who had worn them, barbed-wire and the
battered shafts of trees.

Within less than five hundred yards were the German lines, and
somewhat nearer were the enemy outposts, flat and motionless against
the beaten ground. These men, it was the sniper's purpose to discover,
and to kill. But the bore of Milner's rifle was as yet unsmoked; and
his eye wandered slowly, not over No Man's Land which he was supposed to watch, but at the trench of his own company. He knew them
all. And his acquaintance with a number of the men long antedated
the period of active service in which he had been with them. For he

belonged to a company of National Guards, recruited from Reliance, Ill., the town in which he lived. They were all good fellows, from the captain down. With some of them he had gone to school. Jeff Downing, now rolling a cigarette in front of the dugout, had been his best man when he married Dorothy. . . . It was much more pleasant to reconstruct the days of happiness as a civilian than to wear out his eyes looking for outposts of the Squareheads.

Beneath him, his box respirator (to be used in case of a gas attack) pressed uncomfortably against his chest, and lifting his hand from the stock of his rifle he unclasped the respirator from about his neck. His movements were cautious, restricted lest he should be observed by a German sniper. Then he stretched out again, his hand sliding back along the stock of the rifle.

He was relaxing into a comfortable attitude when he sensed some kind of activity behind him. His head jerked hastily as his eyes sought out the disturbance, but there was nothing unusual to be seen. A moment later there was a whisper: "P-sst!" and turning, he saw Captain Havermeyer crawling toward him on his belly. He was silent, growing a little apprehensive for fear that captain's approach would draw enemy fire. But Havermeyer reached him without ill luck.

"See anything?" muttered the captain. Milner was flattered. For Havermeyer, in addition to his office, was a damned good fellow. He was the sort of person who quelled the disobedient by hanging his blouse (with its insignia) upon a tree and daring the man in the ranks to fight out the difference, man to man. Nor was this action spurious. He would have fought, and probably would have won. He was not tall, but his shoulders were heavy and compact, his neck was thick, and he held his solid jaw outthrust. That he could stare so menacingly made his frequent smile seem the warmer. Then his full lips would part wide over his strong teeth and perpendicular lines would form on his healthy, ruddy cheeks. His hair was black and of a heavy growth.

"I ain't sure," answered Milner. "A couple a times I thought I did." Milner was long and thin, with solemn brown eyes and a mop of black hair beneath his helmet.

"We'll have a look," said Havermeyer, propping himself on his elbows and unslinging his field-glasses from about his neck. Milner was breathless, alert while his superior surveyed the scene beyond the trenches. Suddenly the field-glasses stopped, fixing on an artless appearing log, perhaps four hundred yards distant, and a little to the right of where Milner and Captain Havermeyer lay. "That's a Jerry," said the officer eagerly. "Here! Look." He passed the glasses to Milner. "Right behind that black log."

Milner placed the glasses to his eyes and swept the ground in the direction to which Captain Havermeyer pointed. In a straight line he saw a post of his own barbed-wire, an old boot and the fallen log. For a long while he looked at the log. Behind it, close to the bark, he saw a round greenish cap and a button. As he watched, he saw the cap rise, showing beneath it the head of a man, young, but empty-faced and gray. And though he had never seen the face before, Milner's hands grew shaky; he felt squeamish at the thought of killing him. Evidently a young man, and even from that distance a certain amount of arrogance was to be noticed in the expression.

"See him?" questioned Captain Havermeyer.

Milner answered slowly: "No, I don't believe I do." He felt cowardly because of his lie. It was not soldierly to see an enemy and not to shoot at him, to deny that the enemy was discovered.

"Here, let me show you," said Havermeyer brusquely. "Pick up your gun and I'll give you the sight."

Milner crooked his elbow under his arm and pressed the cold iron of the bolt against his cheek. He waited, a poor soldier, fearing he would have to shoot, to kill.

"Three hundred and fifty yards ahead; one finger to the right," said Captain Havermeyer. "There's an old log. Got it?"

"Yes," answered Milner.

"All right now. Watch for him about two feet from the left end, and when he sticks his head up knock him out cold."

Milner squinted one eye and stared through the telescopic sight of his rifle. He waited cautiously until the red-ringed cap set in the crotch of the tiny, criss-cross wires at the end of the telescopic sight. The stock of the rifle was held snugly against his cheek, his body was at rest, and for a second he ceased even to breathe.

Behind the front lines of the Germans was a battery of artillery of three-inch guns. And, whether or not it was by accident or design, they chose this particular moment to throw a shell into one of the guns, close the breech and jerk the lanyard. As is the custom of shells so dispatched this one screamed into the air on the first lap of a high arc. Then, like the kind of shell it was, it dropped with a wobbling sound, as if it contained liquid, and struck the earth a few yards to the left of Duncan Milner, bursting with a muffled explosion. Milner winced, burying his face in the elbow which, such a short time before, had been crooked under his rifle. Captain Havermeyer scrambled, and ran recklessly. A piece of shell-casing ripped through the air and Milner's nostrils were bitten by a pungent smell while a saffron kind of liquid was splashed toward him. His eyes commenced to smart. He gasped, gulped and in a terror rolled down the gray waste of ground in the direction of his trench. The shell had contained mustard gas.

Captain Haverymeyer had bellowed: "Gas!" and then noncommissioned officers had taken up the cry, frightening, clipping out the word before they plunged their faces into their box-respirators. In the masks they looked like the ghosts of deep sea divers. Duncan Milner, the rawness and sting of his body increasing, sat on the wet duckboard in the bottom of the trench. Somebody stood over him and motioned for him to leave the trench. He barely comprehended. The figure above him removed the mask enough to shout: "Beat it! Beat it!" Milner got up and followed the tortuously laid duckboards to the communication trench which led him to the first aid station. Already his eyes were swelling shut.

Savenay, so the sick and the wounded said, was a madhouse. It is a small French village several miles up the Loire, and in the spring of 1919 it was overcrowded with men of every conceivable ailment, from flat feet to shell-shock, from a punctured leg to pyorrhea.

By the window of one of the low, wooden buildings Duncan Milner lay in his white cot and explained to the man whose bed was next to his: "That may be so with your outfit, but it ain't with mine. I had a damned good outfit, and all the officers were regular guys. Say, if they had a package of cigarettes and you hadn't any, they'd split with you." He had to stop talking for a while because the gas had seared his throat and made his voice hoarse and weak. "No, buddy, you were jist out of luck, that's all. Your officers might have been bums, like you say they were, but they certainly weren't like mine. Of course that's the way with the army. Those West Pointers think they're hell on wheels." He stopped talking and lay back, looking at the whitewashed ceiling. In spite of his illness he was rather happy and eager about life. For he had recently been examined, and he knew that the next ship to sail with wounded out of Saint Nazaire (the port at the mouth of the Loire) would carry him to America.

For nearly five months he had lain in bed. At first he had been wrapped in bandages and coated with salve. Unable to move, he lay in a torpor so complete that no thought ever entered his mind. It was some time before he regained the use of his eyes. But now the scars were healing. He was well enough to be transported again. Frequently, he thought of Dorothy. She seemed more desirable than ever. The funny part of it was that she still loved him. For they had been married less than a year when his company had been mobilized into national service, sending him away to camp. The last time he saw her was the day that she came down to the train to say good-by. He remembered the leave-taking well: she had worn a small black hat and a tight-fitting dress. Their arms had been gripped about each other's shoulders as they kissed. Two years had passed since that moment, two years since he had kissed her full red lips, and looked into her large brown eyes which had seemed to him so mysterious.

She wrote to him with regularity. He read the letters and felt half-exultant, half-ashamed. She had been forced, she said, to go back to the telephone company to work. And even then there wasn't enough money to support her. Of course she was not blaming him for the small amount he was able to send her each month, but she did think that he could rise to some office which would pay him more. A lot of other men, not half so bright as he, had done it. Why couldn't Duncan? But she always said that she loved him, and was impatient for him to come home.

He had little for consolation outside of her avowed love. He sent her the amount that the government gave him, excepting five dollars, which it was necessary to keep. He could not explain why he did not rise in the ranks. She could not understand that promotions were not given to patients in hospitals. But he did assure her that as soon as he got out of service she wouldn't have to worry any more. He would earn plenty and buy her lots of pretty clothes. It made him very anxious to be discharged so that he could return to his job and get to work. Then he could show her that she hadn't made a mistake in marrying him. Yes sir! He also thought of the man he had so nearly killed. Just a squeeze of the trigger and he would have been a goner. And he, himself, Milner knew in horror, would have been a murderer. Now and again he had the impulse to tell the story of how he had almost killed a Squarehead, but he decided against it, knowing the men would laugh at him if he explained why he had not fired.

In April it was rumored for the fourth time that all of the patients in Milner's ward were to be put on a train and sent to the boat at Saint Nazaire. It became a fact a few days later when the commanding officer of the hospital and two examining doctors passed along the aisle between the two rows of white beds, deciding which patients were to be carried on stretchers, and which were well enough to walk. When the officers stopped before his bed Milner grinned so whole-heartedly that one of them said: "You'll be ready for your discharge by the time you get to the States. I imagine you can walk to the boat." "Yes, sir," answered Milner. It was in his mind to add: "I could walk all the way home if you'd give me my discharge."

The boat—an ordinary transport—sailed at noon a short time later. And throughout the whole twelve days in crossing Duncan Milner never glimpsed the sea. He had come aboard while the boat lay in the mouth of the river, and by the time the screw was throbbing in the hull, he was stretched out on one of the lower bunks, made of rough wood and running in a maze through the bowels of the ship. The place was crowded and constantly hot. For twelve days he stayed in his bunk, with nothing but a blanket between him and the wood, while the occupants retched, gagged, and cursed. A negro, he heard indirectly, fell down the hatchway and was killed. Another time some one announced that a ship bound eastward was being passed. But the patients could neither affirm nor deny. If some one had stated that the sun had turned green they could not have proven its absurdity. They remained below decks, negroes, whites, the gassed, the wounded, the victims of dysentery, all packed together.

Ambulances waited for the ship at the Hoboken docks for the white, unshaven faces. The patients jostled down the gangplank and over the concrete flooring, where a few women stood with bars of chocolate. Duncan Milner did not want chocolate, he wanted to send a telegram, but the officer in charge told him to wait until he reached the hospital.

The hospital, he discovered, was like nothing so much as a strictly-governed but over-crowded concentration camp. Except for the patients in bed, who received the care of nurses and doctors, no medical attention was paid to the hordes of new arrivals from overseas. Milner was consigned to ward 30A; he had to find it himself. That was the way with everything: whatever he wanted he had to find for himself or go without. Sometimes, after his quest had been rewarded, he would be informed by a guard that what he was about to do was against hospital camp orders. It was like his experience in sending a telegram to Dorothy. At the boat the officer in charge had charged him to wait until he reached camp before sending the wire. At camp he was told by the guard that the only place from which wires could be sent was out of the camp limits, and leave was only permitted on Wednesdays and Saturdays. An officer, however, going into town promised to send the wire for him, and three days later he had a letter from his wife.

He read it eagerly, and from the first sentence he knew she was glad that he was back in America. She called him Sweetheart, and said the loneliest days of her life would be from that moment, and end only when she was in his arms again. More good news was that she had seen Frank Dawson, the superintendent of the factory in which Milner had worked, and that he had said: "Be sure to tell him that he can have his old job back. His salary will be a little bit better, too." After that, Milner thought continuously of getting home. His mind was so taken up with fancies of what he would do that he was impervious to the irritating aspects of the camp. Now and again he would say to some man in his ward with whom he happened to be talking: "If they just let me out of here, that's all I want." That was all he wanted. Afterward he would stand or fall by his own value. Perhaps in time he would have Frank Dawson's job.

He learned of a way by which he could get out of the army. If he was completely well, and was returned to duty, he could be discharged directly from the camp. His burns had healed, and though his voice was still hoarse, and though he was coughing frequently, he was satisfied with his freedom. The government did not need to look out for him: he would take the responsibility for his physical condition.

The hospital was crowded, and more patients were arriving daily. It was agreeable to the staff that Duncan Milner should be returned to duty and discharged. He looked well; there was no reason to believe that he was not. Milner reported to a medical officer whom he told that he had recovered from the effects of gas. The medical officer said "Humpf!" looked sharply at him and signed an order for his transferral to duty.

That day he walked out of the National Army of the United States of America. On his olive-drab uniform he wore four chevrons: on the right sleeve were two of gold, pointing downward; on the left was one of gold, pointing downward, and one of red cloth, pointing upward. In his pocket was a railroad ticket to Reliance, a sixty-dollar bonus and six months' back pay. He was happy in being his own master and in going back to his young wife.

Dorothy was as pretty as his memory had painted her. Her eyes were a soft, melting brown, her lips could pout bewitchingly, and dark ringlets of her hair lay against her fair cheek. Her hats were not of the best material, but so far as she found them suitable to her beauty, they were always in the mode. Her dresses always fitted closely, seemed almost molded to her breasts and hips, which still were like those of a young girl. Often she sat on Duncan's lap in their little house on a shaded street. He liked to hold her close to him and gaze down at her slender feet, black-slippered, and her slim, curving ankles covered with black silk stockings. She was, he told himself, adorable; and he shut his eyes and pressed his face against her fragrant hair.

For the first three days he did not go to work, though he saw Frank

Dawson at the factory and announced that he was ready to begin at any time. It had been the superintendent who had suggested that he wait a few days. "Stay at home with your wife a little while; take in a movie and see some of your old friends. You don't want to jump right into your overalls the first day you get out of the army," Dawson had said. And Duncan was glad to accept the vacation. It seemed as though he could not kiss Dorothy enough. She was awfully sweet; a wonderful girl to have waited for him while he was away, to have worked and supported herself, beside.

They were busy enough that week. Duncan felt suddenly prominent when the reporters from the two local newspapers wrote stories about him, appearing to the public eye under the caption: "Reliance Hero Returns; Boy Who Battled Hun in Argonne Bares Teeth in Smile at Home Town Welcome." It was less than the first returned soldiers received, and more than those who came later were to get. People went out of their way to shake hands with him, and Dorothy begged him to keep on his uniform instead of wearing civilian clothes. He felt her pride in possessorship as she held his arm while they walked down town. Each evening they were invited somewhere to supper, to his or her relatives, or to the house of a friend.

Duncan went back to work on a Monday. He went in early, before the rest of the workmen were there. And when they arrived, they found him in his old overalls, bending over a lathe, the sleeves of his blue shirt rolled above the elbows. He heard someone approaching behind and he turned quickly. It was old De Groat, who said: "Is this the young feller that knocked the stuffin' out of the Germans?" Duncan smiled deprecatingly, and shook hands. Everyone was friendly. Some of the younger men who had been employed during the war said: "Boss, I'm glad you took a good crack at 'em; I wisht I'd of had the chance." "You will, next time," said Duncan, grinning.

Throughout the day he was idle for scarcely a moment. Machines had to be set up, and some needed repair. Now and again he helped with the handling of the heavy bars of steel. It was severely tiring after his five months in the hospital. Yet he got his work done, and when the whistle blew he could leave the long factory room with its low, metal wall and go home to Dorothy.

It was like a honeymoon all over again. He was being paid sixty-five dollars a week, and with that sum he was able to afford a cleaning woman one day a week, and to have the washing sent to the laundry. With the hardest part of the housework done by others, Dorothy could have his dinner ready promptly and be waiting for him in a fresh dress. Under such stimuli his tiredness would vanish with his leaving the bathroom where he finished the job, begun at the factory, of cleaning the oil from his face and arms and hands. To be able to sit down to his own table, on one of his own mission chairs—a part of the dining-room set—was worth a great deal of fatigue.

Summer was half gone when the company of soldiers with whom he had served in France—Reliance's Own—came back. Duncan stopped work early and he and Dorothy went to the train to meet them. The train was late and half the town was gathered at the station. People who hadn't relatives on the troop cars went away, having seen the arrival of plenty of soldiers. But Duncan and Dorothy stayed. The train came in at eight o'clock, the soldiers shouting above the grinding of the wheels. They hung out the windows and crowded close to the bottom steps of the coaches.

Duncan was dazed with the thrill of the meeting. Voices said: "Well, there's old Dunc Milner, damned if it ain't." "How's the old town, boy?" "Who's that pretty girl you got?" and Captain Havermeyer, now a major, his serge coat hung with medals, stopped to shake hands and say: "I'm certainly glad to see you, Milner, old man." He went back home with Dorothy, shaken with gratitude that they should have remembered him. And in bed that night he said to his wife: "Damn best bunch of boys in the world, bar none." "I s'pose so," she answered crossly. "I noticed you hustled me away in a hurry." Duncan sat up, surprised. "Did you want to stay?" "Oh, I like to have a good time once in a while." Duncan couldn't understand. "I came home because I thought you wanted to come," he explained. Dorothy was silent. He said, "Lord," and went to sleep.

It was a hot summer with that breathless, stagnant heat of central Illinois. Inside the factory, where the motors hummed and the leather belts leaped and slapped on the revolving wheels of the machinery, the heat was like steam; and Duncan developed a headache that threatened to become chronic. With it was the feeling of a heavy weight on his chest, a weight that would have to be lifted before he could breathe. It was because of this that in the latter days of July he often stood by the window, staring out over the browning grass and the green, but still-leaved trees, instead of watching his workmen.

In the evenings he was content to sit on the porch of the bunga- low while Dorothy and Mildred Barry, with whom she had worked at the telephone company, went to the motion pictures. Mildred clothed her blondness with a certain flamboyance. She liked bright colors. Duncan did not accompany them for a number of reasons, one of which was his exhaustion and his nervousness, and another was that his coughing disturbed the people who sat near by and drew unpleas- ant attention to Dorothy and himself. It was better for him to stay at home and rest. Then, too, he did not always remain alone throughout the evening. He had joined the American Legion, and though he sel- dom attended the weekly meetings of his post, some of his old friends often stopped on their way past his house to smoke a cigarette and to talk of days gone past, of things present, and to come.

Prohibition was a frequent topic, and Bolshevism was a word that had just been insinuated into the language. They talked also of Major Havermeyer, who had gone back to his practice of law, and was re- ceiving most of the cases which had to do with former service men. With regard to prohibition Jeff Downing said to Duncan: "It may be a dirty trick. It probably is. They slipped one over on us while we were away at war. But it's a law, and we hadn't ought to break it. I don't mean we shouldn't take a drink: for that matter I got a few cases stored away in the cellar; but what gits my goat is that these bootleg- gers are growing rich off of it. And I tell you, they ain't Americans, ei- ther: they're damned immigrants, wops and Jews and Russians. That's what makes me sore." Duncan agreed. It did not seem fair that a few people, particularly foreigners, should profit by the misfortunes of the rest of the country. "Now if we only had Havermeyer in as judge of the criminal court, we'd soon snap these bootleggers out of it," said Jeff Downing. "He could make it if he'd run for it," agreed Duncan. "He could be major if he wanted to," said Jeff, "but if we put him over for judge that'll be enough." He paused and deliberately shot his cigarette out into the street. "I tell you, Dunc, I know you don't git out much, but you might drop a word or two around the shop and kinda git the idea into the heads of the fellahs down there to vote for Havermeyer." "Sure," affirmed Duncan. "I'll be glad to do it."

By September, though the summer heat had vanished, Duncan had fallen into the habit of standing before the window at intervals during the day and staring out at the landscape, softening with the shades of early autumn. His gripping headache, with all the nerves at the back of his neck feeling as if they were tied into little knots that tortured, and his dry cough had now become a part of him. It was a cough that tore at the lining of his lungs, and another employee, standing beside him at the window and hearing him, would say: "You better do something about that cough. It sounds pretty nasty to me." Duncan would answer shortly. It irritated him that the men should slight their work, that they would be so ill-disciplined as to leave their machines so frequently to smoke in the washroom, to look out of the windows, or to talk together in small groups. He knew that it was his fault, that they were only following his own example of laxity.

Production in his department fell below the required average, and the inspectors complained that too much steel was being scrapped by careless workmen. In another week Frank Dawson, the superintendent, came into the room and stopped before Duncan, who stood idly by the window. "Sort of restless, eh, boy?" he said to Duncan, and patted him on the shoulder "It's pretty hard settling back in the old groove after being in the army, isn't it?" suggested the superintendent. Duncan nodded wearily. He feared to tell Dawson that he was ill. If he knew, he probably would hire another foreman. It seemed easier to agree. "Well," said his superior, "I tell you what I'll do: you go back on the lathe for a while and we'll see if De Groat can put some pep into this department."

Duncan waited until pay day to tell Dorothy. Then he said: "I guess you better not have the cleaning woman come any more." His wife stopped polishing her finger-nails and stared at him. "Why not?" He answered slowly: "Because we can't afford it. Dawson put me back on a lathe and gave De Groat my job." Dorothy was silent for a moment, biting her lower lip so that one side of her mouth turned scornfully upward. "That was smart." "No, it wasn't smart," said Duncan wearily. "No, but it was your own doggoned laziness," said Dorothy sharply. He looked at the evening newspaper, the type blurring before his eyes.

Work at the lathe was still more taxing. It caused him to assume continually a stooping position, hunched over the machine. His chest became sore, and the muscles in his back burned steadily. The steel dust from the shaping tool aggravated the condition of his throat. He was now in more pain for forty-five dollars a week than he had suffered heretofore for sixty-five. Old De Groat would, in his ceaseless vigil of the workers, stop beside him and look at the small pile of finished pieces of steel on the floor by the lathe. From his wrinkled, quizzical eyelids he would glance at Duncan and say: "That's not so good. That machine can turn out more than that." Duncan tried to smile as he said: "I'll get back the hang of it pretty soon. All I need is a little time." Once he had been the best workman in the department, better than Old De Groat who was now placed ahead of him.

Those fall evenings he often spent in the workroom that he had made down in the cellar. Somehow he and Dorothy had little to say to each other. The time they spent together in the evening would be used by her in reading a magazine, and by him in reading a newspaper. In addition, Mildred Barry and Dorothy spent much of their time together. They either went to the motion pictures or else, if Dorothy stayed at home, sat talking of affairs of which Duncan had no knowledge. Mildred, by her behavior, showed that she regarded him as some manner of interloper in Dorothy's house. And thus it was much better to spend his time in his workroom at his miniature lathe, or rummaging through his trunkful of scraps in which he had laid away his uniform, his helmet, gasmask and automatic pistol. Picking up these mementoes of days at war, fondling them, trying them on "to see if they still fitted," he sometimes wished he was back in the service of the army.

He lost his job in November. Nor had he any ground on which to blame the factory. Up to the last hour of his employment he did not know that he was not to come back. It was on a pay day, and as he followed the line of men past the cashier's window he received his pay envelope as usual. Unconcernedly, he thrust it in his inside pocket and walked out the wide doors of the building. Frank Dawson, on his way to his automobile, spoke pleasantly to him in passing. During his journey home he thought of the superintendent, and reasoned with himself that to have lost his foremanship was no more than he deserved. Certainly they shouldn't pay him if he did not produce the goods. Yessir, they were a good bunch, a good outfit to work for.

Dorothy greeted him as he entered the house. She lifted her lips to be kissed, but maintained a distance from him so that her dress might not come in contact with his soiled clothing. He smiled and attempted a jest upon his decreased salary: "Well, another day, another dollar." Dorothy practically reminded him: "The grocery isn't paid yet." "You can pay it to-morrow," said Duncan. He went into the bathroom. On his way he took out the envelope and reached for the check. There it was. "Good—Lord!" he exclaimed. It was for twice the usual amount! Had he been given a raise, he wondered. But he knew he had not, and he had a feeling of foreboding as he looked again into the envelope. It contained a blue slip which informed him that he no longer had a job. The extra size of the check was an additional two weeks' pay. "Good Lord!" he said again.

"What is the matter?" came Dorothy's voice.

"I'm—I'm fired," he answered shakily.

"Fired!" echoed his wife in a voice that had suddenly become hard. "Fired? Well, you'll just have to get another job, Duncan Milner."

Yes, there was no doubt of that.

But to want the job was immensely easier than to get it. Duncan found that out during his days of tramping about the streets from factory to office, and from department store to garage. Apparently, there was no work to be had. The factories, the employment offices said, were laying off men, hot hiring them, and the large stores gave him the slight encouragement that they would need more clerks for the Christmas rush. Meanwhile, the snow fell and lay half melted on the streets while Duncan, in his army overcoat and the oiled shoes which he had worn in the shop, tramped the streets, coughing his dry, tearing cough, and feeling the sweat stand out on his skin in spite of the cold.

He was kept going by two forces: he had little money and he knew he must have more in order to exist; and he had heard, in his younger days, that a good man will always make a job for himself. That was what he said to the men whom he asked for work, but while agreeing with the theory, they were skeptical of the practice in the case of Duncan Milner. They did not like the sound of his cough, nor the aspect of his thin, gray face.

Jeff Downing, meeting him on the street, suggested that he apply for compensation from the government. Some of the other men, in much better physical condition than Duncan, were being paid each month, he said. But Duncan scowled and answered: "I'm not asking for charity. All I'm looking for is a chance to make a living." Jeff Downing counselled: "Don't be such a damned fool. You'll like as not cough yourself into your grave before you find it. Take my advice and see the Red Cross. You have a doctor examine you. If he finds you're not fit to hold down the kind of job you had when you went into the service, then the government'll send you to school and pay your expenses while you're learning another trade." That, Duncan admitted, was not such a bad idea.

Since his dismissal from the factory it had become instinctive with him to walk home slowly. For he was in dread of the moment when he would have to admit to Dorothy the defeat of another day. To hear her talk, it seemed a simple matter to find a job, and yet—Well, he would try this other thing; any money would help out in the pinch that he was in. Thinking thus, he opened the door, expecting to see Dorothy in the kitchen. But it was empty, and no fire was lighted in the gas stove. He called: "Dorothy!" and the quality of the echo convinced him of the fact that there was no one in the house. He muttered aloud that for her not to be home when he was so tired and hungry was "A hell of a note."

After waiting a while he made tea, not because he liked it, but for the reason that it was hot. He had never learned to prepare coffee. There was peanut butter in the cupboard, and jam. Of these he made sandwiches to eat with his tea. He was seated at the kitchen table when he heard an automobile stop in front of the house, then heard the chained wheels grind on the ice and gravel as the car sped away. A moment later Dorothy entered, the color high in her cheeks. "Find anything to-day?" she asked.

"No," he said, continuing his meal. "Who'd'ja come home with?"

"Nobody," she answered, removing her outer coat.

"Thought I heard a car out in the front."

"No, I walked." Dorothy passed into the dining-room.

In the morning Duncan awoke early, dressed, and was walking downtown while Dorothy was still in bed. He had a thought to keep out of mind: It was that she had lied the night before. And though he was unable to cease thinking of it, he placated himself with the excuse that there were many automobiles which might have stopped and started near his house, possibly the machine of the family next door. The weather was below zero, and he hurried along the slippery walks, past clerks and shop-girls on their way to work, to the office of the local Red Cross. And though the hour was early a line already had formed beside the open door, through which he could see stenographers clicking the keys of their typewriters and sifting stacks of paper, piled high on their desks.

It was noon before he got inside the door. And that was but the merest kind of beginning, he discovered. Had he ever made application before? Had he brought his discharge papers along? There were many questions asked by the gray-eyed secretary and depending on whether his answers were negative or affirmative he was relayed to this person or that down the long line of desks. Meanwhile, he coughed so alarmingly that one of the Red Cross workers suggested: "I think you had better go to a hospital." He shook his head decidedly. No hospital for him. He had spent enough time in madhouses. He left with the promise that he would be examined for disability within a few days.

Outside the arc-lamps were lighted, and as he walked homeward he wondered whether Dorothy would be in the house preparing supper. She hadn't been home the night before. No, she had gone out. Running around the town. He had a surge of self-pity: confound it! It wasn't right for her to treat him like this when he needed help so badly. She hadn't been this way when he married her, he recalled, and the scenes of his waiting for her in front of the telephone exchange came back to him. He remembered the swish of her stiff silk dresses, the heavy, sweet odor from her neck and hair. She had pressed so closely to him as they walked along the darkened street, and had made him feel that she was dependent on his strength. Oh, well!—Oh, hell!

Dorothy was at home waiting for him. As he took off his army overcoat she looked at him and said: "Nothing to-day, I s'pose?" He thought he detected the accent of a sneer. It hurt him, damned his speech so that whereas he had meant to tell her of how he had spent the day he replied with a bare "No." She placed a scanty supper on the table and then left the room. When she came back she was dressed for the weather. "Mildred asked me to go to a movie. I'll try to be back early." Duncan said: "All right," scarcely looking up from his plate. He didn't want her to know how her going affected him. He could not plead against her hardness, and he felt, since he was not supporting her, that he had not the right to demand that she stay home. After the door had closed he said to himself, through gritted teeth: "But if there's any other fellow, she'd better look out."

It was about midnight when she returned. He heard her climbing the stairs gently, on tip-toe. When she entered the room he pretended to be asleep, looking at her through the lashes of his half-closed eyes. Her hair, he thought, was unnecessarily rumpled, but he lay motionless, watching her slip her dress from her shoulders and then sit on the bench before her mirror while she took off her shoes and long, black stockings. Once he sighed, and Dorothy glanced quickly at him, but that was his last sound or movement until he fell asleep.

In the morning he once more set out to look for a job. The aid from the government was to be accepted only at the final ditch of his necessity to exist. But on that day, and the next, and the day after, his search was in vain. Then he received notice that he was to be examined by a physician. He went reluctantly, fearing what the doctor might discover.

The Reliance Physicians and Surgeons Building was six floors of pale brick, set in the middle of the city. To an office on the third floor of that place was where the Red Cross card directed Duncan. He ascended on the elevator and found not only the door but a large group of waiting people in the reception-room. He gave the stenographer the card and sat down on the radiator, the only vacant place for him to sit. . . .

"Of course I can't say for certain." It was the doctor talking, his plump hand passing over his gray beard. "But I think you are entitled to compensation." Though it was two o'clock in the afternoon Duncan forgot his hunger in his interest in the doctor's words. "If I had my way I would send you to the Soldier's Hospital. But you will have to wait until it is determined whether your trouble is due to a disability received in the line of your duty." That, then, thought Duncan, was the catch. For how was he to prove that this pain in his lungs, this continual coughing, this throbbing headache, had come about from the gas-shell which had sent him flying out of his sniper's hole into the trenches near Verdun? "At any rate, I want you to see some other doctors. And you will have to have some X-ray pictures taken," said the examiner.

From that moment Duncan found himself caught in an inextricable labyrinth, a maze of doctors' officers, of appointments which prevented him from any other activity during the day save that of staying about the large, pale brick building. He could not hunt for a job because at nine in the morning he was required to be at the throat specialist's; at eleven he would have an appointment with the heart specialist; at one a blood test was to be taken, and at three he would have to be in the X-ray room. And as there were many others also waiting, he had to hover near the doctor's door to be enabled to see them at all.

A week went by, and if he had had every dollar he possessed exchanged for silver the bulk would not have filled his pocket. Still his case was undecided, and he grew to know each turn and twist of the corridors of the big building. In the evenings he went home, and, as Dorothy was often absent, he finished his supper and descended the stairs to his workroom, to play with the hand lathe on which he had once made objects for his own amusement.

The workroom was in the cellar, directly beneath the front room. In it he had a bench (on which the lathe rested), a vise, and a few electric batteries. There were also a discarded armchair, his old trunk and—behind the trunk—a pair of rubber boots which he used to wear while hunting. Sitting in the armchair the electric light, which hung from a long cord, was directly above his head, and straight in front of him was one of the rectangular windows of the cellar. Through it he could see his tiny yard, the big shade tree, the sidewalk, and the street. This was the place in which he found whatever solace his life was permitted to enjoy. This was the place, the only place, in which he could escape the caustic eyes and the upbraiding tongue of Dorothy.

He came home one evening, utterly beaten; his mind was black with misfortune and with the misery of constant physical pain. His supper, already cold, waited for him on the kitchen table. And in the front room he could hear Dorothy and Mildred Barry talking. As he sat down he felt like a vagrant who had broken in a house and was stealing food. There was no welcome; the voices went on, uninterrupted by his arrival. After a while Dorothy walked across the floor, through the dining-room and stopped. "Mildred wants me to go with her to the movies." She spoke hurriedly as if she feared Duncan would object, and as if she had determined to frustrate that objection by a hasty departure. The sound of her voice was still in his ears when the front door closed and left him alone in the house.

He finished his supper and cleaned the dishes at the sink, drying them and putting them away in the cupboard. Then he walked downstairs to his workroom, felt about for the electric button, switched on the light and dropped heavily into the armchair. He drew out his pipe and scraped the bottom of his tobacco-can so that he might have a smoke. At first the fumes irritated his throat and set him coughing drily and violently, then they seemed to soothe. There was a lessening of the pain in his head and he was enabled to think: "In a few days now I'll surely know whether my claim has been approved. I suppose I'll get it all right. They say themselves that they don't know very much about how gas affects a person. It ain't very likely that they can beat me out of it. It shows on my record that my health was good when I went into the service, and they know that it's bad now." It was sensible reasoning, and he began to fancy what he would do when he got the money. Maybe the government would let him go to some school and learn a trade or a profession. He had always wanted to do that; he didn't try to belittle what people could learn out of books. A man of thirty was pretty old to be going to school, but he wouldn't mind that. And, by golly, he'd make the most of his opportunities. No slacker in war, no slacker in work. Dorothy might make him feel like a wet dog because he wasn't supporting her, but if she gave him time he would show her yet.

Damn it all, he had been a good man once. In fact, he had done pretty well in the army. There wasn't a court-martial against him, not a spot to mar his credit. The boys had liked him, too. For that matter, they still did. But it wasn't like the old times in France.

Thinking, through the rose-colored window of remembrance, of those haggard days, he stood up and bent over his trunk. There was his old steel Stetson. It still had grease spots on the top from the candles which he had set on it. And the new blouse they gave him at the hospital Q.M. at Savenay. And his gat, a Colt automatic which he had never fired. When he laid it away he had oiled it well; even now it would pass a rigid inspection. Except, of course, he would have to remove the clip of bullets from the butt.

He grew sleepy, but he dreaded to go upstairs. Dorothy might be saving up her wrath only to pour it out on him when she got home from the movies. It was warm enough in the basement; he might as well sleep down here. Standing up, he snapped off the light and settled back in his chair. As the hours passed he fell asleep.

He never knew what woke him up. Perhaps it was the cold, the chill of midnight coupled with the dying fire in the furnace. He came to consciousness with the same sensation as that which he had had when he had been sleeping in the guard-room in France and had been wakened to go on watch. There was the same stale taste in his mouth, and all of his muscles felt stiff. He wondered what time it was, whether it was nearly dawn. And he stood up to look out the window to see if any stars still showed in the sky.

As he approached the window he fancied he heard the sound of voices, low with caution. He looked sharply, his faculties alert at once. Under the shadow of the shade tree, halfway between the thick trunk and the house, two persons were standing closely together. He could distinguish the outlines of their heads, the one bent over the other, kissing. The kiss lasted for a long time and the larger body seemed to envelop the smaller, to draw it into itself. When the embrace ended he heard a small, stifled exclamation, "Oh!" It had once thrilled *him*, for it was Dorothy who had uttered it. And then a guarded, pleading voice of the man: "Darling, come back—" That was all he could make out, all he had time for. Because the words had found an echo in his heart. He fumbled in the dark for the pistol, felt the chill of the steel. Carefully, he crept up the stairs to the side door.

The lock rasped faintly and he turned the knob, stepping out into the sharp air. As he stole round the corner he heard three more words: "One more night," and his body straightened, his chin held high.

"Darling, come back!" he mocked in his hoarse voice. The bodies separated in surprise, and as the larger one backed away Duncan's mind played a sudden trick, and he saw again the arrogant face of the German sniper at whom he was aiming when the gas-shell came. The man stopped, and Duncan lifted his pistol, all cold blue steel. There was a brittle, smashing noise, and the body before him dropped like a stunned cow. The crisp air held the acrid smell of gunpowder. Duncan calmly lowered his pistol as Dorothy screamed.

Now he felt at ease, more so than he had been in months. Dorothy rushed toward him with wide arms, crying: "My God, what have you done?" The pistol was warm in the palm of his hand and he looked at her. "Done? Why I guess I jist shot somebody." His voice was a little bit shaky, but he controlled it better as he continued: "Who was this man? How long have you been running around with him?" Dorothy cried and sought to embrace him, but he was unmindful of her arms. "How does it feel to be unfaithful?" He laughed. "Golly, maybe I've killed the Perfect Lover."

He was still standing there when several of the neighbors, half-dressed, and a policeman with a pistol, reached the yard and separated him from his clutching wife. The policeman jerked him and threatened with his gun, as policemen will, and he said: "You needn't act like a dirty M.P. I'll go along with you." But the policeman blew on his whistle and deputized a neighbor to call the patrol wagon. Dorothy's sobs were endless, and Duncan was glad when the clangor of the bell on the wagon announced the coming of more policemen, and possibly the coroner.

The policeman whistled and the driver of the lumbering, top-heavy car put on the brakes. They gnashed and whined as the car stopped. Four officers filed out of the opening at the rear. More inquisitive neighbors gathered in the little front yard. Duncan heard them asking questions, offering opinions as he was led away.

In the course of the ride to the station he was silent. That the officers rudely forced him into the cell impressed him more than the fact that a steel door was between himself and the world. After he had been searched and his name, address and occupation registered in the desk sergeant's book, he sat down on the iron cot, its hardness softened only by a thin blanket. Tentatively, he rubbed the blanket with his fingers. It felt unclean, and this bothered him. After a time of indecision he lay down and went to sleep.

He was as docile a murder suspect as the jail had ever contained. Some of the prisoners, during the preliminary hearings, the inspections by the captain of detectives and his subordinates, the ferreting of reporters, the visits of friends and the hysterics of female relatives— some of the prisoners grew queer. They sang hymns, or began to pluck at their clothing. But Duncan remained calm. Dorothy often came and he returned her kisses without fervor. He learned that his application for compensation by the government had been approved. He endorsed the first check and gave it to Dorothy. No, he said, he would not have a lawyer. The court provided one for him. He seemed not particularly interested. He had killed a man; well what of it! A lot of men had been killed. To the consequences of the act he seemed blind.

After a long period the date of his trial arrived, and he learned that the judge was Major Havermeyer. "Havermeyer," he said. "He's a mighty good man, fair and honest." He took a pride in the appointment of Judge Havermeyer. He had helped put him on the bench.

The jury had been chosen, and when he was led into the court room he found them seated in the long pews in which the lower half of their bodies was not visible. Judge Havermeyer sat erect in his chair, looking sternly beyond the clerk, thumping with a wooden mallet, at the crowded court-room. Duncan had an impulse to salute, but refrained. Then the trial commenced.

The slain man, so the assistant state's attorney vociferated, possessed an irreproachable character, was respected by his business associates, and had been cold-bloodedly murdered by the defendant. He rehearsed each detail from the time of the shooting until the present moment. He pointed to the criminal's face and discovered for the jury traces of the most heinous nature written on it. He dwelt upon the recent crime wave in which the city, according to the newspapers, was gripped. Men like Milner, he said, were responsible for it. To kill a man without the least provocation except that that man had escorted the wife of the murderer home! He called upon the jury to do its duty as honest citizens and pronounce the defendant guilty.

Duncan's counsel had pleaded that he be allowed to suggest insanity on the part of the prisoner, but Duncan had refused to permit him. An alienist would have saved him in a moment. Without that, the defense had no case. Duncan listened to the State and grew uneasy. The State, he felt, was lying, but he could not definitely discover in what way. When the clerk had said: "You are charged with . . . guilty or not guilty?" he replied: "Not guilty!"

He took the stand, but he could not say what he wanted to say. His voice had become that of another person, and his tongue was uttering words at random. His mind was far away, sometimes in France on a long, gray hill which led to a zig-zag trench. He was lying on the hill, the cool of his rifle against his cheek, and Captain Haverymeyer—now before him—was giving him the range by which he could kill a man.

The clock in the steeple of the courthouse boomed out twice and was still. Half an hour later it boomed once more. At three o'clock the jury filed back into the room, and the twelve men took their places.

The judge addressed them, and after he had finished the foreman stood up. He was a dried-up little man, with a sharp face and a gray suit, spotted with black. He jingled his watch-chain and cleared his throat. The jury, he said, had found the defendant guilty. But they asked for leniency on the part of the State.

Judge Havermeyer nodded slowly, and his mouth became a hard, straight line. He stood up and addressed the prisoner, also standing:

"You have just been proven guilty, beyond the shadow of a doubt, of the most terrible crime that a man can commit; you have taken a human life. You have broken the most holy commandment of your Maker, and you have defied the civilization which has sheltered you. Human life is sacred, given by God. But you took vengeance in your puny hands and snatched that life away. You are a murderer: you gloatingly watched a living, breathing body and with premeditation you raised your pistol and brought that body to extinction." He paused, levelled his forefinger and began again: "You know better. You have known discipline; you have had the benefits of this enlightened age, yet you have deliberately chosen to revert to savagery, to break the sanctity of human life, to be a coward and a scoundrel. . . . And, to make an example of you to men now living and to generations yet to come, I sentence you to hang by the neck until dead."

And Duncan Milner, cold and sweating, his brain gripped in the vise of his doom, found himself in agreement with the judge: there *was* the sanctity of human life.

X

Uninvited

You may be of the opinion that such a job as that of field worker in the United States Registration of Graves Service is a very peculiar one to have. Not only that, but a singular topic to speak of in the beginning of a story. Who knows? Perhaps you hold an irrefragable prejudice against that form of wage-earning. Yet a job is a job. And to deny this is as false, as flatulent as it is to repudiate the fact that American soldiers went to France and were killed. Another square-jawed truth is that these dead had to be buried, not once, but twice and three times. For a soldier, struck down by a searing bullet or a jarring, ripping shell explosion, lies where he is felled. In an attack he is passed by; during a defense he remains, blackening in the sun and foully thickening the air. Whichever the mode of combat, he is, with its cessation, carried by trembling and wearied hands to the driest near-by spot and there, with the rest who went face down, he is interred.

There he lies while black shells churn up the earth about him and violate the three-foot roof of his tomb. Thus sometimes the rough white cross to which his identification disc has been nailed is destroyed. Thus sometimes a roar and a black, pungent cloud of smoke obliterate him like a dream. If not, he is dug up by limberer hands than those which laid him down, and deposited in a coffin. At a designated cemetery he rests, secure.

But to find these dead! To go about with a memorandum: buried at northeast corner of woods, on rise between road and woods, seventeen soldiers of the Blank Division. To discover so great a number does not seem difficult, and yet, not infrequently, it is. For the landscape so changes. Rank weeds quickly rise to obscuring heights and intensity; trees are cut down and new ones are planted; the people who owned the land in the devastated district have come back to live—all often make their discovery by no means easy.

But Oldshaw, who was employed by the Registration of Graves Department, and whose duty consisted of locating the dead and identifying the bodies, Oldshaw, in all the time he had been at work, had not failed at his task. He was a curious man in appearance. The end of his nose was thick and rounded; his eyes were mild gray, and from them peeped at all times an inclination for a decorous but never gratified merriment. His tow-colored hair was thin on his round, calm-browed skull. His shortness was in his legs. Most unexpectedly, he spoke in a deep bass voice.

The wherefore of Oldshaw's taking up this work is as curious as the man himself. He did it out of a sincere patriotism. Even though the war was over he believed it as important to search out these dead as it was imperative, during the war, that men stand up to die. Conscientiously, Oldshaw went about his work, searching for mislaid identification discs. When they were lost, recognition of bodies was difficult, but often there was a letter, a newspaper clipping from the home town paper, a notebook—something which would lead to the lessening of the official "Missing in Action" list.

Now, for the first time, Oldshaw was stumped. Seventeen bodies had been buried in the open field in front of Vierzy, on the twenty-third of July, four days after the Soissons-Château-Thierry salient had been straightened out. They were somewhere along that level stretch between Vierzy and Tigny, a small town a few kilometres up the road. Seventeen bodies which once were men, waiting to be claimed and taken away. But Oldshaw could not find them.

Two days before, he had come there from Paris, fresh and joyous in the middle of spring time. Driving along in a battered but stubborn Ford, he had passed through Meaux, Dommartin, and Châlons. At Châlons he left his three assistants and set off alone under a soft blue and white sky toward the woods of Villers Cotterets and the town of Vierzy, a cluster of gray houses, now rehabilitated, lying in the bowl of a valley. He had walked up the road past the dugout which once was used as a first-aid station and stood on the rim of the valley, looking out over the broad fields through which the road ran to Tigny. Somewhere near-by were the graves. His memorandum informed him that they were about two hundred yards in a diagonal line to the right of the road from Vierzy. The place was easy to reach, but when he arrived there after tramping through the recently cultivated ground, he saw no trace of them. He spent the afternoon in his search. But when evening came he had nothing to show for his efforts, except countless impressions of his shoes in the soft dark earth, among the green sprigs of planted beets.

The next morning Oldshaw's assistants had arrived from Châlons. All day the four men hunted. With spades they dug up the ground in various places, but they uncovered only a hard stratum of stone a few feet beneath the surface. Now and again they struck into a shell which had not exploded. From the sight of it they hastily withdrew. That evening the men had returned to Châlons while Oldshaw crossed over to the small peasant's cottage where he had arranged to sleep and be given his meals.

Now, after his breakfast of bread and chocolate, he sat in the cool kitchen of the house, waiting for his assistants to arrive from Châlons, to and from which they journeyed each day. Madame Thibaudet stooped before the large fireplace, making the coals gleam by her use of a bellows. Madame Thibaudet was old and scrawny, with shrewd black eyes that were much younger than her habitually bent back. Her hair was gray, tightly framing her thin face. But she minded her business and cooked well. Her garden, a big one out in front of the house, produced well-sized, tender spring vegetables. The bed in the room which Oldshaw was renting was comfortable. It was as much as he could ask and more than he had expected. So he was content, except for this inability to bring his job to a successful end. Madame Thibaudet's felt-slippered feet padded warily on the stone floor as she carried a black iron kettle toward the door.

So far as his limited French would permit, he had talked with her in wisps of conversation as she brought him the platter of stewed rabbit or chicken, and the dish of new peas or string beans fresh from her garden. She had, she said, lived in that same house for the most part of her life. She had been there in 1914 when the Germans had first broken through and were threatening Paris. And with the rest of refugees in the advance area the French Government had driven her away from her home so that she might not be taken captive. She had not gone far. At Meaux she found work in a bakery, and there she remained until the latter part of July, 1918, when the Germans were driven from Soissons. She returned to her home as quickly as she could.

That was one thing that made his search seem so hopeless. This old woman had no remembrance of any graves in that vicinity. Except, of course, the old cemetery which belonged to the people of Vierzy. And she had been there constantly, even before the signing of the armistice. There must, Oldshaw thought, be some pretty big mistake. It was inconceivable that Madame Thibaudet would not have seen seventeen white wooden crosses no more than six hundred yards distant.

He said so to the three men who had stopped the Ford along the road and walked up the lane into the house. To which one of the assistants replied:

"It looks to me as if they'd of give us a bum steer."

Two heads were nodded wisely at the assertion. But Oldshaw, though he had been the first to sound the uselessness of further search, and though his judgment abetted his abandonment of the quest, rubbed the knuckles of one hand against the palm of the other, looking dubiously over the field toward Tigny, and said: "No, we better stick around. They may be right under our nose."—His helpers were so accustomed to their business that the observation brought forth no rejoinder.

Then the men set forth, making four wide paths over the ground between Vierzy and the town of Tigny. They eyed every inch of ground, parted clumps of thick weeds, but neither on their approach nor on their return did they notice a solitary cross.

And in the morning Oldshaw, over his large cup of chocolate, gloomily stared into the fireplace in Madame Thibaudet's kitchen. His short, stubby fingers felt the warmth of the cup as he watched Madame Thibaudet moving about on the stone floor. He thought: seventeen bodies was no small number. It meant seventeen fathers and seventeen mothers. There might be among these dead some who had been listed in the "Missing in Action" columns. If he found them, it meant a long wait would be over for some family. The poor boys; at the least they deserved an honest Christian burial. Damn it! He meant to see that they would get it. He wouldn't go back to headquarters and say he couldn't find them. . . . Funny that this old woman had seen nothing of them.

A fat chicken stood on the threshold of the door, slowly turning its head from one side to the other, inquisitively inspecting the room. It would make a mighty tasty meal, thought Oldshaw. He said as much to Madame Thibaudet, who shrugged and said that the *poule* could be served him at an extra cost. Willingly, he agreed. The chicken stalked temptingly near. Oldshaw leaned forward in his chair, balanced and sprang toward the fowl. His hand grazed the scrawny feet as the chicken rose with a tremendous flapping of wings, cawing indignantly. But Oldshaw followed close behind its long striding legs. Around the house it quickly turned, and Oldshaw was moving so swiftly that he ran far outside its path. But he recovered with hope in his eye, for the chicken was making straight for the side of the woodshed behind the house. But once more, as he was close upon it, it turned and stepped nimbly through the half-open door.

"That cooks your goose!" Oldshaw heavily breathed as he closed the door behind him. The chicken scudded into a corner, and Oldshaw pounced upon it, his hands grappling with its beating wings, which sent dust in great clouds up into his face.

Suddenly he stopped, and his hold upon the chicken relaxed as he stared into the corner where the kindling was piled. For there, in a neat heap, was a number of thin sticks, painted white. The crosses! thought Oldshaw.

"What the hell do you know about that?" he asked the ruffled chicken.

But what, he wondered, was Madame Thibaudet's purpose in tearing up these crosses. Why, that was sacrilege! Seventeen crosses, seventeen graves violated to make kindling wood. The old hag! he thought, moving toward the door. He'd give her such a talking to as she had never had before in her life.

Near the door he stopped, asking himself: "But where are the graves?" Would the old woman tell him? More likely, she'd stick to her story and deny that she knew the crosses were in her woodshed. And then there would be a devil of a time finding them. No, he would better keep quiet about what he had discovered. Meanwhile—

With an effort at making his face mask-like he slowly walked back to the house. Madame Thibaudet stopped her sweeping to inquire whether monsieur had decided not to have the chicken for dejeuner.

"It ran too swiftly to be caught," explained Oldshaw. That morning he wrote a letter to his headquarters office at Paris. And after posting it at Vierzy he returned to the bare kitchen where Madame Thibaudet busied herself with household work.

The room was very quiet. Madame Thibaudet sat before the fireplace watching the fat black kettle which hung down over the pale coals. Her back was toward Oldshaw, whose chair was by the round table with the red-and-white cotton cloth. For some time they were silent. Oldshaw drew a cigarette from his pocket, staring at her meanwhile. He took out a match and as he scraped it across the box he fancied she nervously started. Did she know, he wondered, that the crosses had been discovered.

Throughout the morning he continued to watch her. When she went outside to work in her garden he picked up his chair and placed it in front of the house. There were beds of beans, or peas, and lettuce to be cared for, but Madame Thibaudet appeared hesitant today.

After a short while she walked back toward the house. Near Oldshaw she stopped, muttering a question, looking at the ground: "Monsieur would go away now that he couldn't find the buried Americans?"

Oldshaw shook his head. No, he said, it was very pleasant here. He enjoyed it.

Madame sniffed, tossed her head, and went inside.

The next morning Oldshaw asked if she wouldn't make a lettuce salad for his luncheon.

She consented.

"And some green beans?" he asked.

At that she unexpectedly grew angry. "Nom de Dieu—de Dieu—de Dieu—de Dieu!" Could she have nothing for herself? Was this American to eat her out of house and home? "Rien; rien de toute!" Monsieur, if he must stay, would have to find some place else. She had no more to feed him.

"Ah," thought Oldshaw. Perhaps—. He was very sorry, he said, as he walked out of the house toward Vierzy. It was quite probable, he thought, that the directions which he had been given were false in some slight degree. For example, the graves might be on the left of the road instead of on the right. At any rate, he would mark off the paces and see where they would lead.

Where the road led down into the valley of Vierzy he stopped and turned round. With measured pace he walked back along the road, counting one hundred and fifty steps. He stopped and found himself standing on a spot that was even with the cottage, with the bean patch lying on a dead line between the cottage and himself. "Humph!" he said. The mistake was clear to him and easily understandable now. The road which led to Vierzy, in going down the hill, curved sharply. A person standing on the plain might look down and see the houses of the town and believe himself to be on the right of the road when he was really on its left. But this old woman. Her part in the matter puzzled him greatly.

It was in the morning, three days after he had sent the letter, and Oldshaw had brought one of the plain wooden chairs from the kitchen. He sat with the chair tipped back against the smooth gray wall and looked out over the vegetable garden—green with tinges of brown—toward the road along which his assistants were approaching. All three carried spades.

Though Oldshaw watched the newcomers he knew that Madame Thibaudet was standing behind him in the doorway of the kitchen, and he knew she was very angry. He sat still until the men drew near. Then he got up and asked: "Did you bring the order?"

"Yep," one of the men answered. "But you better be sure you got the right dope, Oldshaw. The Frogs raised the devil before they'd give it to us."

Behind him Madame Thibaudet was breathing hard with gathering excitement, outrage, and hatred. Oldshaw, without looking at her, said: "All right; I guess we'd better dig under that patch of green beans first."

He led the way, carefully following the paths which separated the beds.

As the first spade cut into the earth Madame Thibaudet treaded swiftly and vengefully toward them. Suddenly her stiff, straight-set lips parted, and from them flew invective of every kind and manner. They were dogs, these Americans; pigs, suckled by swine, dolts, cowards to uproot a poor old woman's garden. She shook her fists above her head, grasped at the shovels, screaming that they would pay for this. She would have them jailed, the miserable cowards!

Oldshaw unfolded the paper and showed her the order from the French Government which authorized him to search the property.

And now her threats were unavailing. So she pleaded, throwing herself in the way of the busy shovels, clinging to the handles in a distracted fashion. Would they have no pity on a poor old woman! Would they take her food from her mouth?

But they went on digging until Oldshaw suddenly cried out: "Steady! Easy now! Here we are!"

One of the bodies lay partly showing.

Without looking down at the freshly-spaded earth Madame Thibaudet threw herself against Oldshaw. She was distracted: her garden was being destroyed by these intruders from across the sea—and by order of her own government! The garden into which she had put so much work and care. It had been so luxuriantly productive. And it was hers! It was her bread. What were these bodies but those of intruders? She had been driven away from home by the Bosche. She came back to find seventeen white crosses on her disused garden bed. Was she to be evicted again—by the dead, the dead who did not have to eat?—to her they had no business there, graves or no graves. So, one by one, she had pulled them up. Crosses marking up her garden! Hadn't she, then, been troubled enough? Hadn't she seen enough of war? And wasn't the war over?

She grew still and silent in Oldshaw's arms, too sad to cry.

XI

Semper Fidelis

An Interrupted Narrative Regarding Sergeant Major John H. Quick, U.S.M.C.

My excuse for presenting this actual tale is that the first half of it was written by Stephen Crane and—of necessity—left by him unfinished, since the latter part did not take place until eighteen years after Crane was dead. It is about a man whom Crane once saw and whom I knew slightly; both of us had the fortune, at different and widely separated times, to watch him stand for a moment in a light that was glorious, and which but few mortals are given the privilege even of seeing.

The story has its beginning in "Wounds in the Rain," that collection of sketches which Crane wrote about the Spanish–American War. Near Guantanamo Bay, at Cusco, is the setting. White and watchful, the U.S.S. *Dolphin* lies out in the blue harbor with the black muzzles of it guns thrust over the port side, toward the hot sand and the cactus of the island. An advance party of marines are lying on the crest of a ridge, their backs to the hot, cloudless sky. Farther inland, in a tiny valley below, are a house, a well, and a dense thicket of tropical shrub wherein are hidden six companies of Spanish guerrillas. Two hundred yards of sloping sand divide them from the men in khaki. The marines want to rush the enemy out of the thicket, but they are held up by insufficient numbers. So the captain in charge raises his head from behind a broad-leafed plant and calls out for a signalman—a man to inform the *Dolphin* to hurl some shells into that tiny valley.

An automatic rifleman, sprawling on his stomach, announces that he can send the word. He has scant competition. No, nor even a regulation flag. So he tied his blue polka dot handkerchief on the muzzle of his rifle, stands up and moves down the bay side of the ridge where it is comparatively safe. But the flag is a poor makeshift, and the background of the ridge is so dark that the gunners on the *Dolphin* cannot make out the message. There is nothing for the rifleman to do but return to the top of the ridge and outline himself and his flag against the hot blue sky. There he repeats his signal, very conscientiously.

He offers the first good target the Spaniards have seen. Fully appreciative, they blaze away at it, right at the small of the rifleman's back. At last the *Dolphin* catches the signal, replies, and the rifleman throws himself upon the ground. Then the shells from the battleship whirr over the ridge and tear into the thicket.

Now the fight is carried on in earnest. There is no sniping; only a continuous fusillade from a thousand smoking rifles which raise such a clattering uproar that Colonel Huntington from his camp at Guantanamo Bay grows nervous. He sends out detachments to cover the retreat in case the two hundred men are forced to run. In addition, he orders forty men to support the left flank of the ridge. It is very nice, except that the position places these forty men directly in the line of fire from the *Dolphin*. There is no good seeing your own men killed.

The captain in charge of the besieging company barks for another signalman. The *Dolphin* must be told to lift the range at once. But it is not so easy as it was the first time. The air is black and heavy with pieces of flying steel, steel from Mausers, steel from Lees, soft-nosed steel, and jagged steel from the five-inch guns.

A young man, heretofore intent on perforating every shrub in the valley, rises and announces that he is a signalman. From somewhere he brings out a blue neckerchief. He fastens it to the end of a crooked stick. Then, very calmly, he stands on the top of the ridge, his back to those angry Spanish bullets, and begins to wigwag to the *Dolphin*. He is given sole possession of the ridge. Says Crane:

"We didn't want it. He could have it and welcome. If the young sergeant had had the smallpox, the cholera, and the yellow fever, we could not have slid out with more celerity.

"As I looked at Sergeant Quick wig-waggling there against the sky, I would not have given a tin tobacco-tag for his life. Escape for him seemed impossible. It seemed absurd to hope that he would not be hit; I only hoped that he would be hit a little, little, in the arm, the shoulder, or the leg.

"I watched his face, and it was as grave and serene as that of a man writing in his own library. He was the very embodiment of tranquility in occupation. He stood there amid the animal-like babble of the Cubans, the crack of the rifles and the whistling snarl of the bullets, and wig-wagged whatever he had to wig-wag without heeding anything but his business. There was not a single trace of nervousness or haste.

"To say the least, a fight at close range is absorbing as a spectacle. No man wants to take his eyes from it until that time comes when he makes up his mind to run away. To deliberately stand up and turn your back to a battle is in itself hard work. To deliberately stand up and turn your back to a battle and hear immediate evidences of the boundless enthusiasm with which a large company of the enemy shoot at you from an adjacent thicket, is, to my mind at least, a very great feat. One need not dwell upon the detail of keeping the mind carefully upon a slow spelling of an important code message.

"I saw Quick betray only one sign of emotion. As he swung his clumsy flag to and fro, an end of it once caught, on a cactus pillar, and he looked sharply over his shoulder to see what had it. He gave the flag an impatient jerk. He looked annoyed."

My story begins twenty years after Sergeant John H. Quick stood on a ridge near Guantanamo Bay, under full fire from the enemy, and signaled the off-shore battleship *Dolphin* to redirect its target—an act for which he was given the Congressional Medal of Honor.

He was sergeant-major of our regiment when we went over to France in 1917, and the first time I remember seeing him was one rainy, late spring day in a valley of the Vosges. I was on sentry duty in front of Regimental Headquarters, and he was walking toward the door in front of which I stood. He was a tall man with shoulders that sloped a little forward; his hair was raven black except for a patch of gray above the ears; his face had a curious, kindly expression, as if he had seen so many things over which he could not decide whether to cry or laugh that, in indecision, he had taken on a sad and half regretful smile; his nose and mouth were large and roughly modelled, his eyes still had a fine light in them. He may have thought upon his past glories, his Medal of Honor—but none of us ever heard him speak about it. He was a very quiet man.

Then one day the brigade received orders to move, and to move quickly. The Germans had broken through the French lines and were pushing across the Marne toward Paris. Prompt upon the information, one man in my company saved a German bullet and wasted an American one by shooting himself. None of us was exactly pleased with the knowledge of what he had to do. All of us were highly excited.

But the long marches, the bumping, tedious rides in the French camions, presented more immediate troubles. The sight of refugees packing the streets of Meaux gave us a sense of exhilaration. It made us feel very important.

The next night we were lying in front of Lucy le Bogage with our officers walking up and down in front of us, saying we had about one hour to throw up a breastworks before dawn came. We used bayonets, helmets, the lids of our mess-kits. When morning arrived we were looking out over little mounds of freshly dug dirt toward the gray blue woods ahead from which, occasionally, we could see a tired Frenchman running toward us.

That was on the second of June. At five A.M. on the sixth we were still there, trying to keep the enemy from breaking through the line. And it was decided that the best way to do so was to take Belleau Woods, which lay in front of us, and which was filled with Germans. A little town to the right of the woods, Bouresches, would be invaluable in our hands. So a battalion of each of the two regiments started out, across four hundred yards of open wheat field. The plan was to rush the enemy, five hundred men at a time. These men were deployed in four ways; the first reached the woods, plunged in; then the second, the third, and the fourth. Two hours later German prisoners were being sent back to Regimental Headquarters.

But to get the town. It was decided to do it with one hundred and twenty men, two platoons from the Sixth. After a short bombardment they advanced in attack formation, the first and third waves supplied with automatics and grenades, the second and fourth with rifles, across the wheat field. There was nothing to stop them but three-inch artillery and machine-guns!

They attacked, four short waves of sweating men in olive drab, stalking across that unfriendly field. Men dropped without a sound and the four lines merged into three, two, one. When they reached the gray stone buildings of the town there were twenty soldiers on their feet.

Twenty soldiers to rout four hundred! And they did it, somehow. And then Lieutenant Robertson—wounded, but still in charge—settled down to hold the position against the enemy's counter-attack. He sent out runners for reinforcements. They returned with two companies from the Second Engineers and one from their own battalion.

The counter-attack wasn't long in coming. The Germans had a furious desire to retrieve Bouresches. As the first gray line was glimpsed, pouring over the field, Robertson checked up the ammunition. There wouldn't be enough! That night he sent back word to Regimental Headquarters that the men were running short of ammunition. Sergeant-Major John H. Quick and Lieutenant Moore were there when the order came. They said: "We'll take 'em a whole truckload."

They got a team of mules, hitched up a wagon loaded with shells, and started out, over a shell-torn road, under a venomous fire with a highly combustible cargo. Each step that those mules took was brilliantly lighted by enemy flares, popping up now from this side, now from that. German gunners lay in wait, and you could not hear the solitary whining of the sniper's bullet for the tremendous clattering from the German machine-guns. The wagon creaked, it rolled and jostled over those gullies, stones, and craters; and the enemy artillery ripped up the ground in front and at each side, and threw dirt in the men's faces. Onward they went in the face of the rattling machine-guns.

The ammunition truck arrived in Bouresches with its burden. Sergeant-Major John H. Quick climbed down as the besieged men crowded about the precious ammunition. Once more he had performed a great service at great risk; once more he was decorated for bravery. And Quick? He said nothing about it; he had accomplished only his duty; *semper fidelis*, that was all.

Explanatory Notes

The Dedication

John A. Hughes: Nicknamed "Johnny the Hard," Major John A. Hughes (1880–1942) commanded Thomas Boyd's unit—the First Battalion, Sixth Marines—throughout its service in the Great War. An experienced professional soldier, Hughes received the Medal of Honor for courageous action at Vera Cruz in 1914 and the Navy Cross for his leadership during the Battle of Belleau Wood in 1918. In 1919, his health weakened by exposure to poison gas, Hughes retired from the Corps at the rank of lieutenant colonel.

Cornelius Van Ness: A Harvard graduate and antiquarian booklover, Cornelius Van Ness (1894–1952) hired Thomas Boyd in 1921 to manage Kilmarnock Books, Van Ness's bookstore in downtown St. Paul, Minnesota. Boyd worked in the store during the height of its popularity as a hangout for local writers and wrote much of his first novel, *Through the Wheat* (1923), on its premises.

Foreword

Page 5, **"Through the Wheat"**: Published in 1923, Thomas Boyd's first novel follows an autobiographical protagonist, William Hicks, through the battles of Belleau Wood, Soissons, and Blanc Mont. Hicks is a capable Marine infantryman, but by the end of the narrative, which focuses almost entirely on combat, he is left shell shocked and "numb." Some contemporary reviewers, including F. Scott Fitzgerald (1896–1940), detected a note of nobility and heroism in Hick's ordeal. What stands out today is the uncompromising bleakness of Boyd's vision.

"Unadorned"

Page 8, **"Sam Browne belt"**: A leather waist belt worn on top of one's uniform and featuring a distinctive shoulder strap. During World War I, the US Army limited use of the non-regulation Sam Browne to officers in the American Expeditionary Forces (AEF). Thus, the belt became a coveted symbol of overseas service.

Page 15, **"their spring drive"**: Launched on May 27, the third German offensive of 1918 broke through French defenses along the Chemin des Dames, a ridgeline in the Champagne region, and seemed certain to reach Paris. However, the attack stalled at the Marne River, in part because of the tenacity of American divisions, including the Second, which AEF commander John J. Pershing (1860–1948) loaned to the French Army in this moment of emergency.

Page 16, **"the forest in which the Germans were"**: The Bois de Belleau or Belleau Wood, a forested preserve, roughly a mile square, near Château Thierry, a town on the Marne River. The marine brigade's legendary battle to capture Belleau Wood lasted, with a brief intermission (during which ill-prepared US Army troops lost some of the ground seized by the marines), from June 6 until June 26, 1918. Here Boyd depicts the action on June 6, when marine units had to advance over open ground to reach the edge of the woods. Until World War II, this remained the bloodiest day in Marine Corps history.

Page 17, **"gangrene"**: Because antibiotics were not widely available during World War I, wounds commonly became infected, and many patients developed a condition known as gas gangrene (no connection to poison gas), characterized by swelling and tissue decay.

Page 20, **"Mangin's army"**: Although AEF commander John J. Pershing fought to maintain an independent American army in Europe, the crisis presented by the German offensives in the late spring and summer of 1918 forced him to loan American divisions to the French. During the Second Battle of the Marne (July 15–August 4), the Second Division, which contained the marine brigade, served in the French Tenth Army, whose commander was the notoriously aggressive Charles Mangin (1866–1925), nicknamed the "Butcher." Mangin ultimately praised the Americans for their crucial contribution.

Page 21, **"the seventy fives"**: French 75 mm field guns. One of the best designed artillery pieces of the First World War, the French seventy-five (or soixante-quinze) could achieve an astonishing rate of fire, up to thirty rounds per minute, and featured a sophisticated recoil system that eliminated the need for reaiming after each shot. Two American field artillery regiments per division were issued this weapon.

Page 21, **"Non! Non! Vite!"**: "No! No! Fast!"

"THE KENTUCKY BOY"

Page 22, **"S O S"**: Service of Supply. Goodwin's disdain for the logistical branch of the AEF is typical of a combat infantryman. Soldiers at the front line tended to regard supply troops as malingerers and thieves.

Page 22, **"Vaux"**: A town located approximately a mile southeast of the Bois de Belleau.

Page 26, **"red cords"**: The color of the cords worn on a World War I era US Army campaign hat indicated a soldier's branch of service. Red signified artillery.

Page 27, **"'selected men'"**: The bald soldier in this scene appears to be a member of the Seventy-Seventh "Statue of Liberty" Division, a unit comprised of conscripts (what the soldier euphemistically calls "selected men") from New York. Ironically, the speaker has the pecking order in reverse: men in regular army divisions, such as the Second, usually looked down upon draftee divisions—at least until they proved themselves in battle. The AEF's high command held a similar attitude.

Page 28, **"'The First Division of Regulars'"**: Hawthorne belongs to John J. Pershing's favorite division, the first to arrive in France and one of the most bloodied. Nicknamed "the Big Red One," the First Division saw action in every major American battle on the Western Front and was second only to the Second Division in total number of casualties. The bald man in this scene is not only tangling with the wrong soldier, as he is about to discover, but he also has absolutely no idea what he is talking about.

Page 31, "**'Cantigny'**": The First Division's successful attack on the German salient at Cantigny (May 28, 1918) was the first American battle of the war. The most difficult stage of the operation, which Hawthorne goes on to describe, occurred when the Germans counterattacked. The men of the First Division held their ground and then renewed their own attack.

Page 31, "**'up around Château-Thierry'**": i.e. The fighting in and around Belleau Wood.

Page 31, "**'sea-bags, Jack Johnsons, whizz-bangs'**": AEF slang for enemy artillery projectiles. "Sea-bags" and "Jack Johnsons" were massive artillery shells discharged by howitzers, the latter named after the African American heavyweight boxer. "Whizz-bangs" were lighter shells fired at a near-flat trajectory by German .77 mm field guns.

Page 33, "**'a bon sector'**": A good sector. In the imaginations of most American soldiers, Paris was synonymous with debauchery. Civilian organizations attached to the AEF, such as the YMCA and the Salvation Army, did what they could to steer doughboys on leave toward more wholesome activities. Occasionally they succeeded.

Page 33, "**the Café de la Paix and the Folies Bergère, the Apache District**": Legendary landmarks in the City of Light. Located near the Paris Opera and popular among writers and artists, the Café de la Paix was luxuriously decorated and one of the best places in the city for people watching. The Folies Bergère, a music hall then at the peak of its popularity, featured scantily clad dancers in elaborate routines. The so-called Apache District, an infamous slum, drew in the curious through its connection with gang activity and the criminal underworld.

Page 33, "**Ancient in a horizon-blue cape**": An older French soldier called up for service in a noncombat role. The French Army adopted horizon-blue uniforms in 1915 after discovering that the dark blue overcoats and red pantaloons worn by its soldiers at the start of the war made them easy targets.

Page 34, "**'Ticket, comme ça, comme ça!'**": "Ticket, like that, like that!"

Page 34, "**wound chevron**": Wounded members of the AEF were awarded special chevrons, one per wound, which they wore on the lower right sleeve of their tunics. The best-known American decoration for injury sustained in combat, the Purple Heart medal, was not authorized until 1932; thousands of American World War I veterans applied for and received the award.

Page 34, **"No street cars were to be seen. . . . to take the train for Toul"**: In this elegant paragraph, Boyd contrasts Goodwin and Hawthorne's furtive passage beneath Paris as passengers aboard the subway or Metro with the various decadent pleasures enjoyed above their heads by American troops on furlough. The two renegades are bound for the Gare de l'Est, the main rail station on the eastern side of the city and the point of departure for troops returning to the Western Front.

"Responsibility"

Page 39, **"they had saved Paris"**: Belleau Wood marked the German Army's furthest point of advance—just forty miles from the city. However, the marines could not take full credit for stalling the enemy offensive that opened on May 27. The AEF's Third Division helped hold the south bank of the Marne River, opposite Château-Thierry, against overwhelming numbers, earning the nickname "Rock of the Marne."

Page 40, **"G.I. cans"**: A US government-issued trashcan or, as used here, a large German artillery projectile.

Page 47, **"They left Nanteuil one evening"**: At Nanteuil-sur-Marne, marine survivors of the Battle of Belleau Wood recuperated and, as depicted in the story, welcomed the legions of replacement troops needed to bring their battalions back up to full strength. Then, after being relieved by members of Twenty-Sixth Division, the marine brigade travelled in camions to a new frontline position fifty miles northwest of Château Thierry on the left side of a gigantic salient created by the German advance earlier in the summer. On July 19, presumably just a day or two after the action depicted in this story, Thomas Boyd's regiment, the Sixth Marines, went on the offensive again, joining a French counterattack near the town of Soissons.

Page 52, **"Maxim"**: A water-cooled German Model 1908 machine gun. The weapon's central mechanism, which harnessed the recoil energy released by one cartridge to position the next in front of the firing pin, was the brainchild of American-born British inventor Hiram Maxim (1840–1916), who created the world's first modern machine gun in 1883. The device changed warfare forever.

"Sound Adjutant's Call"

Page 61, **"folded ourselves into box cars"**: French boxcars, tiny by American standards, notoriously bore the numbers 40/8. These figures indicated capacity, either forty soldiers or eight horses. Neither soldiers nor horses fit comfortably inside.

Page 62, **"their pair of gas masks, French and English"**: Each American soldier in 1918 carried a French Model M2 Gasmask, which was filterless and lightweight, and a British (or American-made) Model 1917 Small Box Respirator, a more complicated device with a charcoal filter (fitted inside a canvas carrier), hose, and facemask. The M2 was designed to be worn for long periods in places where gas lingered; the Model 1917 provided protection during a full-blown chemical attack.

Page 65, **"that Alabama regiment"**: The Alabama National Guardsmen who made up the 167th Infantry Regiment, part of the Forty-Second "Rainbow" Division, were notorious for their brawling.

Page 65, **"Santo Domingo"**: In 1916, political instability (with American interests at stake) in the Dominican Republic prompted one of many American interventions in the region. US Marines landed in Santo Domingo, the Dominican capital, in May 1916, and within two months took control of the entire country. The United States occupied the Dominican Republic until 1924.

Page 67, **"the tanks that were grunting and grinding into position"**: This battle scene takes place during the second day (July 19, 1918) of the Battle of Soissons, where an assault by the Sixth Marine Regiment resulted in horrible losses. The French Model FT-17 Tanks that accompanied the Marines were part of the problem. The lumbering vehicles (top speed: about three miles per hour) attracted artillery fire, which rained down on the infantrymen as well. Most were blown up or otherwise disabled by the end of the day. Slow, awkward, and unreliable, tanks in World War I were hardly war-winning weapons.

"Rintintin"

Page 70, **"Strange little dolls"**: Rintintin and his companion doll Nénette were good luck charms carried by French soldiers and civilians during the latter part of World War I. According to superstition, the charms only worked if the dolls remained together, linked by a piece of yarn, and were received as a gift. Twenty-first century readers of *Points of Honor* may be more familiar with Rin Tin Tin, the canine hero. This American pop-culture icon has a direct connection to World War I and to the French good luck charms. In September 1918, Corporal Lee Duncan of the AEF rescued a German shepherd and her several puppies from an abandoned kennel on the Western Front. Duncan kept two of the puppies, which he named Rin Tin Tin and Nénette, and brought them back to the United States. The male member of the pair became a beloved movie star in the 1920s, and his male descendents, all performing under the same moniker, appeared in films and on television well into the 1950s.

Page 71, **"A scant handful of the men"**: This passage, like many others in *Points of Honor*, reminds us that the replacement rate in the marine brigade topped 150 percent by the end of the war. Any marine who made it through all five of the brigade's major battles without injury was extraordinarily lucky.

Page 72, **"the new Enfield rifle"**: The American Model 1917 Enfield Rifle, a bolt-action firearm, held up to six thirty-caliber (or 30.06) rounds in its magazine and was effective within 600 yards. A highly skilled marksman could extend that range considerably. By November 1918, more American soldiers carried the Enfield rifle than the better-known Model 1903 Springfield. One of those soldiers was Alvin York, the most celebrated American hero of the war, who demonstrated the Enfield's reliability and accuracy during the feat of marksmanship for which he received the Medal of Honor.

Page 73, **"'Where's the one that goes with it?'"**: Benner does not have both dolls, which would have been customary. This detail is ominous.

Page 76, **"the brigade commander"**: General Wendell C. Neville (1870–1930), a respected and experienced marine officer, assumed command of the marine brigade in July 1918.

Page 76, "'**a message from the divisional commander**'": The marine brigade joined the Meuse-Argonne Offensive on November 1, 1918. By this point, the commander of the Second Division was the legendary Marine Major General John A. Lejeune (1867–1942), after whom the training camp in North Carolina is named. Lejeune played a central role in establishing the ethos and traditions of the modern Marine Corps.

Page 81, "**Ninth Regular Infantry**": One of the non-Marine regiments in the Second Division.

Page 86, "**Ninette**": An Americanized spelling of Nénette.

"A LITTLE GALL"

Page 87, "**the vicinity of Saint Nazaire**": St. Nazaire, a French port where many AEF units landed, served as the headquarters for the Sixth Marines during its frustrating first few months overseas. This story is set in November 1917, when the marines toiled as laborers and feared they would never see combat.

Page 88, "**Ullo corps!**": "Corps" was a nickname for a marine.

Page 88, "**Boulestin**": A brand of cognac.

Page 93, "'**intelligence section**'": A group of soldiers who served as scouts or observers. Today, we would use the word "reconnaissance" to describe their duties.

Page 97, "**calomel**": A powder used as a laxative.

"THE RIBBON COUNTER"

Page 100, "'**Sammies**'": A wartime nickname for American soldiers, derived from "Uncle Sam."

Page 100, "**four major offensives**": MacMahon has survived Belleau Wood, Soissons, the St. Mihiel Offensive, and the capture of Blanc Mont.

Page 101, "**the Kriemhilde Stellung**": The second of three formidable defensive lines, all named after Wagnerian witches, which confronted the AEF during the Meuse-Argonne offensive. Each line maximized the advantages of high ground and featured underground bunkers, concrete pill boxes, acres of barbed wire, and hidden machine-gun nests designed to catch attackers in a cross fire. German ingenuity combined with American inexperience (many AEF units saw action for the first time in the

Meuse-Argonne) resulted in the bloodiest battle in American history. Between September 26 and November 11, 1918, the bitter fighting in the Meuse-Argonne cost the United States 26,000 lives and left more than 100,000 wounded.

Page 105, **"Hotchkiss guns"**: Most American machine-gun units were issued the French Model 1914 Hotchkiss Machine Gun, a reliable air-cooled weapon that fired .8 mm cartridges attached to a metal strip rather than a belt. The American-made Model 1917 Browning Machine Gun did not reach the AEF in large numbers until after the armistice.

Page 107, **"Bosche"**: A corruption of the French word *"Boche,"* a derogatory term for the Germans.

"The Nine Days' Kitten"

Page 113, **"Just a dream of you de-ea-ea-ea-ear"**: A line from the chorus of the popular song of the same name (music by F. Henri Klickmann, words by Chas. F. McNamara, copyright 1912). The complete lyrics are as follows:

Though waking I dream,
In the sunset gleam
Of the fading summer day.
I linger once more
On the dear home shore,
As the falling shadows play.
My thoughts fondly roam
With the white dashing foam
Of the heaving, sobbing sea.
I dream once again
In memory then
Of a face so dear to me.

Just a dream at sunset
In the fading glow
Just a dream of you, dear
When the sun is low.
Just a dream at twilight

Answering memory's call
Just a dream of you, dear
Just a dream, that's all.

In fancy I stand
On the sunlit strand
Where the tide waves
Come and go.
There steals to my ear
Such a sweet voice near
That I loved long, long ago.
The dream is soon o'er,
And the bright sunny shore
Like a mocking vision flies.
The shadows now fall,
Sad memory's pall,
As the day in darkness dies.

Just a dream at sunset
In the fading glow
Just a dream of you, dear
When the sun is low.
Just a dream at twilight
Answering memory's call
Just a dream of you, dear
Just a dream, that's all.

"The Long Shot"

Page 129, **"a company of National Guards, recruited from Reliance, Ill."**: Regiments in the Illinois National Guard formed the AEF's Thirty-Third Division, nicknamed the "Prairie Division." Soldiers in the Thirty-Third enjoyed much better odds than those in the marine brigade, who had the misfortune of being trained and ready for action by June 1918, but the division still suffered heavily: nearly 1,000 of its soldiers were killed and more than 6,000 were wounded. Boyd would have known all about the "Prairie Division" through his friends and relatives in Chicago and Elgin, and the plot of "The Long Shot," which requires that Duncan Milner's wartime commanding officer later become a court judge in the veteran's hometown, simply would not have worked if Boyd had placed his protagonist in the Marine Corps.

Page 135, **"four chevrons"**: The protagonist's uniform features a wound stripe (awarded, in this case, for poison-gas inhalation), two overseas stripes (each signifying six months of duty in Europe), and a red honorable discharge stripe designed to help authorities distinguish between active members of the military and veterans returning home after demobilization.

Page 135, **"a sixty-dollar bonus"**: The only material benefit, apart from being allowed to keep his uniform and equipment (helmet, gas mask, etc.), that a World War I–era serviceman received upon discharge. Sixty dollars in 1919 had the buying power of $860 in today's currency.

Page 137, **"sixty-five dollars a week"**: Duncan's monthly salary of $260, at the peak of his earning power, is equivalent to $3,727 today.

Page 138, **"the American Legion"**: Founded in Paris in 1919 by Theodore Roosevelt Jr. (1887–1944), the American Legion became one of the largest and most powerful veterans organizations in US history. At the height of its popularity in the 1920s, nearly one out of every four American veterans of the Great War was a member. Initially, the legion argued against entitlements for former soldiers; however, as its members became increasingly embittered over lost wartime wages, the organization changed its position. Politically conservative, even reactionary, the legion was also known for violently suppressing labor unions, especially the radical International Workers of the World (IWW). But not all legionnaires necessarily shared the same political views. Some former soldiers joined the organization primarily as a way of remembering and honoring lost comrades. Others joined to partake of the legion's notoriously raucous conventions, where Prohibition was generally ignored.

Page 138, **"Prohibition . . . and Bolshevism"**: This section of "The Long Shot" takes place shortly after passage of the federal Volstead Act, which established the nationwide enforcement of Prohibition, and during the Red Scare of 1919–1920, when Attorney General A. Mitchell Palmer

(1872–1936) led a crack down on political dissent that resulted in the jailing or deportation of thousands of suspected radicals or "Reds."

Page 141, "**The factories . . . were laying off men**": The recession of 1920–1921 resulted from the sudden influx of demobilized soldiers into an economy already shaken by the cancellation of wartime contracts.

Page 145, "**'send you to the Soldier's Hospital'**": The federal Veterans Bureau, established in 1920 and directed by Warren G. Harding (1865–1923) appointee Charles R. Forbes (1878–1952), was notoriously corrupt and mostly indifferent to the wounded veterans it ostensibly served. The process of proving to the bureau that one's medical condition resulted from military service could take months or even years (especially in cases involving exposure to poison gas), and disability pensions, when granted, were typically inadequate. Scandal broke in 1923 when federal authorities learned that Forbes had pocketed millions of dollars through kickbacks and illicit sales of medical supplies (including alcohol). Forbes fled to Europe; two years later he was returned to the United States and convicted on charges of corruption and bribery.

Page 146, "**'they don't know very much about how gas affects a person'**": Ironically, poison-gas exposure during the war apparently contributed to Thomas Boyd's sudden death in 1935.

Page 147, "**gat**": 1920s-era slang for "gun." Duncan's handgun, a Colt Model 1911 Automatic Pistol, was standard issue, with minor modifications, for US Army personnel throughout most of the twentieth century.

Page 148, "**'The Perfect Lover'**": Most likely a reference to Rudolph Valentino (1895–1926), the first male superstar and male sex symbol in American movie history. In 1922, *Motion Picture Magazine* explored Valentino's erotic appeal in an article titled "The Perfect Lover."

Page 150, "**alienist**": Archaic term for Psychiatrist.

"Uninvited"

Page 152, "**United States Registration of Graves Service**": Established in 1917, the Graves Registration Service (GRS) was responsible for the location, exhumation, and proper reburial or transportation of American military remains. In the years immediately following World War I, the organization's duties were complicated by President Woodrow Wilson's (1856–1924) decision in 1919 to allow the families of the fallen to decide whether the bodies of their loved ones would remain in Europe or be returned to the United States. Ultimately, the GRS oversaw the repatriation of more than 45,000 corpses; those left in Europe were moved to eight permanent cemeteries designed by the American Battle Monuments Commission (founded in 1923 and led by John J. Pershing).

Page 153, **"'Missing in Action' list"**: By 1921, approximately 4,500 American soldiers who fought in France or Belgium remained unaccounted for. The names of the missing are listed on plaques contained in the eight overseas cemetery chapels constructed by the American Battle Monuments Commission in the 1920s and 1930s.

Page 157, **"dejeuner"**: lunch

Page 158, **"Nom de Dieu'"**: "For God's sake!"

Page 158, **"'Rien; rien de toute!'"**: "Nothing; nothing at all!"

"SEMPER FIDELIS"

Page 160, **"Wounds in the Rain"**: This collection of Spanish-American War sketches by the brilliant Naturalist and Impressionist writer Stephen Crane (1871–1900) appeared shortly after the young author's death.

Page 160, **"Near Guantanamo Bay, at Cusco"**: The action described by Crane took place in June 1898, as US Marines, hoping to cut off the enemy's water supply, mounted an expedition to seize the freshwater well at Cusco (or Cuzco). Ultimately a victory for the Americans, the Battle of Cuzco Well formed part of the larger military operation to secure Guantanamo Bay. The United States has, of course, held this area of Cuba ever since.

Page 161, **"a signalman"**: A soldier who would communicate with a distant force by (ideally) holding a pair of brightly colored flags in various positions, a system known as semaphore.

Page 161, **"steel from Mausers, steel from Lees"**: The Spanish Model 1893 Mauser Rifle was a sophisticated bolt-action weapon comparable to Mauser designs used later in the Great War. Marines in Cuba carried the most advanced American long arm of the time, the Model 1895 Lee Rifle, which featured an early straight-pull bolt design and, like the Mauser, fired smokeless powder cartridges.

Page 164, **"the Second Engineers"**: A non-Marine regiment in the Second Division.

Page 165, **"semper fidelis"**: The official motto of the US Marine Corp, often shortened to semper fi, meaning "always faithful."